DARKROOM

DARKROOM

Graham Masterton

severn House

This first world edition published in Great Britain 2004 by
SEVERN HOUSE PUBLISHERS LTD of
9–15 High Street, Sutton, Surrey SM1 1DF.
This first world edition published in the USA 2004 by
SEVERN HOUSE PUBLISHERS INC of
595 Madison Avenue, New York, N.Y. 10022.

British Library Cataloguing in Publication Data

Masterton, Graham
    Darkroom. - (Jim Rook series ; 6)
    1.   Rook, Jim (Fictitious character) - Fiction
    2.   Horror tales
    I.   Title
    823.9'14 [F]

    ISBN 0-7278-6053-4

Typeset by Palimpsest Book Production Ltd.,
Polmont, Stirlingshire, Scotland.
Printed and bound in Great Britain by
MPG Books Ltd., Bodmin, Cornwall.

WEST GROVE COMMUNITY COLLEGE
SPECIAL CLASS II

Jim Rook
English and Special Needs

Vanilla King	Freddy Price	Sue-Marie Cassidy	Edward Truscott
Ruby Montes	George Graves	Pinky Perdido	Randy Bullock
Sonny Powell	Brenda Malone	[spare desk]	Delilah Bergenstein
Roosevelt Jones	David Robinson	Sally Broxman	Philip Genio

One

They were laughing so much that Bobby almost fell down the wooden stairs leading up to the beach-house balcony, and twice he dropped the key that opened the living-room door. They were both excited, but nervous, too, and Bobby was feeling the giddy effect of four pina coladas and two beers, as well as a long, deep drag at the joint that Freddy Price had given him, 'to make you invincible, dude.'

Bobby managed to unlock the living-room door and slide it open. The net curtain billowed out into the evening wind and wrapped itself around them like a shroud. Bobby held Sara's face in both hands and kissed her, and kissed her again, and almost lost his balance.

'You know something, Sara Miller? You are a . . . princess. A princess in *pink*. And red! With yellow spots, too.'

'You're not so bad yourself, Bobby Tubbs.' She kissed him teasingly on the tip of his nose, and then his eyebrows, and then his lips. Enfolded in their shroud, they held each other close for a moment and stared at each other wide-eyed, unblinking, as if it was a challenge to see who would burst out laughing first. Only a hundred yards away, in the breezy darkness, the ocean slapped against the pier, and slapped, and slapped, so that the yachts and rowboats knocked against each other at their moorings, as hollow as coffins.

'It's incredible,' Bobby decided.

'What's incredible?'

'Fate. That day you first came trucking into the classroom, with that tight white T-shirt and that short denim skirt on – I thought, *bavaroofi!*'

'Is *that* what you thought? *Bavaroofi?*'

'*Bavaroofi*, that's exactly what I thought. But I never would have believed, not in a million, grillion years—'

Sara smiled and pressed her fingers against his mouth. 'Ssh. You *have* to believe it, otherwise it won't happen.'

'You're right, you're right,' Bobby replied, trying hard to sound serious. 'Like, anything you *don't* believe in . . . it just doesn't exist, right?'

'Let's go inside,' said Sara, struggling free from the curtain. 'Do your parents have any booze?'

'Are you kidding? My parents don't give blood, they give dry Martini. They always keep loads of stuff in the icebox. Wine, beer. And rum, too. My dad loves his rum. He says rum puts hairs on your chest, and makes you talk like Johnny Cash. Well, like Johnny Cash *used* to. You know – before he cashed in.'

'In that case, I think I'll stick to wine. Is there a *light* in here?'

Bobby stumbled over an armchair, knocked a brass ashtray on to the floor, and only just managed to catch a standard lamp before it fell over. At last, however, he found the light switch. 'There,' he said. 'Welcome to my humble abode. Well – my parents' humble abode.'

His parents' beach house had rough, white-painted walls. The floors were laid out of wide, bleached planks salvaged from the SS *Narwhal*, and the living room was furnished with natural linen chairs and couches and loose-woven slip mats. All around hung oak-framed prints of sailing ships and storms at sea, as well as nautical knots and compasses and maps.

'My dad said he would have been the skipper of a three-masted schooner if he hadn't been a movie accountant. Skipper of a three-masted schooner, my rear end. He gets seasick washing his hair.'

'*My* dad always wanted to be a professional card sharp,' said Sara. 'You should see him whenever he plays poker with his friends. He wears one of those green eyeshades and bands on his sleeves and smokes a cigar out of the side of his mouth. It's pathetic. Like, if he wanted to be a professional card sharp so much, why didn't he just go to Las Vegas and *be* one?'

Bobby made his way through to the kitchen, and switched on the light there, too. 'I'll tell you something – me, I'm going to be exactly what I want to be. No compromises.'

He opened the icebox and took out a bottle of Stag's Leap Chardonnay. It had been opened already, but it was still three-quarters full. He pulled out the cork with his teeth.

'So what *do* you want to be?' asked Sara.

'A falconer.'

'A *what*?'

'You know . . . one of those guys who goes around with a falcon on his wrist.' He crooked up his arm by way of illustration.

Sara frowned at him. 'Is there any money in that?'

'I don't know. I just like the idea of doing it. Somebody's dog comes yapping at you, biting at your ankles, and all you have to do is whip your falcon's hood off. The falcon swoops on the dog, *neeeeoooowwww*, flies up into the air with it, hovers for a while, sixty feet up, *flap-flap-flap*, and then drops it into the nearest dumpster. *Wheeeee-splotch-woof!*'

Sara nodded, but didn't say anything. Bobby wasn't the only student in Special Class II who had slightly off-center ideas about what they were going to do when they left college. David Robinson seriously thought that he would make a good Pope, while Sally Broxman had set her sights on training miniature ponies for the blind.

Sara wanted to be a masseuse to the stars. She had written it on her college registration form. 'Masseuse to the Stars.'

3

Bobby sloshed out two large glasses of wine. 'Here's to things that exist,' he said, and they clinked glasses.

'Here's to things we believe in,' said Sara.

She had never taken a whole lot of notice of Bobby, not before tonight. He was tall and skinny and loose-jointed, like a life-size marionette, with startling blue eyes and sticky-up hair with bleached-blond tips. He always seemed to be smirking at some private wisecrack. Even when he asked to go to the bathroom he sounded as if he were telling a joke. He would put up his hand and say, 'Please, ma'am, I really, truly, have to . . .' and everybody in the class would collapse.

He had read out part of *Hamlet* in class last Thursday, and by the time he had come to the lines about 'the dread of something after death . . . the undiscover'd country from whose bourn . . . no traveller returns,' everybody had been crying with laughter, including their substitute teacher, Mrs Lakenheath.

But tonight, thirteen of them had gone to Papa Piccolino's Pizza House for Kerry Lansing's nineteenth-birthday party, and for no particular reason except that he had been sitting right opposite her, Bobby had caught Sara's attention. She had suddenly seen how alert he was to the people around him, and how hard he worked to make sure that everybody had a good time. He was always smiling at people and teasing them and giving them silly compliments, and if a girl looked as if she were being left out of the crowd, he had made a point of going over and talking to her. He made people feel happy. He was quite good-looking, too, she thought, if you didn't mind sharp, pointy noses.

Sara hadn't dated since she had split up with Brad Moorcock during the winter holidays. Plenty of guys had asked her out, because she was one of the prettiest girls at West Grove Community College. She was petite and perky, with messy brown hair and brown eyes as big as a cartoon character, and she always wore huge dangly earrings and bangles on her wrists. She had a figure that made boys walk into lamp posts. After Brad, however, Sara had felt like a break from serious romance. Brad was handsome, no question about it. He was broad-shouldered, jut-jawed, curly-haired, confident, and captain of the most successful football team that West Grove had ever fielded. But he was also vain, and obsessively jealous, so that Sara hadn't even been able to talk to another boy about her English coursework without Brad muscling in and threatening to break his legs in fifty-four places. She was still enjoying the relief of being free from him.

'Let's have some music,' Bobby suggested. 'What do you feel like? "The Absolute Dregs of Perry Como" or "Songs for Harpooning Whales To"?'

'Why don't we make our own music?' said Sara, putting her arm around him.

'You mean, like a duet?'

'Yes. Like a duet.'

They kissed again, and this time they went on kissing until Bobby had to put down his glass of wine in case he spilled it. Without a word, he took hold of Sara's hand and led her into the master bedroom. This was decorated on a nautical theme, too, with a huge brass bed and a deep-blue bedcover with a seagull motif. On the walls hung pictures of bare-breasted mermaids with blue nipples and seductive smiles, surrounded by lustful lobsters waving their claws.

'Sorry about the pictures. That's my dad's idea of porn. Prawn porn.'

Bobby fell back on the bed and Sara climbed on to it next to him. She kissed him and kissed him again. He tugged up her tight pink T-shirt and pulled it over her head. She was wearing a white lacy see-through bra, but Bobby immediately shut his eyes.

'What's the matter?' she asked him.

'I'm closing my eyes in case this isn't really happening.'

She laughed and kissed him and started to unbuckle his

belt. 'You ought to open them. You wouldn't want to miss anything.'

He looked up at her and his eyes were bright with pleasure. 'You're right. Who cares if it isn't really happening? It *looks* real. It *feels* real. Nothing else matters, does it?'

'No,' she said. 'It's just you, and me, and this big blue bed.'

'Oh, God,' he exclaimed, suddenly sitting up and looking around him. 'My parents!'

'What about your parents? Your parents are in Phoenix for the weekend, aren't they?'

'No, but this *bed*. My parents have you-knowed in it.'

'They've *what*?'

'You-knowed. *You* know. They've done that thing you can't believe your parents still do but they do.'

'What do you care? If you go to a hotel it's even worse. Total strangers have you-knowed in your bed. Hundreds of total strangers. People you wouldn't even want to sit next to on a bus.'

Bobby looked dubiously down at the dark blue throw. 'I guess you're right.'

'Come on,' said Sara, and sat astride him, pushing him back on the bed. 'I thought you were going to show me that there *is* life after Brad Moorcock.'

Bobby reached around and unfastened the clip of Sara's bra. He fondled her and nuzzled her ear, tugging gently at her earrings with his teeth. 'I'll show you just how great you make me feel,' he whispered. 'You make me feel like King Bobby the First.'

He rolled her over, touching and stroking her hair, and then he felt in his pocket. 'Condom,' he said, holding up the packet. 'I've been saving this one in case I ever got ravished by the most gorgeous girl in Special Class II.'

'Only in Special Class II?'

'I'm sorry. I meant the universe. Easy mistake to make.'

He found the zipper at the side of her short white skirt

and was just about to pull it down when he stopped, lifted his head, and listened.

'What's the matter?' asked Sara.

'I don't know . . . I thought I heard something.'

'The wind, probably. Or maybe the curtains. You left the door open, didn't you?'

Bobby kept on straining his ears. He could faintly hear the ocean, slapping against the pier, and the boats knocking, but he was sure that he could hear something else, too. A soft, complicated sound, like an insect. *Ker-chikk*. And then a long silence. And then *ker-chikk*.

'You can't hear that?' he asked Sara. 'It sounds like some kind of bug.'

Sara listened, gripping Bobby's hand. There was an even longer silence, but then it came again. *Ker-chikk*. And this time, inexplicably, it sounded much closer.

'It's the faucet dripping in the kitchen,' said Sara.

'I don't think so. I'm sure it's a bug.'

Sara grabbed hold of him and bounced up and down. 'What does it matter? If it's a bug it's only a bug, and if it's the faucet dripping, it's only the faucet dripping!'

Ker-chikk. This time it sounded as if it were right outside the bedroom door. Bobby grabbed Sara's wrists to stop her from bouncing, and said, 'Ssh!'

'Oh, come on,' she protested. 'It's nothing.'

'There's somebody in the living room.'

Sara immediately grabbed her T-shirt and covered her breasts. 'You're kidding, right?'

'I don't know for sure. Ssh!'

Almost half a minute went by. The ocean went slap, slap, slap. Then *ker-chikk*. The noise was quite distinct this time, more like precision machinery. It certainly wasn't a bug.

'*Hey!*' Bobby shouted out. 'This is private property and if you don't get out of here right now, I'm within my rights to shoot you!'

They waited. No response. Sara leaned close to Bobby

and murmured, 'I don't think there's anybody there. It's something blowing in the wind, that's all. But why don't you go take a look?'

'Yes,' said Bobby without moving.

'Well, go on then. Take a look. I bet you it's only a lamp-shade, or something like that.'

'Yes,' said Bobby. 'You're probably right.'

He was about to climb off the bed when they heard it again. *Ker-chikk*. And this time, abruptly, all the lights went out.

'Who's there?' Bobby shouted, and his voice sounded much more shrill than he had meant it to.

A moment's pause, then he shouted out again. 'Who's there? I'm warning you, I have a shotgun here. If you don't get the hell out of this house right now, I'll be shooting to kill.'

Again there was no response. The bedroom was seamlessly dark. Bobby squeezed Sara's hand and then said, 'I'm going to go for the light switch.'

'Don't!' said Sara, and now she sounded seriously frightened. 'Why don't you call nine-one-one?'

Bobby crawled awkwardly across the bed and located the nightstand. He groped around his father's bedside clock until he found the phone. He picked up the receiver but as he did so he heard *ker-chikk* and the line went dead.

'Phone's cut off,' he whispered.

'Don't you have a cellphone?'

'I left it in the kitchen. What about you?'

'In my purse. In the living room.'

'Shit.'

The bedroom was so black that Bobby was beginning to see dark crimson shapes swimming in front of his eyes. They looked like squid and jellyfish from the depths of the ocean, where the sun could never penetrate, and the pressure was so intense that a man would be flattened. He groped his way back to Sara and found her shoulder and her back.

'I still don't think there's anybody there,' Sara whispered. 'This is just a power outage, that's all.'

'If you don't think there's anybody there, why are you whispering?'

'In case it *isn't* a power outage, and there is.'

'This is crazy. I'm going to go for the light switch.'

'Bobby, be careful.'

Bobby felt his way off the edge of the bed, holding on to the brass rails to guide himself, and swinging his left arm from side to side to feel his way.

'Are you all right?' asked Sara. 'How can it be so dark? You'd think that there'd be *some* light, coming from the highway.'

'I'm almost at the door,' Bobby told her. 'I can feel the door frame. I can feel the light switch.'

He clicked the light switch up and down, but nothing happened. The beach house remained totally black, without even a chink of light from the shuttered windows. Normally, the sky was filled with sodium light from the Pacific Coast Highway, but not tonight.

'Maybe the circuit-breaker's gone.'

'But if there are no lights *anywhere*, it must be the power company.'

Ker-chikk. Now it was really close, only inches away from Bobby.

'I'm warning you!' he yelled. 'I have a shotgun here and I'm going to count to three and then I'm going to fire!'

'It's no good shouting at it if it's an insect,' said Sara.

'It's not an insect! I don't know what the hell it is! It's right here! It's right in front of me!

He waved his arms wildly from side to side but he couldn't feel anything. 'There's nothing here! There's nothing here! Oh *shit*, Sara, there's nothing here!'

'Stop it!' Sara screamed at him. 'Stop it, you're scaring me!'

Bobby took two or three steps backwards and collided

9

with the bed. He negotiated his way around the brass bed rails and climbed back on to it, reaching out for Sara's hand. He was panting with terror.

'If there's nothing there,' said Sara, 'there's nothing for us to be scared of.' She didn't sound at all convinced.

'There's something there, but it's *nothing*.'

'What do you mean, it's nothing?'

'I don't know. But it's there. I mean, we can *hear* it, right? Even if we can't feel it.'

They waited for over a minute. Normally, they would have expected their eyes to grow accustomed to the darkness, but even after all this time, they couldn't see anything at all. It was almost like being buried alive.

'What the hell's wrong with the power company?' Bobby complained. 'Why don't they put the lights back on?'

But then, very faintly, they saw a shimmering shape in the doorway. It shifted and rippled, as if they were viewing it through running water.

'What is that?' Sara whispered. 'It looks like a moth.'

Bobby stared at the shape intently. It had two white blotches on either side, which could have been wings. But as it gradually brightened, he realized that they weren't wings at all, but eye sockets. The shape was a human face, except that it looked like a photographic negative, with white hair and black skin and shadows in varying shades of white and gray.

'Oh my God,' said Sara. 'What is it? It's not a ghost, is it?'

'OK, whoever you are!' said Bobby in the most challenging tone he could manage. 'I can see you now, OK? And you have to get the hell out of here, because this property belongs to Mr and Mrs John D. Tubbs and you don't have any right to be here. So just go.'

There was silence, but then there was a soft *ker-chikk*, and the face was suddenly much closer. Because it was negative, it was impossible to tell it if was young or old.

But its white eyes were wide open and staring at them, and its black teeth were bared.

Sara was gripping Bobby's hand so tightly that her false fingernails were digging into him. 'What is it?' she gasped. 'Oh God, make it go away!'

But Bobby couldn't speak. The face brought back all of the nightmares that used to wake him up when he was younger. It was the face of everything terrible that hid during the day, but came out of concealment as soon as it grew dark. The things that hid at the end of the alleyway, inside the rusty old water tank. The strange faces that looked at him from passing buses; or disappearing round the corner; or reflected in storefront windows. You turned around, and they were gone; or else they had never been there. But they were frightening beyond all reason because they *knew* you, and they knew where to find you, and they knew what really scared you.

There was another *ker-chikk*, and the face jumped right up to the end of the bed. Bobby couldn't stop himself from jerking backwards, his heart thumping like a rabbit.

'*Go away!*' screamed Sara. '*Go away and leave us alone!*'

The face stayed where it was, staring at them. But then they heard a slurred, muffled voice, like somebody talking in another room.

'*Thought you could walk away, did you? Nobody walks away. Not without regretting it. Not without paying the price.*'

'What are you talking about?' Bobby demanded. 'We don't even know you!'

'*Oh, you know me better than you think. And now you're going to suffer for it.*'

'What do you want? Just tell me what you want. You want money? My parents have money. Just take what you want and get out of here, please.'

'*You know what I want. I want to see you pay the price.*'

'Price? What price? What are we supposed to have done?'

11

'*The price of disloyalty, my friends. The price of contempt.*'

There was something in the voice that Bobby recognized. He peered at the face more intently, and then he sat back on his heels. 'This is a trick, isn't it? This is a goddamn practical joke.'

'What?' said Sara.

'They've fooled us.' He waved his hand in front of the face, and it didn't even blink. 'This is some kind of projection. I'll bet Dudley set it up. They're watching us now and they're probably wetting themselves. "The price of contempt," my ass.'

'Are you serious? This is just a joke?'

'Of course it is. Look at it.'

'But how did they know we were going to get together tonight? How did they know we were going to come here? How have they managed to make it so *dark*?'

'I don't know. But I'm sure going to find out when I sit on Dudley's head.'

'*You think this is a trick?*' asked the negative face.

'Yes, as a matter of fact. For the simple reason that I don't believe in ghosts or demons or . . . or faces that hover at the end of the bed. Are you getting this, Dudley? I'm going to have your guts for a golf bag, I warn you.'

'*You think this is a joke?*' the face persisted.

'Yes, I do.'

'*Then smile.*'

Bobby was just about to say something when the entire world went white. The bedroom was blotted out with intense, dazzling light, as if a hydrogen bomb had gone off. He felt a shock wave of unbearable heat that scorched him all over, and as he tried to twist himself away from it, the last thing he saw was Sara with her hair on fire and her face charred black.

Two

Jim walked into Special Class II without even looking at the fifteen students who were there, sitting with their feet on their desks, tossing paper darts, listening to garage music on their earphones, phone-texting their friends in other classrooms, reading *X-Men* comics, fixing their lip gloss, and practicing their dance steps.

He sat down at his desk and laid both hands on it, palm-down, like a lounge-bar pianist who doesn't think he can face playing 'Strangers in the Night', not again. He looked tired and gaunt, and he had two days' growth of stubble on his chin. His mousy hair was messed up as if he hadn't bothered to comb it, and his blue check shirt was crumpled as if he hadn't bothered to press it. His tan corduroy pants had a stain on the left leg that could have been anything from tomato catsup to cat food.

He opened his briefcase by untying the string that held the broken catch together. He took out a dog-eared book, opened it and started to read it in silence. One after another, the students became aware of his presence, and even though they didn't all stop what they were doing, they turned their eyes on to him, and spoke more quietly, and gradually the dance steps petered out.

It was ten minutes before he said anything. 'Today,' he finally said, taking off his thumb-printed glasses, 'we're going to talk about *time*. What time is, and what time does to us, and how we express our feelings about it.'

'About time,' said Freddy Price, and everybody laughed.

'Well, I'm sorry if I'm two weeks late,' said Jim. 'I hope that Mrs Lakenheath kept you entertained. I wasn't really expecting to come back here at all, as a matter of fact. But that's time for you. You stroll off into the future, whistling to yourself, and before you know it, you're right back where you started from.'

Sonny Powell raised a long black arm. 'Pardon my saying so, sir, but it don't seem to me like you is exactly over-joyed to be back.' Sonny was 6ft 7in tall and everybody called him the Shadow because of his obsession with his Saucony Shadow running shoes, and because he overshadowed everybody else in the class. 'Like, if you don't feel like learning us or nothing, we don't mind just carrying on doing what we're doing. Let sleeping dogs sleep, if you know what I mean.' He bounced his basketball three or four times just to make the point.

Jim stood up and walked to the classroom window. 'Tempting, I have to admit. But the trouble with *that* idea is, I came back here to West Grove Community College because I need to find out something about myself. *I* need educating, even more urgently than you do. Now, none of *you* may be interested in learning anything, and quite frankly I don't care if you don't. If you want to stay ignorant and illiterate, that's entirely your choice. But *I* need to learn something, and I'm sorry if it's an inconvenience, but I need your help to do it.

He turned around to face them. 'This class may be called Remedial English, but it isn't going to be all about spelling, or reading, or writing. This class is going to be all about living in a world that doesn't give anybody an even break; and what to do when your luck runs out – if you had any luck to begin with – and all of the tricks and traps and petty cruelties that make you wonder if it's worth getting out of bed in the morning.

He had his students' attention now. Even Vanilla King had stopped in mid-nail-polishing, her brushful of Tangerine Sparkle poised in the air.

Jim said, 'This class is going to be all about survival.

14

How to stay alive and well on a highly dangerous planet.'

'What, you going to be learnin' us road safety and like that?' asked Roosevelt Jones, from the back of the class. Roosevelt was short and stocky, with a shiny shaved head and mirror sunglasses.

Jim shook his head. 'I'm not going to be telling *you* anything. You're going to be telling *me*. If you must know, I've forgotten how to keep going. I've lost my faith that everything's going to turn out for the better. I don't believe that it's going to be another bright sunshiny day.'

'We can't learn you nothing, man,' said Shadow. 'You the Teach. *You* suppose to be learning *us*.'

Edward Truscott put up his hand. 'Actually, you don't "learn" somebody something. You teach them. Otherwise, think about it, you wouldn't call him the Teach. You'd call him the Learn.'

'Are you messing with my head again, geek?' Shadow demanded, with exaggerated anger. 'If education turns a person into *you*, you pasty white string of spaghetti, then I don't want none of it.'

Jim said, 'Like I said – if you don't want to be educated, that's your concern entirely. But you're wrong when you say that you don't have anything to teach me. You do. You're young, you're fresh, you're unsullied. You still have confidence in who you are, and what tomorrow's going to bring you, and that's what I want to learn.'

'You was here before, sir, wasn't you?' asked Ruby Montes. She had a mountain of black wavy hair and earrings like Christmas trees.

'Yes, I was. Three years ago. But I was offered a very interesting job in Washington with the department of education, and I went.'

'So why'd you come back?' asked Roosevelt. 'Wasn't the pay no good?'

'The pay was fine. The job was fine. Something happened, that's all.'

'Like what? You was caught in the stationery closet with some foxy teacher?'

Jim gave him a weary smile. 'Let's put it this way . . . Something bad happened. Something tragic. Something that made me realize that you can run away from everything in this life, except yourself.'

'That's very true,' said George Graves. He had very badly chopped hair and a long, horse-like face. 'No matter where you wake up in the morning . . . well, you're always there, aren't you?'

'Where else would you be, fool?' asked Shadow.

Freddy Price said, 'I don't know. I woke up the morning after my New Year's party and I *definitely* wasn't there.'

Nervously, hesitantly, Sue-Marie Cassidy put up her hand. She had long, straight, gleaming blonde hair, and a face that could have been classically beautiful if she hadn't applied so much eye make-up and so much lipstick, and her mouth hadn't pouted so much. For her last birthday, her mother had paid for collagen injections for her lips. Now she looked more *Baywatch* than Botticelli.

'What was it exactly that happened to you in Washington?' she asked in a husky voice. 'I mean, you say it was tragic.'

Jim said, 'It was, yes. But it was something I'd rather not talk about, just at the moment. I want to move on . . . so I'm going to make believe that I never went to Washington. In fact, I'm going to make believe that I'm still thirty-four years old and that I never left West Grove at all.'

'Shouldn't you, like, face up to it, whatever it was?' asked Delilah Bergenstein. Her real name wasn't Delilah but she had dark, cat-like eyes and a beauty spot on her cheek and she liked to think she looked like an Old Testament seductress.

'Are you interested in psychiatry?' asked Jim.

Delilah nodded with enthusiasm. 'That's what I eventually want to be, a psychiatrist. But – you know – my English needs a little work.'

16

'Yeah – like you can't spell psychiatrist,' put in Randy Bullock, who sat right in front of her.

'I'll bet money that *you* can't spell it, either,' said Edward Truscott scornfully.

'Like, I don't need to, genius. I'm going into fast food, me.'

'Looks like the fast food went into *you*, fatso.'

Jim returned to his desk. 'OK, that's enough free association. If you're going to teach me anything, we're going to need some structure. Some starting points for discussion. Let's start by defining time.'

Special Class II looked at each other in bewilderment. George Graves noisily blew his nose on a crumpled-up scrap of toilet tissue and Ruby Montes flapped her hand at him in disgust. 'I just had breakfast. I really want to hear your snot bubble, you know?'

'OK,' said Jim. 'What do we mean by time? Can anybody tell me what it is?'

Roosevelt leaned back in his chair and said, 'Time is like what allows you to stop doing something, say like eating pizza, and do something else, say like crashing out in front of the TV. I mean, if it wasn't for time, you'd be eating pizza over and over, because it was never time to do nothing else, and you'd be sick to your stomach of eating pizza. You'd also start looking like Randy over there, you know, like three people rolled into one.'

'Hey,' Randy protested. 'Just because you look like a famine appeal.'

David Robinson stood up, right at the back of the class. As he did so, the sun lit up his bright red crewcut and his scarlet ears. He said, 'Time is the difference between human beings and God.' Then he hesitated and looked around. The rest of the class were all noisily pretending to yawn.

'Go on,' Jim encouraged him.

'Well, *we* grow old, don't we? but God never does. That's why God knows so much more than we do. We spend our whole lives learning stuff, but when we die, everything we ever learned, it's all forgotten.'

'That's totally right,' Shadow interrupted, with a mock serious frown. 'Like, what is the point of going to all that stress of filling up your head with how to spell psychiatry and what the capital of Paris is, when you're only going to end up dead, and what good is all that information then? They don't have no spelling bees in the boneyard.'

Jim opened the dog-eared book on his desk. 'I'm going to read you a poem,' he said. 'It's all about time, and fate, and I want you to think about it and tell me if it affects your view of things. It's called "The Clock and the Cake" by James McFadden.

> At five the clock strikes five
> And, just as yesterday, the cake is cut
> And handed round amid the conversation and the smiles
> The cake is like the clock and each slice disappears
> Like time, and life, and all the passing miles'

Vanilla King started polishing the nails on her right hand, her tongue stuck between her teeth in concentration. Randy Bullock twisted his finger in his left ear and then examined it. There was a lot of coughing and shuffling and somebody at the back was having an intense, whispered conversation, but Jim carried on.

> 'At ten the clock was speechless
> Not yet wound up, and waiting for its key
> The showers had passed and sunlit glistened on the path.
> The clock was like a friend who chose to wait
> While we caught up, and we caught up at last.
>
> 'At four the clock struck slowly
> Its spring so slackened it could barely chime
> I woke, and heard it like a warning from the years to pass

18

"Your bed will soon lie empty and your bones
Will soon be lying sleeping in the grass."

'At two the clock struck two
Just as the christened child began to cry.
And cake was cut, and passed around to family and friends
The cake is like the clock, and each slice disappears
Until our plate is empty, and it ends.'

He closed the book and looked around. 'Was anybody listening to that?'

'*I* was listening to it,' said Edward.

'You was *listening* to it, geek,' Shadow challenged him. 'But did you *hear* it?'

'How about you?' Jim asked him. 'Were *you* listening?'

Shadow was taken aback. 'I wasn't listening *specifically*. Not to every single individual word. But I was digging it.'

'OK, if you were digging it, what do you think it meant?'

Shadow sniffed, and shrugged. 'I wasn't digging it *that* much.'

Jim slowly walked the length of the classroom. When he came to Sally Broxman's desk, he picked up a velvety doll of SpongeBob SquarePants and turned it this way and that. SpongeBob SquarePants was the hero of a Nickelodeon cartoon about creatures who lived under the sea. 'You like SpongeBob SquarePants?' Jim asked her.

Sally blushed and looked embarrassed. She was very fair, and plump, with wild bunches of hay-colored hair. 'He's kind of my mascot.'

'"Absorbent and yellow and porous is he,"' Jim quoted, from the SpongeBob SquarePants theme song. He held up the doll so that everybody in the class could see it. 'See this guy? Absorbent. How about you following his example? *Absorb* things. Absorb everything. Just because you think you don't like something – just because you think it's boring, or you can't understand it, or you don't *want* to understand it – that doesn't mean it isn't going to give you the key to getting the most out of your life.'

He walked back to his desk. 'That poem that I read you is all about time, and what time means to you. And I mean you personally. You were all born, but even when you were lying in your cribs, you were already lying in your coffins. You are all going to die. You are, and *you*, and *you* are, too. You can't place any bets against it, because it's going to happen to you, each and every one of you – and me, too. In a hundred years' time this classroom may still be here, but we'll be gone, and forgotten, all of us, and whoever walks in here, no matter how hard they listen, they won't be able to hear us.'

Every student in Special Class II was silent now, and staring at Jim with their mouths open. 'Was this *news* to you?' Jim demanded. 'Did you actually believe that you were going to live forever?'

'Shit,' said Freddy Price. 'I woke up this morning feeling on top of the world. Now I feel like hanging myself.'

On his way to the faculty room, Jim was stopped by Sue-Marie. 'I just wanted to say welcome back, sir,' she said, showing him a mouthful of perfect white teeth.

'That's very nice of you. Rosemary, isn't it?'

'Sue-Marie.'

'I'm sorry. Give me a couple of days and I'll have all of your names off pat.'

'What you said in class today . . . it really made me think. You know, about life, and death, and stuff like that.'

'I hope you didn't find it depressing.'

Sue-Marie shook her fine blonde hair. 'Oh, no. It was like *karmic*, you know? I felt like you really understand me.'

'Well, I'm pleased about that. At least I understand *some-body*.'

Sue-Marie looked into his eyes and slowly blinked, and

her eyelashes were like two black hawkmoths settling on her cheeks. 'You're still feeling pain, sir, aren't you?'

'I'm sorry, Sue-Marie. Like I said in class, that's something I'm not ready to discuss, right at this moment.'

'If there's anything I can ever do to help . . . If you just need somebody to listen . . .'

'Sure,' said Jim. 'That's very . . . considerate of you.'

He watched Sue-Marie walk off along the corridor to join her friends, wiggling her bottom in her little blue pleated skirt. She looked back once and smiled at him coquettishly. He smiled back at her in what he hoped was a mature, trustworthy way, as if she could sit on his knee and blow in his ear and still be confident that he wouldn't compromise the teacher–student relationship. Actually, he wasn't at all interested in flirtatious students, not at the moment. He was more concerned about putting together the bits and pieces of his disassembled life, and finding himself someplace to live.

He pushed open the door to the faculty room. It was crowded with beaten-up armchairs and sagging couches and teachers that he didn't know. His old favorite armchair by the window was occupied by a large black lady in a print frock covered with African zigzags. She was talking to Hector Lo, the deputy head of business studies, and jabbing her finger into the armrest with every point she made.

'We have to make it clear to *all* of our students – white, black, Asian, lesbian or gay – that they have a *right* to be rich!'

Hector Lo was nodding in the calm, appreciative way he always nodded. Jim knew from experience that he wasn't even listening.

He was making his way toward a chair in the opposite corner when a voice called out: 'Jim! Hey, Jim! You finally made it!' He turned around and it was Vinnie Boschetto, from the history department. Vinnie looked more like an extra from *Miami Vice* than a teacher of nineteenth-century politics. He had black, fashionably gelled-up hair, a deeply tanned face with a bulbous nose, and he was wearing one of his trademark Hawaiian shirts, all orchids and humming-birds and pineapples.

He threw his arms around Jim and clapped him on the back. He smelled strongly of Armani aftershave. 'When you didn't show up last week, we thought you'd chickened out. Wouldn't have blamed you, not one bit! This place hasn't changed. It's still the blind leading the dumb, closely followed by the very stupid.'

'Good to see you, Vinnie. How's Mitzi?'

Vinnie gave a theatrical cough into his fist. 'Ah-hem! Mitzi was three partners ago, I'm ashamed to admit. Or was it four? Lovely girl, Mitzi. *Great* girl. Unparalleled legs. Well, they *were* parallel, but there were no legs like them. But you know how it is. We didn't see eye to eye on matters pertaining to the U.S. Constitution. Such as my constitutional freedom to play poker with the boys every Friday night.'

'So who is it now?'

'Alana. She's gorgeous. We'll have to go out together, you and me and Alana. I've found this really terrific Namibian restaurant on Pico. You don't have any qualms about eating ants, do you?'

'Ants? What do you think I am – an aardvark?'

'Oh, come on. I'm not talking about those teensy-weensy little guys you find swarming out of the cracks in the side-walk. I'm talking about big fat ones, specially fed on sugar. They're terrific with a chili dip. They just go *pop* in your mouth. Delicious!'

'I think I'll stick to burritos, if it's all the same to you.' Jim sat down, opened up his cellphone and took out a crumpled piece of paper. 'Right now I'm trying to find myself an apartment. All my books are in storage and my cat has probably forgotten who I am.'

'You want someplace to live? Search no further! My

uncle passed away last month and his apartment is standing empty. I've been planning on letting it out, but I haven't had the time to get it organized. Alana, you know . . . she's kind of demanding. What am I saying, *kind of* demanding? Ha! She won't give me a moment's peace! You'll love this apartment! It's fully furnished; all it needs is cleaning and airing and maybe a lick of paint.'

'Where is it?' asked Jim dubiously.

'Venice, only a couple of blocks from where you used to live before. The Benandanti Building. It's great. You'll love it. Four bedrooms, a hu-u-uge living room, a dining room, a kitchen and a bathroom like Emperor Nero's.'

'Sorry, Vinnie. A place like that has to be way out of my price range. I can only afford eight hundred dollars a month, at most.'

'Don't be stupid! You can have it for seven fifty! So long as you pay me in cash, no paperwork, no questions asked, and you keep the joint in good repair. At least I'll have a tenant that I can trust.'

'Seven fifty?' Jim closed his cellphone. 'Do you think I could take a look at it?'

'Sure thing. How about tomorrow at twelve?'

'Absolutely.'

Jim was about to ask him about all the changes that had taken place at West Grove College in the past three years. But then the door of the faculty room opened and Mrs Frogg, the principal's secretary, peered in. She caught sight of Jim and beckoned, furtively, as if she didn't want anybody else to see her. 'Excuse me a minute,' he told Vinnie. 'Medusa calls.'

They called Mrs Frogg Medusa because of her gray, snake-like hair and her pale-green bulging eyes. Vinnie reckoned that all of the white marble figures that supported the front of West Grove Community College were former members of staff who had dared to talk back to Mrs Frogg, and whom she had instantly turned to stone.

'Something I can help you with?' Jim asked her.

'Dr Ehrlichman wishes you to come to his office, Mr Rook. There is a police detective who would like to have words with you.'

'A police detective? What about?'

'Not for me to say, Mr Rook.'

Jim turned and gave a brief wave to Vinnie, tapping his wristwatch to indicate that he was definitely going to keep their appointment tomorrow. Mrs Frogg wordlessly led the way along the corridor, her rubber-soled shoes squelching. She made Jim feel as if he were thirteen years old again, summoned to the principal's office for blocking up the water fountains with blotting paper.

Mrs Frogg knocked and an irritable voice called out, 'Yes, yes! Come on in!' When Jim went in, Dr Ehrlichman was sitting at his desk in his shirtsleeves, his bright-green necktie askew, looking troubled. He was small and bald. He wore old-fashioned, heavy-rimmed spectacles, and he had a large, hooked nose and a little bristly moustache. He looked as if he had bought spectacles, nose and moustache, all joined together, from a magic store. But it was the man standing by the window with his back turned who immediately caught Jim's attention. He was almost square – with shoulders so broad that they had strained the stitching of his crumpled tan coat – and short, stocky legs. He had a wiry tangle of sandy-colored hair and dandruff on his collar.

'Well, well,' said Jim. 'Lieutenant Harris. I thought I read in the paper that you retired.'

Lieutenant Harris turned around. Although Dr Ehrlichman's office was air-conditioned, his face was crimson and he was sweating. 'I decided to stay on for another three years. If you knew my wife, you'd understand why. How about you, Mr Rook? I thought you'd gone for good.'

'I went to Washington, yes, but things didn't really work out.'

'Sorry to hear that. I can't truthfully say that I'm delighted to see you back.'

'Thanks. Good to see you again, too.'

Lieutenant Harris managed a sweaty smile. 'Nothing personal, Mr Rook. It's just that whenever you're around ... it seems like spooky things start to happen.'

'Spooky things happen all the time, Lieutenant. *Life* is generally spooky. Maybe you're more aware of life's general spookiness when I'm around, because you think *I'm* spooky.' He paused, and when Lieutenant Harris didn't answer, he said, 'What's the problem this time?'

Lieutenant Harris took out his notebook, licked his finger and turned over two pages. 'Two students of yours – Robert Tubbs and Sara Miller ...'

'I'm sorry – this is my first day today. I haven't had the chance to get to know any of my students yet, not by name.'

'These two, you never will. At nine thirty this morning they were both found dead.'

'Oh, God. I'm sorry. How did it happen?'

'Very spookily, which is why I wanted to talk to you.'

'Why me? I never even met them.'

'I know. But I think you might be able to help us.'

Jim held up his hand. 'Listen ... before you continue, I don't get involved with any of that stuff any more. I came back to West Grove to lead a normal, boring, underpaid, ordinary life. I'm very sad to hear that two young people have died, but as far as I'm concerned it's your problem. Not mine.'

Lieutenant Harris took a stick of chewing gum out of the breast-pocket of his coat, unwrapped it, and thoughtfully folded it into his mouth. With his eyes lowered, he fashioned the silver foil into a tiny model airplane.

'The *Spirit of St Louis*,' he said, holding it up. 'I can make the *Enola Gay*, too, but that takes at least four wrappers.'

'How did they die?' Jim asked him.

'I thought you weren't interested.'

'Of course I'm interested. It's just that I don't want to find myself all tangled up in anything weird. Especially anything *dangerous* and weird.'

Lieutenant Harris cleared his throat. 'Robert and Sara were found in a beach property at Santa Monica that belonged to Robert Tubbs' parents. Mr and Mrs Tubbs had no idea that they were there, and Robert wasn't allowed to use the property without their specific consent. They weren't even aware that he had a key. The Tubbs' maid found them. She was supposed to clean the place up for a dinner party they were holding this weekend. She smelled something as soon as she opened the door. When she went into the bedroom she found their bodies, burned.'

'Terrible,' said Dr Ehrlichman. 'Absolutely terrible. Their parents are devastated.'

'Was it an accident?' asked Jim. 'Were they – what? – smoking in bed or something?'

Lieutenant Harris shook his head.

'So what was it? Murder?' Jim paused and frowned. 'Don't tell me they set fire to themselves deliberately.'

'No, no, it doesn't look like a suicide pact. There was no accelerant on the premises, anyhow – nothing they could have used to burn themselves with. It's kind of hard for me to explain it to you.'

'I'm not so sure that I want you to.'

'Look, I can totally appreciate why you don't want to get involved, Mr Rook – and if you insist that you don't want to help, then I'll have to accept your decision, won't I? But there are certain aspects of this case that even the Crime Scenes Unit can't make head nor tail of, and neither can I.'

'And what makes you think that I'll be able to? I'm not a detective.'

'I know you're not. But you're au fait with all of this supernatural stuff, aren't you?'

Jim took off his glasses and rubbed his eyes. 'Lieutenant, when I was ten or eleven years old I suffered from pneumonia and I nearly died. Ever since then, I've had a heightened sensitivity to what you might call *presences* – spirits, or souls, or whatever you want to call them. I can see things that other people can't see – or don't notice, to be more accurate. But that's the whole story, and it doesn't make me the world's expert on everything bizarre. I'm sure you'll find that there's a perfectly logical explanation for the way these two young people got themselves burned, even if it isn't immediately obvious.'

'You haven't seen the crime scene.'

'I don't want to, either.'

'Well,' said Lieutenant Harris, 'it's your decision. But I can't see any logical explanation for what happened to Robert Tubbs and Sara Miller – none whatsoever – and I'll bet you a double enchilada at Tacos Tacos that you can't, either.'

Three

Jim followed Lieutenant Harris down the ramp that led to the beach, and parked his aging gold Lincoln Continental on the sand. It was a warm, windy afternoon, and the seagulls hung suspended in the air as if they had been captured in a still photograph. There were already four squad cars parked outside the beach house, as well as an ambulance from the coroner's department, two sport-utility vehicles from the Crime Scenes Unit, and satellite-transmission vans from three different TV news stations.

As Jim and Lieutenant Harris walked toward the beach house, a crowd of reporters and cameramen came hurrying toward them over the sand.

'Lieutenant! Can you give us any more details about the way these kids died? The ME says they were seriously burned. How seriously is seriously? Do you know if the fire was deliberate? Was it arson, or was it a horrible accident?'

Lieutenant Harris stopped and raised both hands. 'I'm sorry, people. Right now, I can't give you any more information over and above what the coroner and the fire department investigators have already told you. As soon as I know anything more, believe me, you'll know it, too.'

'Who's *this*, lieutenant?' asked Nancy Broward from CBS News, pointing at Jim.

'Mr Jim Rook from West Grove Community College. He's agreed to assist us with our investigation. Mr Rook is Bobby and Sara's class teacher ... or he would have been, had they survived.'

'How are you spelling that? Rook as in bird?'

'Rook as in chess castle,' Jim corrected her.

'In what way exactly are you going to be helping the police?' asked Nancy Broward.

Lieutenant Harris looked uncomfortable. 'Mr Rook has some specialized abilities which may enable us to determine exactly what happened here.'

'Specialized abilities? Of what nature?'

'I can't tell you any more than that,' said Lieutenant Harris. 'Now, if you'll excuse us—'

But Jim interrupted him. 'I've been teaching young people for nearly nine years. Teaching means giving them guidance, as well as facts. There may be some evidence here to tell us if Bobby and Sara had any particular problems. Like drugs, maybe. Or a falling-out with their parents. You know, one of those Romeo and Juliet-type situations.'

'So you think it could have been a teenage suicide pact?'

'I don't think anything yet. I haven't seen them.'

'OK,' said Lieutenant Harris, taking hold of his arm. 'That's enough for now. You've already given them a goddamned headline.'

He led Jim up the wooden stairs to the living room. A uniformed officer was keeping guard on the door, and the beach house was jostling with crime scene specialists and photographers and fingerprint experts, as well as fire officers and people who seemed to have nothing better to do than shout into their cellphones.

'It's never like this on TV,' said Jim as a broad-shouldered blonde woman with a digital camera pushed her way past him, and he was unapologetically elbowed by a young black man in a Tyvek suit.

'That's because the TV production people are always trying to economize on extras. This particular crowd scene, on the other hand, is paid for out of your taxes.'

Jim looked around him at the nautical decor – the ropes

and the anchors and the paintings of four-masted clippers. 'Jesus. Who lives in a house like this? Long John Silver?'

Lieutenant Harris led the way through to the bedroom. Jim had been preparing himself to see two burned bodies, and he knew from experience that it was going to be horrifying. He had seen a burned-out Winnebago once, on the San Diego Freeway, with dad and mom still sitting in their seats. The seats had been reduced to their springs, while dad and mom looked like charred stick people. What was worse, the heat had left them grinning, as if they were still having fun.

Here, however, he couldn't understand what he was looking at, not at first. The bedroom walls and ceiling were covered all over in a fine film of waxy yellow soot. The carpet was black and crunchy when he walked on it. The bed itself was nothing but smoking layers of incinerated fabric, like a huge burned cake, and it stank of wool and latex and shriveled-up nylon.

As he approached the bed, Jim saw a tangle of bones lying on it. They were scorched, like barbecued ribs, and they were so mixed up together that it would have been impossible at first glance to tell that they were the remains of two separate people – except that there were two skulls, with their foreheads poignantly touching, staring into each other's empty eye sockets.

All around the scattered bones lay heaps of damp gray ashes. A criminalist was scooping up samples with a spoon and dropping them into clear plastic bags.

'Harris!' A big man with a big Roman nose and silver Roman-emperor curls came barging around the bed to greet them. He was wearing baggy blue coveralls with FORENSICS printed across the back.

'How's it going, Jack?' Lieutenant Harris asked him. 'Jack, this is Jim Rook. Mr Rook, this is Jack Billings, head of the crime scene unit.'

Jack Billings nodded to Jim and wiped his sweaty forehead with the back of his glove. 'They were cremated,' he said in a thick, harsh voice, as if he had a cold. 'In fact, they were more than cremated. Your average crematorium oven burns at two thousand five hundred degrees Fahrenheit for more than four hours to reduce a human body to this condition. I would say that the temperature in this bedroom reached well over five times that, even though it happened over a very short space of time. Possibly in seconds.'

'How the hell did that happen?' asked Lieutenant Harris.

'I was hoping that you were going to tell me. As I told you before, there's no evidence of arson . . . no indication that any kind of accelerant was involved, such as gasoline or kerosene or turpentine. No spent matches, no cigarette lighter. It couldn't have been a gas explosion, since the house isn't fitted for natural gas or butane. An arc welding torch can reach twenty thousand degrees Celsius, but the burning would have been concentrated in a very small area – unlike here, where we have soot spread evenly all over the walls, and the carpet evenly charred all over, and the same with the bed.'

'A bomb?' suggested Lieutenant Harris.

Jack Billings shook his head. 'There was plenty of heat, but there was absolutely no explosive force. Look at these remains, these ashes, they're just lying here in a pile. Any bomb that was capable of generating this much heat would have blasted them over a five-mile radius. We would have been picking up selected bits of them in Anaheim.'

'Lightning?'

'That's an outside possibility. But it doesn't seem very likely that lightning could have incinerated two people who were lying on a well-insulated bed. Apart from that, there were no electric storms reported along the coast last night.'

'So that's it? You don't have any other ideas?'

'Not so far. But you know me. I'm not defeated yet, not by a long chalk. Oh, but there's this to consider.'

'What's that?' asked Lieutenant Harris.

Jack Billings beckoned them through to the dressing room. There were white louvred closets on the left-hand wall, which backed on to the bedroom, and a built-in dressing table on the right, with bottles of perfume and hand lotion on it. The end wall was mirrored from floor to ceiling, so that their reflections entered the room at the same time as they did. Jim thought he looked crumpled and washed-out. He needed a break. He needed the love of a good woman and three weeks on Oahu.

'OK,' said Lieutenant Harris. 'What's to see in here?'

Without a word, Jack Billings opened the closet doors. 'We only found this because we were trying to see if any of the power cables had shorted out.' All of the clothes that had been hanging on the rail had been pushed right over to one side, so that the back wall of the closet was exposed.

'My God,' said Jim. He moved closer to the wall and took off his glasses. Lieutenant Harris came and stood close behind him, shaking his head in disbelief.

Printed directly on to the paint was a life-size black-and-white image of Bobby and Sara. They were lying side by side on the bed, both of them half-naked. Sara had her right arm raised as if she were trying to protect her face, and her hair was on fire, so that a shower of tiny sparks was spraying out of the top of her head. Bobby had his eyes squeezed shut and his teeth clenched. It was difficult to tell, but it looked as if his ears were already burned off.

'This is like a photograph,' said Jim with undisguised wonder. 'It *is* a photograph.'

Jack Billings coughed and nodded. 'I'd say that this is an exact image of the moment that Bobby Tubbs and Sara Miller were killed.'

'What's this wall made of?' asked Lieutenant Harris, knocking it with his knuckle.

'Seasoned pine – two-and-a half inches thick, painted with regular white emulsion. We've taken samples, but it doesn't appear to have been treated with any kind of photo-sensitive chemicals.'

Jim stepped back. 'This is exactly what you would have seen if you had been standing at the foot of the bed when Bobby and Sara were killed. It's like somebody took a photograph the instant it happened, and then brought it in here, and printed it on to the wall.'

'But *who*?' asked Lieutenant Harris.

Jack Billings shrugged. 'I don't personally know of any photographic technique that could have been used to produce an image like this. But here it is in front of our eyes, so there must be *some* way of doing it, and that's what we have to find out. If you ask me, Lieutenant, once we know how, it won't take us long to discover who, or why. This is highly advanced, highly specialized stuff . . . There can't be more than a handful of people who have the technology to produce this kind of imaging.'

Jim couldn't take his eyes off the picture of Bobby and Sara. They didn't have the terrified expressions of people who suddenly realize they're just about to die. They were simply reacting to a devastating blast of light and heat – eyes shut tight, face muscles clenched, hands protectively lifted. When this picture was taken, it was already a split-second too late to save them.

He went back into the bedroom. The acrid reek of burned bedding made his sinuses run. He discovered a paper napkin from Roy's Rib Shack in his pocket, and wiped his nose. The napkin smelled strongly of barbecue sauce.

'Sense anything?' asked Lieutenant Harris hopefully.

Jim shook his head.

'No spiritual vibes or nothing? No ghostly echoes? No auras?'

'No, nothing like that.'

'You ever hear of anything like this before? People getting cremated while they're lying in bed.'

'I've heard about spontaneous human combustion – people catching fire for no apparent reason and burning to ashes. Scientists call it SHC or "ultra-rapid holocaust."'

'Do you think something like that might have happened here?'

'I don't know,' said Jim. 'It's quite a famous phenomenon. Even Charles Dickens wrote about it. There's a character in *Bleak House*, a rag-and-bone dealer called Krook, who gets burned to a pile of ashes while he's sitting in his chair by the fire. But I don't think there's a whole lot of serious research to back it up.'

'What about that picture on the closet wall?' said Lieutenant Harris. 'Damned if I know what to make of that.'

'Damned if I know, either. Sorry.'

'Well, if you think of anything at all – if you get any hunches, or funny feelings – you know how to get in touch with me. Just don't talk about any of this to the media, *please*. Especially that picture. I don't want to get the lunatic fringe excited. You know the ones I mean – those people who see images of the Virgin Mary reflected in the windows of Toys R Us.'

'You got it,' Jim agreed. 'But you'll keep me up to speed, won't you? If any new evidence comes up . . . well, it might help me to get a handle on how those poor kids were killed.'

He walked back across the beach and climbed into his Lincoln. The reporters and the cameramen immediately surrounded him, pushing microphones close to his face.

'Did you see the bodies, Jim? How do you think they died? Will you be talking to Bobby's and Sara's parents? How are their classmates taking it? Pretty badly, I'll bet.'

Jim started the engine, jammed his foot down on the gas, and immediately the Lincoln's rear wheels buried themselves in the sand. He tried revving the car forward, and then back, and then forward again, but the wheels spun deeper and deeper. In the end he had to turn around to the reporters and cameramen and give them a look of utter defeat.

'OK, OK. I give in. If you people help to push me out of this sand, I'll give you a quote.'

'Oh, yeah? How do we know we can trust you?' challenged Roger Frick from CNN. 'We might push you out of the sand, and then you might just drive off.'

'I'm a college teacher. If you can't trust a college teacher, who can you trust?'

Six or seven reporters gathered around the front of his car, as well as two cops. They all leaned forward, and when Jim shouted, 'Push!', they pushed. He revved the engine, spraying everybody with twin fountains of sand, but suddenly the Lincoln surged backward and bounced up on to the concrete ramp.

'Thanks!' said Jim. 'Thanks, you're terrific! Thank you!'

Nancy Broward came up to him and held out her microphone. 'OK, Jim. How about that quote?'

'Of course. Never let it be said that I didn't keep my side of the bargain.' He waited until all of the reporters were gathered around him, and then he said, '"Men talk of killing time, while time quietly kills them." Dion Boucicault, 1820 to 1890.'

'Huh?' said Roger Frick.

'I promised you a quote . . . that's a quote.' With that, Jim backed the Lincoln up the ramp, slewed it around, and drove back on to the Pacific Coast Highway.

He walked into Special Class II five minutes late for their last session of the day, which was supposed to be creative writing. All of them were busy, although not one of them had a book open. Shadow was bouncing his basketball from the bridge of his nose to the top of his head and back again, while Brenda Malone was hunched in front of a magnifying mirror, squeezing out her blackheads, and Randy Bullock was eating his way through the largest submarine sandwich that Jim had ever seen. Jim almost expected to see cows' legs hanging out of the side of it.

The classroom was filled with the *chikkity-chikkity* sound of dance music, coming from half a dozen headsets. It sounded like a cornfield full of crickets.

Jim dropped his books on to his desk and then stepped forward to the front of the class. 'Everyone – I need your attention, please.'

Shadow went on bouncing his ball and Randy Bullock went on chewing and Ruby Montes went on swaying and miming the salsa music she was listening to.

Jim waited for a while with his head lowered. Edward Truscott was giving him a dutiful frown, but George Graves had his back turned, and Vanilla King had almost disappeared inside her huge woven bag, rummaging for something critically important, like a lost eyebrow pencil probably.

After almost half a minute, Jim went up to the chalkboard. In large, clear letters he wrote BOBBY TUBBS AND SARA MILLER ARE DEAD.

The class fell silent almost immediately. CD players were switched off. Shadow scooped up his ball and gripped it between his knees. Jim turned back to face the class, dusting his hands. 'The power of the written word,' he told them. '"Thoughts that breathe, and words that burn."'

'Is it true?' asked Pinky Perdido in her squeaky little voice. 'Bobby and Sara – they're dead?'

Jim nodded. 'They died together sometime last night at the beach house belonging to Bobby's parents. I'm very sorry. I never had the chance to get to know them, but Dr Ehrlichman tells me that they were very well liked, both of them.'

'What happened?' asked Freddy Price, and it was obvious that he was worried. 'They didn't OD or nothing, did they?'

'So far as we can tell, their deaths were not directly caused by drugs or alcohol. There was a very fierce fire. The police don't yet know how it started, but they didn't stand a chance. They were probably overcome by fumes before the flames got to them.'

'Oh, man,' said Philip Genio. He was thin and Latin-looking, with a high shiny pompadour and a pale-pink silk shirt. 'I was messing around with Bobby only last night.'

'Sara was my best friend,' wept Sue-Marie, with mascara running down her cheeks. 'We've been best friends ever since grade school. I couldn't understand why she didn't text me this morning, when she didn't show up.'

Jim cleared his throat. 'I'm sorry I had to bring you such bad news. You can all leave college early today. I guess you don't feel like remedial English, just at the moment.'

'They weren't *trapped*, were they?' asked Sally Broxman breathlessly.

'I don't think so,' said Jim. 'It looked as if it happened very quickly.'

'You *saw* them?'

Jim nodded. 'The police wanted me to visit the scene of the fire, just in case I could shed some light on what happened. But . . . I don't know. I couldn't really tell them anything very helpful.'

'Was it really gross?' asked Randy Bullock. 'I mean, were they all, like, roasted and everything?'

Jim shook his head.

'Did they look peaceful?' asked Sue-Marie. 'They didn't suffer, did they?'

Jim thought of Bobby and Sara's skulls, staring into each other's sightless sockets. 'Yes,' he said, 'I guess you could say they looked peaceful.'

For a long moment, nobody spoke, but nobody stood up to leave, either. Sue-Marie mewed quietly into her handkerchief, like a lost kitten, and there was a chorus of emotional sniffs from most of the other students. David Robinson had his eyes tightly closed, and his hands pressed together, and he was rapidly mumbling in prayer.

Jim said, 'It's always a terrible shock when somebody dies so young, and so suddenly. You ask yourself, don't you, what kind of a world can this be, when people with so much promise can have their lives snuffed out, just like that. This is what we were talking about this morning, wasn't it? Time. Bobby and Sara had the greatest gift of all taken away from them. Time to grow up, time to fall in love, time to enjoy all the pleasures this life has to offer. For Bobby and Sara, time has stopped forever, while all the rest of us go rushing on – minute by minute, day by day, week by week, and every second that passes leaves them further and further behind.'

He went to the chalkboard again, and underneath BOBBY TUBBS AND SARA MILLER ARE DEAD, he wrote: So WHERE ARE THEY NOW?

'Since none of you seem to feel like leaving early, and this *is* a writing class, I suggest that we try some creative therapy. Try to express what you feel about Bobby and Sara on paper. You can write anything you like – an essay, a poem, a song lyric, if you want to.' He tapped the chalkboard with his ruler. 'All I expect you to do is to answer this question.'

'Maybe they're ghosts,' said Edward Truscott.

'There's only one spook in this class and that's you,' retorted Shadow.

Jim sat down. 'If you think they're ghosts, say so. Write whatever you like . . . so long as it's thoughtful, and honest, and it comes from the heart.'

Vanilla King put up her hand. 'Mr Rook, sir. Do *you* believe in ghosts?'

Jim looked at Vanilla for a long time, with his hand partly covering his mouth, saying nothing. She was just about to ask the question again when he gave her an almost imperceptible nod.

Four

'**Y**ou are going to *so* love this place,' said Vinnie as he parked his bright-red Pontiac GTO and switched off *Nessun Dorma*, which he had been playing at full volume all the way from West Grove to Venice.

Jim climbed out of the car and looked up at the gloomy 1930s apartment building which took up the entire block between Willard and Divine. When he had lived on Electric Avenue he had driven past this way almost every day, but he couldn't remember having noticed this building before, in spite of its monstrous bulk. It seemed to keep itself aloof from the busy, brightly colored neighborhood around it. It was five stories high, built of dark reddish-brown brick, with tiny diamond-leaded windows and twisted barley-sugar pillars. When he looked up, Jim saw dozens of gargoyles leaning over the parapets, and the chimneys bristling with elaborate lightning rods, as if the residents were trying to protect themselves from the wrath of God.

A discolored bronze plaque over the main entrance announced Benandanti Building, 1935.

'Forty years my uncle Giovanni lived here,' said Vinnie, bounding up the front steps and pushing open the heavy oak doors. 'He was old and he was sick, and his apartment was way too big for him, but he absolutely refused to move. He said he had to live here until he died. He never told us why, silly old coot.'

As the oak doors swung shut behind them, Jim was overwhelmed by the sudden silence. It was total. He listened and listened, but he couldn't even hear a TV playing or the sound of the traffic outside. 'It's like a church,' he said, stepping forward into the hallway. His footstep echoed, and re-echoed.

The hallway looked like a church and it even smelled like a church. It was octagonal, with pillars of streaky red marble, and a matching marble floor. The walls were paneled in decoratively carved oak, with bunches of grapes and wild roses and human faces, all of them Italian-looking men with hawk-like noses and highly disdainful expressions. Even the elevator doors were covered in bas-reliefs of trees and brambles and pictures of distant castles.

At one side of the hallway stood a creamy-colored statue of a naked man, about three-quarters of life size, with one hand raised in front of his eyes as if he were trying to stop himself from being blinded by the sun. In his other hand he was holding a square box, about four inches along each side.

'Interesting statue,' said Jim. 'Any idea what it's supposed to be? Michelangelo's David is Deeply Disappointed with his Bar-Mitzvah Present?'

'I don't have any idea. All I know is that my mother always kept her back to it when we were waiting for the elevator. I think she was embarrassed by the size of his schlong.'

'Well, he *is* pretty well endowed, isn't he? But there's an inscription on the side here. LIGHT SNARETH THE SOUL. What does that mean?'

'Don't ask me,' said Vinnie. 'I asked Uncle Giovanni about it once, and all he said was "don't ask questions you don't want to know the answer to."'

'How were you supposed to know you didn't want to know the answer unless he told you what it was?'

'That's what *I* said. But all he said was "shut up, kid, and eat your linguine."'

The elevator arrived with a startling bang, and the doors

40

shuddered open. Inside, the elevator car only had room for three or four people, but it was mirrored on all sides, so that it appeared to be crowded with dozens of Jims and Vinnies.

'It's the fourth floor,' said Vinnie. He pressed the button but nothing happened. 'It's old, this building,' he apologized. 'But – you know – it's cramful of character.' He pressed the button again, and this time the doors shuddered shut, and they were winched unsteadily upward. Jim was sure that he could hear the cable pinging, strand by strand.

They walked along the fourth-floor corridor for what seemed like miles. The carpet had once been maroon, but now it was mostly string and holes and rumpled-up hillocks. When they reached Uncle Giovanni's apartment, Vinnie fumbled for the key and eventually unlocked the massive oak front door. They groped together into a gloomy lobby area which smelled strongly of shoes. Eventually Vinnie found the light switch and said, 'Presto!'

On the right-hand side of the lobby stood a large mahogany hall stand which was clustered with more than two dozen men's hats – fedoras, trilbies, skimmers and derbies. There were probably six or seven overcoats hung up, as well as scarves for every conceivable occasion, from motorcycling to the opera, and a thicket of walking sticks and umbrellas.

The left-hand side of the lobby was a mountain range of discarded footwear – sandals, two-tone Oxfords, patent-leather evening pumps, tasseled loafers, bedroom slippers. It looked as if Uncle Giovanni had kept every pair of shoes that he had worn since he came to California.

'Sorry about the whiff,' said Vinnie. 'My mom used to call him Gorgonzola feet.'

He led the way through to the living room, and Jim could see that he hadn't been exaggerating about the size of the apartment. It was vast, almost baronial, but it was shabby and airless, and thick with dust. The living room was still decorated with the original 1935 wallpaper – faded green with wavy brown patterns – although there were so many pictures hanging everywhere that the wallpaper was barely visible. At the windows, nearly twenty feet high, moss-green velvet drapes hung rotting on their rails. The room was dominated by a huge marble fireplace, its grate over-flowing with half-burned letters and documents. Assembled around it was a yard-sale collection of furniture: sagging couches covered with sun-faded brocade; 1930s Lloyd Loom chairs, painted turquoise; antique Spanish side tables and studded leather stools. In one corner stood a tall-backed chair that looked more like a throne, and on either side of it stood two torchères, those tall twisty pillars for statuettes or trailing plants.

Over the fireplace hung a large, dark oil painting of a man in evening dress. He was standing in front of a mirror, but he had a black cloth draped over his head. The painting needed cleaning, which made it look yellowish and even more sinister than it was probably supposed to be. It reminded Jim of the surrealist paintings of René Magritte – portraits of men looking into mirrors and seeing nothing but the backs of their heads.

'That is seriously creepy.'

'Yeah . . . that used to scare three colors of shit out of me when I was a kid. I never knew why he had to have that cloth over his head. Was he so homely that he didn't want anybody to look at him? If he was, why have his picture painted at all? I always wanted to know what he looked like, under that cloth, and I used to rest my head against the painting and try to peer up underneath it.'

'You asked your uncle?'

'Of course.'

'And he said "eat your linguine"?'

'No, surprisingly, he didn't.' Vinnie put on a thick, Neapolitan accent. '"You watch out for dis fellow, kid. You ever see dis fellow, you don't talk to him, you don't look

42

at him, you don't stand still for one-a second. You come run to me, so fast you shoes catch fire.'

'Didn't he tell you who he was?'

'Nope. But I always felt that he had hung up this picture like one of those wanted posters. He used to sit in that chair and smoke cheroots and just stare at it.'

Jim approached the fireplace and peered at the signature in the bottom right-hand corner of the painting. Sebastian Della Croce, 1853. 'Well, whoever this guy was, it's pretty certain that he's gone to higher service.'

Vinnie held up his left hand against the side of his face so that he wouldn't have to look at the painting directly. 'I really hate that painting, you know. I should smash it up, or burn it, or throw it in the nearest dumpster. The nightmares it used to give me! I would be lying in bed, right, and I'd imagine that my door was suddenly thrown open, and this guy would be standing in the hallway, with that black cloth over his head. I would be so frightened that I couldn't even scream. I would just lie there and stare at him. Then he would step into my room, and as he came nearer, his legs would get longer and longer, like telescopes, and he would be leaning over my bed and I just knew that he was going to kill me.'

Jim stepped back. The picture was eerie, but it was so well painted that he could almost see the black cloth moving up and down, as if the man beneath it breathed.

'No, you shouldn't destroy it, Vinnie, it's a good piece of art. Let me find out more about it. A friend of mine works in an auction house. She can tell you how much it's worth, and she can probably sell it for you, too, if you don't mind paying commission.'

Vinnie pulled a face. 'Be my guest. But if it turns out that it isn't worth nothing, you'd be doing me a favor if you burned it.'

Jim looked around. Although the walls were so crowded with pictures, the man over the fireplace was the only painting. All of the rest of them were photographs, mostly black and white, except for half a dozen hand-tinted in a very faded color. All of them were either framed in ebony or tarnished silver. They were strange photographs for anybody to hang on their living-room walls. Disturbing, even. Ramshackle barns, somewhere in the mid-West, with frowning farmers standing beside them. Three cyclists on a deserted road in Iowa, one of them wearing an ill-fitting suit apparently made out of brown paper. A plump young woman in nothing but a tightly laced corset, her breasts bulging, standing by a window in Paris with the Eiffel Tower in the background, its upper levels hidden by fog. A cross-eyed boy with bare feet sitting in a ditch next to a dead, half-rotted dog, its stomach teeming with maggots.

'Pretty unusual taste, your uncle,' said Jim.

'I know. But I guess they meant something to him.'

Jim walked down to the far end of the living room. There were double doors here, metal-framed, which gave out on to a narrow balcony. It looked as if the doors hadn't been opened in years, and the balcony was cluttered up with dead eucalyptus leaves. The only furniture out there was a cast-iron table and a deckchair with no canvas.

The balcony overlooked a central courtyard, in which there was a dried-up fountain and five or six old-fashioned bicycles, all stacked together. He was reminded of Italian art movies of the 1960s. *The Bicycle Thief, 8½.*

'This place is in a time warp.'

'Yeah, it is, in a way. It still belongs to the Benandanti Trust, the people who originally built it. They're based in Italy – Piedmont, I think – so I guess they don't bother about it too much, except to collect the ground rent. There's a super, who can unblock your toilet if you bribe him enough, and a Lithuanian woman comes around twice a week to beat up all the dust which has settled since the last time she beat it up.'

Vinnie led Jim through to the dining room, where there

was a dining table with twelve mismatched chairs, and an oak sideboard that was almost a building in itself. The dining table was stacked high with books – some of them old and bound in leather, some of them dog-eared paperbacks. There were also two battered boxes marked DAGUERROTYPE PLATES. The room smelled sour, like a second-hand bookstore, although there was another smell, too, like chemicals, which reminded Jim of something but he couldn't immediately think what.

Jim picked up one of the books and took off his glasses to read the cover. *Extinct Tribes of Southern California*, by Charles Oppenheimer and Leonard Flagg. He flicked through to the middle, where there was a section of photographs. The Serrano tribe, 1851; the Luiseño tribe, 1854; the Daguenos, date unknown. The Indians were all in their finest traditional dress, and the Luiseños were proudly displaying their hand-woven baskets. Most of them were smiling at the camera, but some of them looked dubious and bewildered, while a few of them had their hands raised to shield their faces.

Jim lowered the book with a frown. He couldn't help thinking of the naked statue in the hallway downstairs, with its hand raised in just the same way. LIGHT SNARETH THE SOUL.

'You want to see the bathroom?' asked Vinnie. 'The bathroom, believe me, is something else.'

'Sure,' said Jim, putting the book down on the table.

Vinnie was right. The bathroom was like a green-tiled cathedral, with a frieze of dolphins all the way around the ceiling. The windows were glazed in green, too, so that Vinnie and Jim looked as if they had been dead for weeks.

'What do you think of the shower?' asked Vinnie. 'My mother used to call it the Iron Maiden.' Jim could see why. The shower enclosure was like an antique torture chamber, constructed of chrome and dusty glass, with a bewildering array of handles including 'Monsoon', 'Bracing' and

'Arctic.' The bathtub itself had feet like bears' claws. The enamel was stained with rust, as if the faucets had been steadily dripping blood, but the tub was large enough for five people to share, or for two people to drown in.

The toilet stood on a plinth, three steps up, and was flushed by an elaborate handle which reminded Jim of the gearshift in his grandfather's 1948 Packard.

The bathroom, like everywhere else, was utterly silent, except for the *plink-plink-plink* of a leaky washer.

'Terrific room for singing opera,' said Vinnie. The toilet cistern gurgled as if it agreed with him. *'Nessun dorma! Nessun dorma-a-ah!'*

'You're sure I can stay here for seven fifty?'

'Absolutely. You can see how much remodeling it needs. Try it for six months and if you don't like it we'll simply call it quits.'

Jim held out his hand. 'OK, it's a deal. I'm going to feel like Miss Havisham, living here. Or Dracula. When can I move in?'

Vinnie held up the keys, dangling on a key fob in the shape of a miserable clown's mask. 'Why not today? No time like the present.'

Jim drove to Sherman Oaks to pick up his cat, Tibbles Two. He had arrived back from Washington last Saturday afternoon, and since then he had been staying at the Grand Studio Hotel on Hollywood Boulevard, which was very much less than grand, and had nothing to do with any of the movie studios, and which didn't allow pets. He could have stayed with friends. He could even have stayed with Karen, he supposed. But he needed time to think about the way that his life had suddenly broken into pieces, and so he didn't think he would be very amusing company at the moment.

He parked outside the neat yellow suburban house belonging to his friend Dennis Washinsky. On and off, he and Dennis had kept in touch since they were freshmen at college together. In those days, they had both been convinced that they were going to be the greatest screen-writers of the twentieth century. Watch out, William Goldman! Eat your heart out, Joe Eszterhas! To be fair, Dennis had written three episodes of *Star Trek: Voyager* and a made-for-TV thriller called *X Marks the Spot*. But now he was teaching screenwriting over the Internet to housewives whose chances of having a script accepted by a major studio were only marginally better than being struck by a meteorite, while Jim was teaching Special Class II, and the twentieth century was something you watched on the History Channel.

Jim rang the door chimes and Dennis's wife Mary snatched the door open as if she had been standing there waiting for him. She was pale and flat-faced and she was always worried about something, so that she had a habit of stopping in her tracks – *screech!* – and about-turning like Olive Oyl, because she thought she might have left her house key dangling in the front door or forgotten to put the ice cream back in the freezer or turn off the gas under the saucepan of milk.

'Jim! How nice to see you! Come on in! I'm just about to start supper. You like meat loaf, don't you? Meat loaf?'

'I can't stay,' Jim told her. 'Wish I could. I came to collect Tibbles, that's all.'

'Won't you have a beer? Oh, dear!' *Screech!* About turn! 'I don't think I put any more beer in the fridge. Or maybe I did! Did I?' She opened the icebox and the bottom shelf was stacked with at least two dozen cans of Pabst Blue Label. 'There! I thought I must have done! You've come for Tibbles? Have you found yourself someplace to live?'

'Yes, I've really lucked out. One of the teachers at West Grove has a vacant apartment on Saltillo Street.'

'That's Venice, isn't it? Venice? You like Venice. Will you be sharing?'

'Only with the ghost of the previous occupant. You should see this place. It looks like a set from *The Haunting*.'

Jim saw Tibbles's bowl on the floor in the laundry room, and it was licked clean, so she must have been eating well. 'Tibbles give you any trouble?'

'I wouldn't say *trouble* exactly. But she's a *very* queer cat, isn't she? For a cat, I mean. For a cat.'

'She's idiosyncratic, I'll give you that.'

Mary blinked, and Jim realized that she probably didn't know what idiosyncratic meant. 'Quirky,' he added.

'Quirky! You can say that again! Look, I'd better find her for you. Come on out back. Dennis has his screenwriters' chat room at six, so he's making sure that he's well prepared.'

She led Jim through to the small back yard, which had a red-painted picket fence all around it, a single row of sunflowers and a lawn covered with that bright green dichondra that used to be popular in the '60s. It looked like a child's drawing of a back yard rather than a real one. Dennis was sitting on the sun deck, apparently asleep, with his hands folded over his belly. His face was covered with a floppy cotton hat, like a wilted cabbage, and he was wearing a red and yellow striped shirt.

'Dennis!' called Mary. 'Look who's here!' *Screech!* About-turn! 'Did I put the washing on? Dennis has to have a white shirt for tomorrow.' She hurried back into the house.

Dennis raised the hat off his face and sat up. 'Jim! How's things?' He was a bulging, overweight man with sun-reddened cheeks and a Jimmy Durante nose and wildly overgrown eyebrows. But his eyes were so intensely blue that Jim always felt there was a mischievous child hiding inside him, peering out.

'Come to take Tibbles off your hands,' said Jim.

'Hey – soon as you like. Gives me the willies, your cat.'

Jim sat down and took a mouthful of cold beer. 'She hasn't been misbehaving herself, has she? Hasn't made any mess?'

'Oh, no, she's a very *clean* cat, I'll have to admit that. But she's a very *strange* cat, isn't she?'

'What happened?'

'You won't believe this. Sunday night we were sitting in the parlor watching TV when she walks in, takes a sniff around, then jumps up on to the table where we keep all the family photographs.'

'I'm sorry. She didn't break anything, did she? She's not allowed to jump on the furniture.'

Dennis held his stomach for a moment, and burped. 'Sorry. Too much beer. But I can never do that chat room thing unless I'm halfway drunk.' He adopted a monotonous, nerd-like voice. '"Dear Mr Washinsky, I've written a terrific new action-adventure movie, *Dead From The Neck Upward*, especially for Bruce Willis. Please give me Mr Willis's address so that I can deliver it to him personally in a brown-paper bag. I just know that once Mr Willis has had the chance to read it he'll insist on starring in it."'

Jim smiled. 'Come on, Dennis. You have to let people have their dreams. They know as well as you do that they're never going to come true.'

'Jim – you always were soft. You should see some of the scripts my students send me, complete with totally impossible camera directions and casts of thousands. Scene one: exterior; a high aerial shot; the Battle of Gettysburg; day.'

Jim laughed. 'So tell me about Tibbles.'

'Oh, yes. Tibbles jumps up on to the table and starts to nose at the photographs. Then suddenly she knocks one over, with her nose. It's a picture of my half-sister, Isabelle.'

'You should have whacked her. Tibbles understands whacks.'

'Well, whatever, Mary shoos her off, and stands the picture up again. The next thing we know, she jumps up again and knocks it over a second time. So this time Mary takes the picture and puts it up on the fireplace. Tibbles doesn't try to get up on the table again, but later on we go into the kitchen, and we hear this crash. Tibbles has only jumped up on to the fireplace and knocked the picture into the hearth.'

'I'm really sorry. Like you say, she can act a little strange. I think she's probably descended from a long line of witches' cats.'

'You're not kidding. A half-hour later Isabelle's husband Michael calls up and says that Isabelle has fallen down the front steps and broken her hip.'

'Coincidence,' said Jim.

'You can call it what you like. I call it weird. Tibbles knocks the same picture over, three times; and how many steps does Isabelle fall down? Three.'

Mary appeared, with a long-suffering Tibbles hanging from her arm. 'I found her under the bed. Her, and seven dead spiders.'

'Yes,' said Jim. 'She likes chasing spiders. She kind of – well, she *collects* spiders, live or dead.'

Dennis shook his head. 'Why doesn't that surprise me?'

Five

From the moment he dropped her on to the threshold, Tibbles sniffed at their new apartment with deep suspicion. She smelled the shoes heaped up in the entrance hall and violently sneezed, and when she walked into the living room she stopped and looked around, and her tail slowly lifted as if she could sense something there that she didn't like at all.

Jim went through to the kitchen with his bags of groceries, but then he came back to see what she thought. 'Well, TT, how does it grab you? It's kind of well-worn, I'll admit. Decrepit, even. But it has *atmosphere*, doesn't it?'

Tibbles padded across the hearthrug and looked up at the painting of the man with the black cloth draped over his head. She stared at it, unmoving, although both of her ears were pricked up.

'Don't worry about that,' said Jim after a while. 'I'm going to see if Genevieve Frost can sell it for me.'

Tibbles turned around and looked at him, and gave him a querying *miaow*.

'OK, we can leave it up if you like. But Vinnie says it gives him nightmares, and it'll probably give me nightmares, too, especially after six beers and a *quattro staggione* pizza with extra jalapeño peppers.'

Tibbles gave a more dismissive miaow, as if she didn't want to discuss what Jim was like after six beers and a *quattro staggione* pizza with extra jalapeño peppers. Then she jumped up on to the sagging brocade couch and sniffed distrustfully at the cushions.

'That's OK,' said Jim. 'That can be your couch.' He went across to the throne-like chair which was standing in the far corner of the room. 'This one's going to be mine.' He confidently tried to pick it up, but it was carved out of solid Spanish oak and he couldn't even lift it off the floor. In the end he had to drag it and push it and walk it on alternate feet. He maneuvered it to one side of the fireplace and smacked its seat cushion in a cloud of dust. Its purple velvet upholstery was faded and threadbare, and half of its buttons were missing, but it still had grandeur. Jim sat down on it and said, 'There . . . King Jim and Queen Tibbles in their royal palace. No serfs, admittedly. No minstrels, no dancing girls. But what do you expect for seven hundred and fifty bucks a month?'

Tibbles didn't stay on her couch for very long. While Jim watched her, she jumped off it again and started to explore the rest of the living room. 'You hungry?' Jim asked her, but she didn't respond. 'I bought anchovies. Mmmm, anchovies! No? How about a saucer of milk?'

When she didn't respond, he went back into the kitchen and took a cold can of beer out of one of his grocery sacks and wrenched open a giant-size bag of pretzels. 'Beer and pretzels, the food of real men everywhere!' He unpacked Tibbles's bowl and set it on the floor next to the antiquated fridge. 'You're sure you're not hungry?' he asked her. 'I bought spaghetti shapes, too. Simpsons spaghetti shapes, your favorite!'

He opened the fridge. It was reasonably clean inside, even if it smelled a little like sour milk and the light kept flickering, as if it were trying to warn him of something. He took out the salad tray, sniffed it to make sure, and then filled it up with green capsicums and beef tomatoes and a cucumber. He had made up his mind that he was going to eat much healthier food now that he was back in Los

Angeles. When he was in Washington he had been too harassed and overworked to cook for himself, and he had lived mostly on cheeseburgers and fried chicken. He hadn't put on very much weight, because he had been too stressed out, but he had always felt slightly nauseous, as if he had just staggered off a fairground carousel.

He was stacking blueberry yogurts in the fridge when he heard a screech of agony. For a split second, horrified, he thought that it was human. He dropped one of the yogurts and it splashed across his foot. 'Tibbles!' he called. 'Tibbles, are you OK? *Tibbles!*'

He pushed his way through to the living room. The spectacle that greeted him made him stop dead, and he felt as if cockroaches were running down his back. Tibbles was perched right on top of one of the torchères. It was over five feet high, and how she had managed to jump up on top of it without knocking it over he couldn't even begin to imagine. Her eyes were like slits and her lips were stretched back over her gums, baring her teeth. Just above her head, a twist of brown smoke was lazily unwinding, and the room was thick with the stench of badly scorched fur.

Tibbles had been burned all over, so that she was crusty black instead of tortoiseshell, and she was still smoking. Tiny orange sparks winked in the fur around her neck and her haunches.

'TT! What's happened? Jesus Christ, TT – you're on fire!'

He dodged around the couch, holding out both of his hands to her, expecting her to jump down from her perch. 'Come on, baby! Come on, Tibs!' But she spat at him, and cackled, and lashed out with her left paw to warn him off.

He stopped. 'Come on, TT. We need to get you into some cold water, pronto. Come on, baby.'

He edged closer, but she remained rigid and wild-eyed, hissing at him with total hostility. He tried to soothe her.

'Come on, baby, everything's going to be OK. What have you been doing, playing with matches? You remember what happened to Harriet, when she played with matches?'

He was close enough to reach her, but he held back and waited, hoping that she would start to relax. '"Then how the pussy cats did mew; what else, poor pussies, could they do?" Come on, TT. I only want to help you.'

She didn't blink. He waited nearly half a minute more. At last he said, 'OK, you want to stay there, smoldering? Have it your way,' and he pretended to turn away. Immediately, he turned back and tried to grab her by the scruff of the neck, but she hissed and reared up and lashed out at him. The torchère tipped sideways, Tibbles dropped to the floor, but as she fell her claws tore the skin across the back of his hand, and the next thing he knew he was spraying spots of blood across the carpet.

He sucked his hand and shook it. 'Jesus, Tibbles, that hurt! What's got into you?'

Tibbles had scrambled under the couch. Jim knelt down and peered underneath it. Tibbles stared at him out of the shadows, one lip caught in her tooth so that she looked as if she were sneering.

'Tibbles, it's no use hiding under there. You need treatment.' He waited, and waited, but she didn't show any signs of coming out. After a while he straightened himself up and checked around the room. He couldn't understand what could have burned Tibbles so badly. There were no candles anywhere. No naked wires. The grate was clogged up with paper ash but that had all gone cold, long ago. Even the sunlight that filtered through the grimy French windows was as weak as watery tea.

Jim bent down again. Tibbles had retreated even further, where the springs were showing through the sagging hessian. Maybe it was better to leave her. As far as he could see, her burns were mainly superficial, and maybe she needed some time to herself, so that she could recover from the shock.

He waited for a while longer, and then he stood up and went back into the kitchen for his beer. He caught sight of himself in one of the glass-fronted cabinets and thought he looked like one of the photographs in the living room. *Mystified Man in 1930s Kitchen.* Well, he thought, I *am* mystified. Cats don't spontaneously catch fire, do they? If you brush a cat the wrong way, briskly enough, static electricity can build up in its fur, and you can sometimes produce a crackling noise, or even sparks. But enough sparks to set it alight? That didn't seem at all likely.

He suddenly thought of Bobby Tubbs and Sara Miller. Another case of spontaneous combustion. Or what had *looked* like spontaneous combustion. He couldn't seriously compare what had happened to Tibbles to the way in which those two had been totally incinerated, down to the bone. But it was coincidental, wasn't it? Two unexplained burnings in two days.

He went back into the living room. To his surprise, Tibbles had emerged from under the couch and was sitting right in the center of the rumpled-up hearthrug. She was no longer smoldering but her fur was badly charred and in some places it was burned almost down to the skin. She was shivering, almost imperceptibly, as though suffering from a chill.

'Hey, TT . . . How are you feeling, baby?' As bedraggled as she was, Tibbles didn't seem to be listening to him and she didn't deign to look at him either. She continued to stare at the painting over the fireplace, and when Jim came closer he could hear her soft, harsh, strangulated breathing.

Jim glanced up at the painting. The man was still standing in front of the mirror with his black cloth draped over his head. Not that Jim seriously expected him to be doing anything else.

'Listen, Tibbles. It's only a picture. Paint and canvas, that's all. I'll tell you what I'm going to do. I'm going to take it down, right now, and put it out in the corridor. Then tomorrow morning I'm going to put it in the car and take it along to the auctioneers to have it valued. And sold. Then it'll be gone, OK, and it'll be somebody else's problem.'

Tibbles still didn't move, or even acknowledge that he was there. Jim made no more attempts to pick her up. She had been in weird moods before, particularly after he had boarded her at the Paws-a-While cattery in Anaheim, and he had learned to keep his distance when she was feeling resentful or out of sorts. Once – when he was first dating Karen – he had left Tibbles alone in his apartment for two days, and as soon as he had opened the front door she had sprung up at him like a jack-in-the-box and furiously scratched his cheek. All the rest of the staff at West Grove had assumed that Karen had done it, and he had been forced to endure days of winks and nudges and 'got too fresh, did you, Jim?'

Grunting, he dragged the throne-like armchair across the hearthrug, and pushed it as close to the fireplace as he could manage. He climbed up on it, his shoes sinking into the threadbare cushions. 'Look, TT, I'm taking the picture down, OK?'

It was easier said than done. The painting was titanically heavy, and he struggled for three or four minutes just to lift it off its hook. 'Come on, you bastard,' he grunted, but the wire kept catching, and in the end he had to go through to the dining room and fetch a chair that was higher, with a harder seat. Tibbles watched him with half-closed eyes, as if he were the local retard.

At last, his teeth clenched, straining every muscle in his arms, he lifted the painting off the wall and lowered it down to the floor.

'There,' he panted, and he had to lean against the side of the fireplace to get his breath back. When he looked up, he saw that the painting had left a large unfaded square on the wallpaper where it had been hanging for so long. The pattern had been surprisingly bright and jazzy. He could almost hear the Charleston, and the chatter of bright young things.

The back of the picture-frame was woolly with dust, and

there was a deeply discolored label on it, with italic hand-writing in brown ink. *Mr Robert H. Vane, Daguerrotypist, September 17, 1853. In mourning, after the occasion of the Dagueno Tragedy.*

Jim cocked his head so that he could look at the painting more closely. Daguerrotypist, huh? He knew that daguer-rotypes were an early kind of photographic plate, in the days before film had been invented. Several famous daguer-rotypists had roamed California in the middle of the nine-teenth century, taking pictures of mountains and valleys and Indian tribes.

But who was Mr Robert H. Vane, and what was the Dagueno Tragedy? And why had he chosen such a bizarre way to display his grief, with a black cloth draped over his head?

Tibbles let out a high, sharp wheeze, more like a cough than a miaow. She was still shivering, so Jim went through to the big gloomy bedroom, opened the immense mahogany blanket press and found her a blanket. It was thick and prickly and it faintly smelled like some kind of horse lini-ment. He knelt down and carefully draped it over Tibbles, and this time she didn't seem to mind at all. She didn't even protest when he bundled it right around her, picked her up and laid her gently on the couch. He didn't quite know what you were supposed to do when a cat went into shock, but he guessed that keeping her warm was pretty much top priority.

'Just relax, TT. Your fur will grow back before you know it.'

Tibbles looked up at him as if she wouldn't trust a human as far as she could throw him.

When he was sure that Tibbles was settled, Jim turned his attention back to the painting. He couldn't lift it, so he grad-ually dragged it across the living room and into the lobby. He stumbled over the shoes, and gave them a furious kick.

After he disposed of this painting, the next thing he was going to get rid of was Vinnie's uncle's stinky old collection of footwear.

Sweating and swearing, he managed to open the door and maneuver the painting into the corridor. There, panting, and nursing a badly bruised elbow, he leaned it up against the wall. If anybody stole it, too bad. In fact, they would be doing him a favor.

He was just about to go back into his apartment when the door opposite opened and a young woman stepped out. She was tall, with long, glossy black hair, cut very straight and severe, and she was wearing a tight black sleeveless sweater with silver sequins in it, and black slacks, and very high black strappy sandals. She had a squarish face, with arched eyebrows and deep-set eyes. Jim's first impression was: Lady Vampire.

'Hi,' she drawled.

'Hi.'

She double-locked her door, then looked at the painting leaning against the wall. 'You can't leave that there.'

'I'm taking it down to the auction house tomorrow. I just moved in.' He wiped his hand on his jeans and held it out. 'Jim Rook.'

She ignored his hand and said, 'Glad to know you. Eleanor Shine. But you still can't leave that there. Fire regulations.'

'It'll be gone by tomorrow morning.'

'And what happens if the building catches ablaze tonight? Which it's not going to, I know. But we can't have anarchy, can we – everybody doing whatever they damn well please. Next thing we know, people will be throwing champagne parties in the elevators, and keeping pet lions.'

'You think so?'

'I *know* so. I know people better than they know themselves.'

'Well . . .' said Jim, looking at the painting. With each passing moment, he had become increasingly aware of

Eleanor Shine's perfume. It was like lilies, combined with a fear of heights.

'I'd help you carry it,' she smiled. 'But my nails . . .'

'Sure. Don't worry about it. I dragged it out here; I can drag it back in.'

He lifted the painting away from the wall. She peered over so that she could see it. She stared at it for a very long time, one hand lifted to hold her gleaming black hair away from her face. At last, she looked up at Jim and she was frowning.

'What a strange picture.'

'It is, isn't it? It doesn't belong to me. It came with the apartment. The label says it's of some daguerrotypist.'

'Some what?'

'Daguerrotypist. A daguerrotype was a kind of photographic plate they used before camera-film, and a daguerrotypist was . . . well, somebody who took daguerrotypes.'

'Oh.' Pause. 'Why is he wearing that cloth over his head?'

'He's supposed to be in mourning.'

As Jim shifted the frame around, Eleanor Shine followed him, and examined the painting even more intently. 'My God,' she said. 'Wait a minute . . . Can you keep it still, please? This is *very* unusual indeed.'

'Something wrong?'

She held out her hand, almost touching the surface of the painting but not quite. She was right to be cautious about her nails. They were ridiculously long, and polished silver. 'This is not just a painting,' she said emphatically.

'What do you mean?'

'This has such *power* . . . I can feel it. This is like a man's soul, rather than a painting.'

'Is it? I'm not too sure I understand what you mean.'

'Can't you feel it for yourself? Whoever this man was, something of his personality is concealed inside this painting. And I don't just mean his likeness. I mean *him*.'

Jim looked at her warily. 'I still don't get it.'

Eleanor Shine leaned closer to the painting, and steadily drew in her breath. 'He's here, I can *smell* him. Either he's hiding, or he's been imprisoned. But he's here.'

'My cat really hates this picture. So does my friend – the one who owns the apartment.'

'Your cat? What cat? You're not supposed to have cats here, you know. Tropical fish, they're permitted, so long as you have flood insurance for a broken tank. Birds, too, so long as they stay in their cages. But not cats.'

'She's very quiet. Very clean. Very well behaved. She's practically human.'

'All the same, the regulations are absolutely specific. Pussies are *verboten*.'

'What about this picture?' asked Jim, changing the subject.

'I don't know. It's very strange indeed. You were going to sell it?'

'That was what I had in mind.'

Eleanor Shine clasped her hands together. She had rings on every finger, including her thumbs. They were all silver, or platinum, or white gold, and they were all studded with various semi-precious stones – garnets, and sapphires, and moonstones.

'I don't think you should sell it. Not without warning the next person to own it.'

'Warning them? Warning them about what?'

'That it's more than just a painting, of course. You don't know what they might do with it. More important, you don't know what it might do to *them*.'

Jim glanced into his apartment. Tibbles, in her blanket, appeared to be sleeping. He looked back at Eleanor Shine and he didn't know what to say. She was obviously eccentric, but Tibbles had been perched directly in front of this painting when her fur caught fire, so maybe there *was* something more to it than met the eye. But how could a man's personality be concealed in oils and canvas and a grimy gold frame? It didn't make any sense.

'Maybe you could explain this to me,' Jim suggested.

'Not now,' said Eleanor Shine. 'I'm always late, but today I'm later than ever.'

'Well . . . when you come home, why don't you knock on my door?'

'All right,' she agreed. 'But in the meantime . . .' She nodded toward the painting.

'OK, I'll take it back inside and I promise I won't sell it. But I'm going to cover it up, whether there's anybody's soul inside it, or not. I just don't want to look at it, that's all.'

'Oh, I'd cover it up, too,' said Eleanor Shine. 'But only to stop it from looking at me.'

Six

Next morning the air was stained with yellow smog. When Jim looked out of the leaded windows of the Benandanti Building, he felt as if he had woken up inside a nineteenth-century photograph. He went into the kitchen and made himself a mug of murderously strong black coffee and then sat down at the kitchen table and tried to think what he ought to do today, to start putting his life back together. Meet some old friends for a pizza? ('Do you really want to know what happened to me in Washington? Three young people died, horribly. How about another slice of meat feast?') Start writing a diary? ('Dear diary, last night my cat caught fire but I met a very sexy woman from the next apartment.') Book a session with a psychoanalyst? ('This very sexy woman from the next apartment thinks a painting has a real man inside it, and I'm worried that I might believe her.') Get drunk? ('Karen, darling, you're the only woman I ever wanted.') Stay sober? ('Of course, Karen, it never would have worked out between us.') Go for a nine-mile run? ('Cough, pant, cough, cough, pant.')

He couldn't help feeling that he was doing little more than picking up one piece of his life at a time, turning it over and dropping it again, like an auto mechanic who doesn't have a clue how to reassemble the car that he's taken apart.

Maybe the best thing for him to do – maybe the *only* thing – would be to concentrate all of his attention on the students of Special Class II. Maybe *they* could show him which bits of his life were still worth salvaging, and polishing up, and which bits ought to be tossed away for scrap.

He finished his coffee and stowed the mug in the dishwasher. Tibbles was under the sink, wolfing down her breakfast of economy tuna. She was still patchy and scruffy, and she walked as stiffly as if she had rheumatism, but if her appetite was anything to go by, she seemed to have recovered from the shock of her burning.

'I don't know how you can eat that stuff at six thirty in the morning,' said Jim, wrinkling up his nose in disgust. Tibbles briefly glanced up at him as if he had no taste at all, and went back to her bowl. Cheap, slushy, rank-smelling tuna – nothing like it.

'Listen, TT, I'm going to work now. Behave yourself. Don't start yowling, because you're not really allowed to be living here. And if you think I'm going to give up this apartment just because of you, forget it.'

He stopped by the front door. 'If you catch fire again, dial nine-one-one. Or jump in the shower and turn on the faucet marked "Deluge".'

Behind the heaps of Vinnie's uncle's shoes, the portrait of Robert H. Vane was propped against the wall, covered by a gray blanket with red stitching. The blanket had slipped at one side, and Jim tugged it back into place. He didn't even want to see an inch of Robert H. Vane's black funereal pants.

He closed the front door behind him and stood in the corridor and waited and listened. He was hoping that he might bump into Eleanor Shine again, but he couldn't hear any sound from her apartment. She hadn't knocked on his door yesterday evening, even though he had spent nearly half an hour tidying up and dusting and trying to make the place look reasonably presentable. *And* bought some flowers, *and* some ruffle-cut potato chips, *and* a bottle of Chardonnay.

When the clock had dolefully chimed midnight and he had known for sure that she wasn't going to knock, he had realized – to his genuine surprise – that he was disappointed. There was something about her. Her face. Her liquid black hair. Her extraordinary notion that Robert H. Vane was hiding inside his own portrait. Or trapped, maybe. Or a bit of both.

She was a real original, Eleanor Shine, and he hadn't met an original in a long, long time.

Except Pinky Perdido, maybe. When she stood up in class to read her tribute to Bobby Tubbs and Sara Miller, she was wearing black ribbons in her strawberry-pink bunches, a black T-shirt, a pink lace skirt and black pantyhose, with pink-and-white trainers. Pinky had a freckly nose, spiky eyelashes, and a voice so squeaky that it sounded like a dog's rubber toy.

'They woke up and Bobby blunk his eyes and said where are we what happen and Sara said what is this place it's all sunny and roses everywhere so many roses it smells like that sashay I put in my underwear drawer. So an angel all dress in white Armani came to them and said you are in wedding land and I will take you to the chapel of weddings where you will be married with bridesmaids and champagne every day this is your reward for loving each other in the real world a wedding every day even a stretch limo and wedding gifts. Sara said this is bliss this is what I always wanted a wedding that goes on for ever amen.'

There was a smattering of applause. Pinky sat down, her cheeks all fired up. Jim nodded, and said, 'That was excellent, Pinky. It was tender, wasn't it? It was full of imagination. But it wasn't all cotton candy, was it? It also posed a very poignant question. 'Poignant – meaning what?' he asked, looking around the classroom. 'Anybody?'

Edward put up his hand. 'Affecting the emotions, or relevant, or intense. From the Latin *pungere.*'

'Yes, like you is an intense poignant in the ass,' put in Shadow.

Jim gun-pointed his finger at Shadow, and mouthed the word *pow!* as a warning. Then he said, 'If Bobby and Sara were to find themselves in Pinky's version of paradise, what would it be like? They would have wedding cake and champagne and all the toasters they could wish for, for all eternity, but they would never grow older. They would never know what it's like to have children and to travel the world. Every day, for ever, they would have to go through that same wedding celebration, over and over, like in *Groundhog Day*. Maybe that's heaven, or maybe that's another kind of hell. What do you think?'

'I went to my dad's wedding last year,' said Edward. 'That was definitely my definition of hell. I mean, my stepmom's cool. She used to be a pole dancer. But you should have seen her family. Talk about cave dwellers. One of the cousins had a circular target tattooed on his forehead. He said he wanted to be like Kurt Cobain, but he didn't have the guts actually to blow his head off, so that was the next best thing.'

'Who is *you* to diss anybody, you geek?' Shadow challenged him. 'That guy probably went home and told his friends that you was the biggest freak since Pee Wee Herman.'

Jim walked toward the back of the classroom. As he made his way between the desks, cellphones and comic books and Snickers bars miraculously vanished out of sight. He stopped, and turned around, and caught Randy with his cheeks bulging. 'Hands up how many of you believe in an afterlife?' he asked. There was a moment's bewildered pause. 'I mean, are we still conscious after we die, or not? Can we see, think, feel . . . or have we gone for ever?' One by one, hesitantly, eleven hands were raised.

He stopped by Brenda Malone's desk. Brenda was plump and pale and asthmatic, with coppery-colored hair that frayed like electrical wire, and a slight squint. 'Brenda? It is Brenda, isn't it? You don't believe in an afterlife?'

Brenda shook her head so that her pigtails swung. 'When you die, that's it.'

'So you don't believe in any kind of heaven, or hell, or

continuing existence? When you die, that's it, the lights go out, and you're gone?'

Brenda nodded. 'My sister died and before she died I made her promise to send me a message when she got to heaven. She was supposed to pick three petals from a daisy that I had in a vase on my windowsill.'

'But she didn't?'

'No.' Brenda started biting at the edge of her thumbnail.

'Did it occur to you that maybe she couldn't do anything physical, like picking off petals, once she was a spirit?'

'Unh-hunh, she's gone,' Brenda insisted. 'I can't even feel that she's close.'

Jim looked around the classroom. Some of his students had grown tired of holding their hands up; others were propping up their elbows with their other hand. It was then that he saw a young girl standing in the doorway – a girl wearing a long, pale-green nightdress. She wasn't a pretty girl. She had a plump, plain face and bushy red hair, which was pinned behind her ears. But she was smiling optimistically, and she was holding a red long-stemmed daisy in her hand.

Jim smiled back at her. He knew who she was, and what she was doing here. He also knew that nobody else in the classroom could see her, not even Brenda. Especially not Brenda.

He hadn't had a visitation like this for over two years, and he found it unexpectedly welcoming. The afterlife was crowded with people who were furious that they had died before their time; or vengeful; or couldn't believe that they had died at all. But there were contented spirits, too, and this girl was one of them.

'How old was your sister when she died?' Jim asked Brenda.

'Twelve-and-a-half. She had leukemia.'

'What was her name?'

'Mary.'

Jim laid his hand on Brenda's shoulder. 'Mary hasn't left

you, Brenda. She still watches you. She still loves you, and cares about you.'

Brenda stared up at him suspiciously, as if she might have expected her family priest to make an assertion like that, but not her remedial English teacher.

'You don't believe me?' Jim asked her.

'I've never felt her. Ever. And she didn't give me a sign.'

Jim beckoned, and Mary left the doorway and walked across the classroom toward them, passing right through Vanilla King and George Graves as if they didn't exist. Vanilla must have sensed her, though, because she suddenly said, 'Oh!' and looked around as if somebody had touched her. George was too busy doodling Gothic-style gravestones in his notebook, with RIP inscribed on them.

Mary came right up to Jim, still smiling. 'I never left her,' she said. She sounded distant, as if she were speaking in another room, and in a way she was. 'I never left Brenda for a single minute.'

'Couldn't you show her?' asked Jim. 'It would make her very happy.'

'What?' asked Brenda.

Mary plucked three petals from the red daisy that she was carrying and dropped them into the palm of Jim's hand. Jim closed his fingers and said, 'Thank you.'

Brenda frowned at him. 'Thank you for what?'

Jim opened his hand. Brenda stared down at the three red petals in disbelief. She opened and closed her mouth, and then she said, 'How did you know the daisy was red?'

'I told you, Mary's close by. She didn't leave you, when she died, and she never will. She's your sister.'

Brenda's squinty eyes filled up with tears. 'It's a trick, isn't it? You're playing a trick!' George turned around in his seat and frowned at her, and then at Jim, but when he saw that nothing particularly interesting was going on, he returned to his doodling.

Jim laid a hand on Brenda's shoulder. 'Do you think I'd

be so cruel to you?' He tipped the petals on to her work-book. 'Here, take them. Mary wants you to have them. She said that she'd give you a sign, and she has. She just needed somebody like me who could help her to do it.'

Brenda pulled out a crumpled Kleenex and dabbed her eyes. Jim said, 'Listen, talk to me after class. I'll explain it all to you then. You're excused now, if you want to be.'

'No, no. I want to stay. I thought she'd left me. I really thought she'd left me.'

Mary was still standing so close to Brenda's desk that if she had been substantial, Brenda could have reached out and touched her face. She waited for a moment, but her smile gradually faded because she knew that Brenda would never be able to see her again. She looked up at Jim regretfully and then she vanished.

Jim gave Brenda's shoulder a reassuring squeeze and walked back to the front of the class. 'OK,' he said briskly. 'Freddy, how about you – do you believe in an afterlife?'

'Sure,' said Freddy. 'Whenever I'm playing cards, my grandpa whispers in my ear and tells me what the other players are holding in their hands, which is cool.'

'How do you know it's your grandpa?'

'I can smell him. Rebel Yell whiskey, and cigars, and garlic breath, that's what he used to smell like.'

'Well, if it's true, that's very interesting, because many people report that they can smell spirits even when they can't see them. Spirits seem to be capable of making their presence known by arousing our nasal receptors, which are much more sensitive, say, than our eyes or our ears. Ruby?'

'I don't know,' said Ruby, flashing her gold charm bracelets. 'I believe that we go on living so long as there's at least one person left who remembers us. People live in other people's minds. If somebody can remember a song, and pass it on to their children, then why can't a person's soul get passed on that way, too?'

'Randy? You don't believe in an afterlife?'

Randy wobbled his jowls. 'All we are is meat, right?'
'Absolutely,' said Shadow. 'And some of us is ten times
more meat than others.'

'I'm going to sit on your head and fart *Camptown Races*
in your ear,' Randy warned him.

'Enough of that,' Jim warned him. 'What's your point,
Randy?'

'The point is that when our meat dies, right, our brain dies,
and when our brain dies, that's it, no more us. How many
pigs get slaughtered, right? Millions of them, every day. But
we don't get haunted by millions of pigs, do we? You never
hear them going oink-oink in the middle of the night.'

'That's because animals don't have souls,' put in David
Robinson. 'Only humans have souls, because animals can't
tell the difference between right and wrong, or have faith
in our Lord, like we can.'

Jim wondered what his class would have made of Mary,
picking the petals off her red daisy. He still didn't understand spirits himself – why some spirits chose to appear
and others didn't, or why some spirits were seething with
resentment, while others appeared to be so placid. Maybe
there was no real mystery about it. Maybe they were just
the same as living people.

'All right,' he said. 'I want to hear another piece about Bobby
and Sara. Roosevelt, how about you? What did you write?'

Roosevelt awkwardly stood up, his head gleaming as
brightly as his mirror sunglasses. He shrugged his shoulders two or three times and then he held up a scruffy square
of paper, sniffed, and announced, 'This is like a pome. This
express exactly what I feel for Bobby and Sara and how
they pass away:

'Bobby and Sara they wanted to do
What *everybody* do when they feel the urge
To get their souls together and their bodies to merge
Like two waves surging on the verge of the shore

69

Like crashing and smashing with the foam all splashing.
But the fire of their desire it became a pyre
They was torched and scorched and instead of *mated*
They was both *cre*-mated
Their lust it turned into ash and dust
So the wind it blew them both away
And we won't see them no more till the dawn of Doomsday.'

'Roosevelt, that's very good,' Jim told him. 'A little macabre, maybe. But I guess we have to face the fact that they both met a terrible death.'

His attention was caught by a sharp reflection outside, between the trees. Lieutenant Harris's car was coming down the driveway toward the college entrance. Jim turned back to the class, and said, 'OK, we'll get back to Bobby and Sara tomorrow. Meantime, I have a project for you. No groaning, if you don't mind. This should be a very interesting and worthwhile project, but it will require a little *work*.' More groans.

He turned to the chalkboard and wrote the word DAGUER-ROTYPE.

'Anybody know what this is? A daguerrotype?'

'Is it like a terrorist?' asked Philip.

'Inspired guess, but no. Edward?'

'It's an early sort of photography, sir. Invented by Louis Daguerre.'

'That's right. Before film was invented, photographers had to use metal plates which they made sensitive to light with chemicals. It was a very messy business, and they had to carry a whole lot of stuff around with them – cameras, tripods, bottles of mercury. But they took some incredible pictures. Mountains, lakes, railroad locomotives. The battlefields of the Civil War. They even took saucy pictures, too. Oh yes, they had porn, even in 1850.'

He chalked up the name ROBERT H. VANE.

'This is the man I'm interested in. He toured Southern California around 1853, and I believe that he took pictures

70

of Native American tribes. I want you all to see how much you can find out about him, and see if you can locate any of his pictures. You can use the library, the Internet, whatever you like.'

'Is there some kind of point to this, sir?' asked George solemnly. His hair was sticking out at the back, as if he had just got out of bed.

'Yes, George. We're going to be writing an imaginary diary of what it was like to wander around California in the pioneering days, taking daguerrotypes.'

'Er . . . what for?'

'I'll tell you what for. So that you can use your imagination to describe California as it was in the middle of the nineteenth century, and how new and wonderful it must have appeared to visitors who came from the east. So that you can describe the technical process of taking a daguerrotype in clear, easily understandable English. So that you can tell me which pictures *you* would have taken to show the people back in New York what California was like, and why it was worth them making a hazardous three-thousand-mile journey to settle here.'

Jim stuck up four fingers, one at a time. 'One, you'll be demonstrating how good you are at describing scenery and people. Two, you'll be showing that you can understand the way somebody else thinks – even somebody who lived a hundred and fifty years ago. Three, you'll be making it clear that you can grasp a technical process and explain it in non-technical language. Four, you'll be displaying your powers of persuasion, your salespersonship. You may think this is a history project, but believe me, all of those four skills will help you to find a modern-day job. Any job.'

'Even if you want to work for Radio Shack?' asked Edward.

'Especially if you want to work for Radio Shack.'

Shadow puffed out his cheeks and Jim could tell how daunted he was by the thought of writing more than two coherent sentences.

71

'You got a problem, Sonny?'

'Kind of. Maybe I misinterpretated it – but didn't you say yesterday that you wanted us to teach you?'

'Yes, I did. But think about it. How can you teach me anything if you don't *know* anything?'

'Hmm,' said Shadow. He wasn't convinced.

Jim smiled at him. 'You find out all about this Robert H. Vane character, believe me, I'll sit and listen to you. And I won't file my nails, or pick my nose, or send suggestive text messages to my girlfriend. I won't even bounce a basketball on my head. Is that a deal?'

Lieutenant Harris was waiting for Jim outside the main entrance, along with two detectives. They were all standing in the shade of the college's pride and joy, a hundred-foot cedar of Lebanon, which was allegedly planted by Tom Mix, the great silent-movie cowboy, in 1923.

'We have an eye witness,' called Lieutenant Harris as Jim came walking across the grass.

'Oh, yes?'

'Detectives Mead and Bross have interviewed dozens of bums and itinerants who spend their nights by the seashore. One of the bums was camping less than fifty yards away from the Tubbs' beach house.'

Detective Mead flipped open his notebook. He was black and handsome as a TV actor. He wore a gray lightweight suit, immaculately cut, and a red and yellow silk necktie. 'Hayward Mitchell, aged 48, unemployed dishwasher of no fixed address. Says he was settling down for the night when he saw two young people coming down the ramp to the beach. Says they were laughing and joking and generally horsing around.'

Detective Bross was well over 6ft 5in tall, with a head that looked as if it had been sculpted out of raw granite with a jackhammer. He had a gray buzzcut and deep-set eyes, and a hook-shaped scar around the side of his mouth. He said nothing, but he stared at Jim as if he were trying to remember his face from a recent armed robbery.

Lieutenant Harris took two color photographs out of his pocket and held them up. 'Mitchell admitted that he was nine parts intoxicated, but he identified both Bobby Tubbs and Sara Miller. He gave a reasonable description of what they were wearing and we don't see any reason why he should be shooting us a line.'

Detective Mead turned over another page. 'The vics went into the beach house, and about ten minutes later Mitchell says he saw a third individual coming down the ramp. Says this individual appeared to be dressed in white and gray. This individual climbed the steps outside the beach house. When he reached the verandah, he turned around, as if he was making sure that nobody was watching him. Mitchell says he was definitely African-American, no question about it. Possibly late middle-aged or elderly, too, because his hair was white. We took Mitchell down to the station and had him sit with our best composite artist. The artist used ImageWay computerized ID and came up with this . . . which Mitchell agrees is a very accurate likeness.'

Jim took the paper and opened it out. Looking back at him was a square-jawed black man with a shock of white hair and white eyebrows.

'Ever seen him before?' asked Lieutenant Harris.

Jim shook his head. 'Nope. Never have. It's not the kind of face you'd be likely to forget, is it? You don't mind if I keep this, though? Maybe something will come to me.'

'According to Mitchell, this individual was very well-built,' said Detective Bross, in a thick, concrete-mixing voice. 'About the same height and weight as me.'

Jim looked Detective Bross up and down. He must have weighed all of 275 pounds. 'Well-built? You don't exaggerate, do you?'

'Let's just say that his mother must have made him eat his greens.'

Jim stared at the ImageWay picture closely. He found it

oddly unsettling. It was like seeing a friend in a mirror for the very first time – a friend whose face you know well, but when his features are reversed left-to-right, looks unfamiliar, even creepy.

'Mitchell says he never saw this individual leave the beach house, although obviously he must have done. He probably waited until later, when Mitchell was asleep.'

'So it looks like Bobby and Sara might have been murdered?'

'Almost certainly. So, if you can get something out of that face that we can't, don't hesitate to call me.'

'Sure thing,' said Jim.

He nodded goodbye to Detectives Mead and Bross. He could tell that they were deeply unimpressed by his psychic abilities, but that was their problem. He had picked up no vibrations from the crime scene, nothing at all, even though today's visitation by Brenda's sister Mary had shown him that he was still capable of seeing spirits. He couldn't identify the suspect in the ImageWay picture, either. At least it wasn't the college janitor, Walter. He, too, was black, with snow-white hair – but he was only 5ft 5in tall and skinny as a spider.

He was walking back toward the main entrance when Karen came out, with Perry Ritts from the science department. Perry was deeply tanned, with thinning blond hair that waved in the wind like a flag, and one of those wholesome-guy faces with plenty of teeth and eyes that were always a little too wide, as if everything surprised him. Karen was wearing a pink check blouse that he had never seen before, and she was laughing. She looked a little older, of course, but it suited her, and he had forgotten how pretty she was.

Jim veered sharply right toward the side entrance. He wasn't ready to confront Karen yet. He was even less ready to nod and smile at her as she walked past him with Perry Ritts. He had made up a rhyme about Perry Ritts – it wasn't clean and it wasn't at all complimentary.

Seven

Jim went for a drink after college with Vinnie and Stu Bullivant from the arts department. Stu looked more like a Minnesota logger than an art teacher, with a massive brambly beard and a red checkered shirt and jeans that could have comfortably accommodated Jim and Stu in each leg. Stu had a theory that *everything* was art, particularly after seven beers. A shopping cart was art, because you filled it with things that revealed your soul.

'Stand behind any woman at the supermarket checkout, and look at what she's buying. She wouldn't let you read her private diary, would she? But she's spreading out her shopping in front of you, and that's much more intimate than any diary. What does it say about her, if she's buying twenty-four bargain-price toilet rolls, and six loaves of medium-cut white bread, and four gallons of milk, and thirty cans of dog food, and a box of incontinence pads, and a dozen Hungry Man TV dinners, and a can of drain unblocker, and a copy of *National Enquirer*? It says everything. It's a searingly honest self-portrait. Searingly honest! Just because she happens to have created this self-portrait in consumer goods, instead of paint, that doesn't mean it's any less meaningful. It's still art!'

'I think I'll stick to Rembrandt,' said Jim. 'At least Rembrandt didn't show you his sprinkled donuts and his wart cream.'

When Stu had gone to the rest room, for the ninth time, Vinnie lit up a cigarette and said, 'How are you settling in? Everything OK?'

Jim hesitated for a moment, but he decided not tell Vinnie what had happened to TT. After all, he wasn't supposed to have a cat in his apartment at all. 'Fine,' he said. 'That shower's something, isn't it? It's like going over Niagara Falls without the barrel.'

'You . . . ah . . . you *slept* OK?'

'Fine. It's kind of creaky at night, that's going to take me some time to get used to. But I love that bed. There's room enough for me and a dozen passionate women.'

'Well, if you can only find eleven passionate women and you need somebody to make up the numbers, you know my cellphone number . . . Thirteen in a bed, that's supposed to be very unlucky, isn't it?'

'I don't know about unlucky. *Exhausting*, yes.'

When Stu emerged from the rest room, Jim drove him home to Westwood. Stu told him over and over that he was so happy to see him back at West Grove College because there were no genuine people left in Los Angeles, only fakes and liars and snake-oil salesmen.

'Let me tell you something, Jim, some people are so dishonest these days they'd even buy things they don't really want, like pâté de foie gras, and dictionaries, so that when you look at their shopping you think they have taste, and education, when they don't have dick.'

'Sleep well, Stu,' said Jim, and waited patiently outside his house while Stu jabbed his key at his front door again and again, as if he were trying to pin the tail on the donkey.

Jim stumbled over Vinnie's uncle's shoes yet again before he found the light switch in the lobby. The living room was dark and silent, except for the ticking of the bronze Italian clock on the mantelpiece.

'Tibbles?' he called. 'TT?'

He went to the side table and switched on one of the lamps, and then another, and then another. 'Tibbles, are you OK? Where are you hiding yourself, baby?'

It was then that he saw Tibbles sitting in the very center of the hearthrug, utterly still. She was staring up at the wall above the fireplace. And hanging on the wall above the fireplace was the painting of Robert H. Vane, with his black cloth draped over his head.

Numbly, Jim lifted the blue canvas satchel off his shoulder and laid it down on the couch. His feeling of dread was so overwhelming that he could have believed his hair was crawling with lice. He approached the fireplace and looked up at the painting in disbelief. It must have weighed well over 120 pounds. Who could have lifted it up and re-hung it? Who would have *wanted* to? And why?

He looked down at Tibbles. She must have been washing herself today, because she looked a little sleeker, even if she did have five or six raw patches.

'What's going on here, TT? Did somebody come in here while I was away? Huh? Who did this?'

Tibbles briskly shook her head, but that was all.

Jim took two or three steps back. He didn't know what to think. He was so nonplussed that he laughed, but then he immediately stopped. This simply wasn't funny, even as a practical joke.

'So, Mr Robert H. Vane!' Jim challenged him out loud. 'Do you want to explain how you got yourself back up there, you bastard?' He waited, but underneath the black cloth that covered his face, Robert H. Vane remained as silent and mysterious as ever.

Jim walked through to the kitchen and took a beer out the fridge. He came back into the living room and stood in front of the painting again, just like Tibbles, and stared at it. He knew that the supernatural was a day-to-day reality. He had spoken with ghosts and he had seen a kitchen table rotating of its own accord. But there were limits to what spirits could do, and re-hanging an oil painting, in his opinion, was way beyond those limits.

Maybe Vinnie's uncle had a cleaning-lady, who had

thought that she was supposed to dust the painting and put it back up again? Maybe the super had replaced it, thinking that Jim had been unable to do it himself?

He looked around and saw that the gray blanket with which he had covered the painting was neatly folded on one of the chairs. Spirits don't fold blankets, do they? This must have been done by a human. One of Vinnie's relatives, possibly? Maybe Vinnie hadn't told the whole family that he had rented out his uncle's apartment, and one of them had called by to inspect it.

Eleanor Shine? She had seen the painting, after all, and come to the conclusion that there was something strange about it, something powerful. But why would she hang it back up, even if she were strong enough to lift it, which she probably wasn't? Maybe she had decided that it was against the co-op's rules and regulations for paintings to be taken down if they had been hanging for longer than a certain number of years. If you started letting people take their paintings down, what next? Champagne parties in the elevators, and pet lions?

Jim approached the painting as close as he could. Like Vinnie had done when he was a child, he leaned his head against the canvas and looked upward, at an angle, as if he could see the man's face under the cloth. Of course, it was impossible; but the unsettling thing was that he felt that there *was* a face, covered by the cloth, and that in some extraordinary circumstance it might be possible to see it. If and when the painting itself chose to reveal it.

He stepped back. What he hadn't noticed before was Robert H. Vane's left hand. On the wedding-ring finger, instead of a wedding band, he wore a heavy silver ring with a crest on it. The crest was painted in some detail, but Jim couldn't decide what it was. A shield and two crossed daggers? A skull and crossbones? It was impossible to tell.

'Still . . . we're not scared, are we, TT?' said Jim. '"The sleeping and the dead are but as pictures. 'Tis the eye of childhood that fears a painted devil."'

Tibbles squeezed her eyes shut, and yawned.

'Shakespeare, *Macbeth*, act two, scene two,' Jim informed her. 'And put your paw in front of your mouth when you yawn.'

Jim cooked himself a stir-fried supper of strips of beef and red and yellow pepper confetti, pungently flavored with chilis and cumin and garlic. He hadn't eaten anything all day except for half a chicken sandwich, but once he had turned his wok out on to his plate, he suddenly didn't feel hungry. In fact, he felt slightly sick, especially since the kitchen was still filled with smoke.

He sat at the kitchen table, prodding at his supper with his fork. You shouldn't let this get to you, Jim. Are you listening to me? There has to be a rational explanation for how the painting got back up on the wall, and when you find out what it is, you'll feel like a total idiot.

Tibbles came limping into the room, sniffing. She hated garlic, so he knew that she wouldn't want to share any of his supper. He played with it a little more, and then he said, 'It's no good, TT. Unexplained events play havoc with the appetite.' He pushed back his chair and stood up, putting his plate into the microwave oven so that the flies couldn't walk all over it.

He was just closing the oven door when there was a brilliant flash of bluish-white light. He jumped back, thinking that the oven had shorted out, but then he realized that the flash had come from behind him. Not just behind him, but from the living room, next door. Tibbles had jumped, too, and was hiding herself under the sink, where her bowl was, and staring at him wide-eyed.

Jim waited and listened. It couldn't have been lightning, because it hadn't been followed by a peal of thunder. But it had been bright enough for lightning – brighter. Even though he had been standing with his back to the door he still had a green image of the kitchen clock swimming in front of his eyes.

He picked up his largest kitchen knife and cautiously went back into the living room. Nothing had visibly changed, although he thought he could smell overheated metal, like an empty saucepan left on a hot electric hob. He prowled around the room, prodding at the furniture with the point of his knife, but there was nobody here, and no clue as to what might have caused such a dazzling flash.

He deliberately kept his eyes away from the painting of Robert H. Vane. He wasn't even going to speculate on how it managed to get back on the wall. He had too many other things to do, like putting his life back together. His career was OK, even if he had taken a step backward. He had a reasonable place to live, with a sexy lady living across the corridor. Tibbles looked like somebody had attacked a Davy Crockett hat with a flame-thrower, but her fur would probably grow out in a week or two.

Had the painting suddenly jumped up on to its picture hook all by itself? Or had it slowly and eerily risen off the floor, as if it were being lifted up by unseen hands?

He was still circling the room when the doorbell made a weak buzzing sound like a blowfly in an empty matchbox. He stood very still for a moment, with his knife lifted. He wasn't expecting anybody, was he? Maybe it was the super, coming to tell him that he had re-hung the painting for him, and expecting a tip. He went to the front door and peered through the spyhole. Before he could see who it was, the blowfly buzzed again.

He opened the door. It was Eleanor Shine. Her hair was tightly braided so that she looked like a princess from a medieval storybook, and she was wearing a black satin dress, very short, and black suede pixie boots. She was wearing that vertigo perfume again.

'I promised I'd call,' she announced.

'Oh, sure. Come on in.' What else could he say? She had told him that she was always late, hadn't she? But twenty-four hours late . . . that was *late*, no question about it.

'Mind the—' he said, after she had tripped on Vinnie's uncle's shoe mountain.

'My God. Who do you share with? Imelda Marcos?'

'No, no – these belong to the owner. The late, deceased owner.'

'Mr Boschetto, yes. Very nice man, from what I saw of him. Always beautifully dressed. Always polite. Lifted his hat, opened the elevator door for me, said "*buena sera, signora,*" and all that. But he always kept himself to himself. Hardly ever came to co-op meetings, and when he did he never spoke.'

She strode long-legged into the center of the living room. 'This is amazing. I was never in here before. My heavens – that must be the original wallpaper, is it? And these photographs! Amazing! What is this one?'

Jim went over and took a look. 'A woman in an Amish costume, on stilts.'

'Yes, but the stilts are on fire!'

'Yes, so they are. What does it say? *Religious obser-vance, Pennsylvania, 1937.*'

'But what do you think happened to her? It's dreadful! Everybody's just standing around, staring at the camera! Do you think anybody saved her?'

Jim shook his head. 'Most of the pictures in here are like that. Kind of . . . you know . . . disturbing. Look at this one.'

Eleanor peered at a tiny photograph of a small girl with bunches and a grubby face. She couldn't have been more than four years old, but she was holding a huge nickel-plated .44 to her left temple. The caption read: *Monica, Russian Roulette, Arkansas, 1924.*

'It's awful,' said Eleanor. 'Do you know who took them? It wasn't Mr Boschetto, was it? I always thought he was such a gentleman! I mean, these are quite *perverted,* aren't they? I don't mean sexually perverted, but . . .' She stopped. She had caught sight of the painting above the fireplace.

'You put it back up! I thought you were going to hide it away!'

'I ... ah ... I thought I might as well re-hang it. You know, so that you could see it better. Would you like a glass of wine?'

She turned to him. Her eyes were extraordinary, as if they were specially made out of green and white glass. It was a long time since he had met a woman whose sexuality was so tangible. She seemed to be charged with static electricity, as if she would make angora sweaters rise like thistledown, and make iron filings swirl into patterns, and actually crackle if you touched her.

'A glass of wine? Yes, why not?'

He went into the kitchen and she followed him. 'You've been cooking. I didn't interrupt your supper, did I?'

'No, I – lost my appetite, kind of.'

'You're worried about something.'

He took the bottle of Chardonnay out of the fridge and peeled off the foil around the neck. 'I'm ... I've had a difficult couple of years, that's all. Let's just say that I have a tendency to attract trouble.'

Tibbles was still under the sink. She looked up at Eleanor and mewed.

'That's your cat? She can't stay here, you know. The board is very Hitlerian about animals.'

'Well, I'm sure that we can work something out.'

Eleanor hunkered down and made cheeping noises. 'Here, puss! Puss-puss-puss! What happened to you, puss? You look like you've been sitting too close to the fire!'

'That's one of the things I wanted to talk to you about,' said Jim. 'It happened last night, directly after we'd moved in. I heard her yowling, so I went into the living room, and there she was – perched right on top of a torchère, *smoking*.'

'Oh, no!' said Eleanor. 'Is she badly hurt? Poor pussycat! Look at her fur! Do you know, my rabbit-skin coat looked like that, after the moths got to it! Well, that's when I used to wear fur. Just think of all the rabbits who are hopping about today, happy and free, because I won't wear their skin any more!'

'Yes,' said Jim, trying to think about something else altogether.

Eleanor stroked Tibbles under the chin, which she could never resist. 'Poor pussycat! How did it happen?'

'I don't have the first idea. There were no candles in the room, no bare wires. The fire wasn't lit.'

Eleanor gave Tibbles one more stroke and then she stood up. 'Do you think the painting could have had anything to do with it?' Her tone of voice was not only serious, but demanding, as if he was obliged to answer her, by law.

'I can't understand how. But the way that Tibbles was looking at it, you'd have thought that she blamed it for setting her alight. She hid under the couch for a while and she wouldn't come out. I mean, she was very, very scared, and however she got burned, it was the painting she was scared of – no doubt about it.'

'Does it scare you?'

'Well . . . not really. But like you said yesterday, it does have a certain . . . I don't know . . .' He flapped his hand, trying to think of the right word.

'Power?' said Eleanor.

'I don't exactly know if I'd call it power. In my experience, some objects appear to have a power of their own, when they don't, really. Not in themselves. It's only the way they make people feel. Voodoo masks, witch doctors' bones, crucifixes, things like that. They strike certain primitive chords.'

Eleanor was staring at him.

'What?' he asked her.

She came closer, still staring at him. He wondered if he had a zit on his nose.

'You can *see*, can't you?' she asked him.

He knew what she meant, but he pretended he didn't.

83

Over the years, his sight had caused him so much pain, and so much fear, and so much heartache. He wished more than anything else that he could be blind to the afterlife, so that when he walked along the street he couldn't see the dead any more, or the hideous things that crawled out of the human imagination, like boogie men, and ghosts, and creatures that hid beneath the bed, waiting to bite at children's ankles. Because they were really there, to those who could see them.

'Let's go through,' he suggested, and led the way back into the living room. But Eleanor refused to be put off.

'You can *see*,' she insisted.

'All right,' he confessed. 'I can see. How can you tell?'

'Because I'm sensitive myself, that's why.'

'Oh, yes?'

'I've been sensitive ever since I was a little girl. I can't actually see spirits, not the way that you can, but I can tell when they're close by, and I can usually tell what they're thinking, especially if they're unhappy.'

Jim took off his glasses and rubbed his eyes. In the past five or six years he had come across dozens of psychics and so-called 'sensitives,' but only one or two of them had proved themselves to be halfway genuine. The rest had been fruitcakes or dangerous frauds.

He liked Eleanor. He thought she was the kind of woman who could easily help him to get over Karen. Sexy, smart, elegant, eccentric. But if she was going to make out that she was a sensitive, that could give present a serious problem, especially if she was a fake.

'Why don't you sit down?' he asked her.

Eleanor looked around. 'I can sense a presence in this apartment. Here and now.'

'Really?'

She frowned, and cupped one hand around her ear, listening. 'Two presences, in fact. Well, more than two – many more – but two that are really important.'

She plonked herself down on the couch, very abruptly, as if she were playing a game of musical chairs. Her dress was really very short.

'You don't believe me, do you?' she demanded.

'I didn't say that.'

'No, but you were thinking it,' said Eleanor. 'But answer me this: if I don't have the gift, how could I possibly know that you can see?'

'How should I know? Maybe Vinnie told you. Most of my friends know about it. Some of my students used to know about it, too. It isn't that easy to hide.'

'I've never even met Vinnie. Who's Vinnie?'

'Mr Boschetto's nephew. He inherited this apartment. Well, along with two of his sisters.'

'Jim, I'm telling you the truth. I can feel two strong presences here, but they're keeping themselves very well hidden, because they're worried that you'll see them – and that you'll want to talk to them, and that you'll find out what they're doing.'

'So who are they? And what *are* they doing?'

Eleanor put down her glass of wine on the side table and pressed her fingertips to her forehead. Jim noticed for the first time that, deep between her breasts, she was wearing a large silver pendant. It was emblazoned with a bland, round face, rather like the face of the moon in medieval paintings. It was the face of a fool, but a sly, cruel fool.

Eleanor closed her eyes and tilted her head back. Jim waited patiently, occasionally glancing around the room to see if there was any visible sign of her 'presences'. The Italian clock ticked away each minute as if it could barely summon up the energy. Eleanor's lips were moving slightly, but Jim couldn't hear what she was saying. He was tempted to look up at Robert H. Vane, but he found the strength of will not to. He wasn't going to allow a nineteenth-century daguerrotypist with a cloth over his head to win a 'made-you-look' contest.

He was just about to pick up his glass of wine when Eleanor clutched at his wrist and almost broke his watch strap.

'They're *good* spirits,' she said hoarsely. 'They're very good spirits. I can *feel* their goodness.'

'Where are they?' Jim asked her.

Silence.

'Eleanor, where are they?'

'He came . . .' she continued. 'There was something – something about a wedding. A wedding, that's it! And he was there, but he wasn't related – or a guest, or a friend of the family. He was all dressed in black . . . and *she* said—'

'She? Who's she?'

'*She* said, "he looks like a mortician," and she didn't realize then how true her words were.'

Jim laid his hand on top of Eleanor's. 'Eleanor, can you hear me? Listen, Eleanor, I need to know who they are, these spirits. Ask them what their names are.'

'They're *good* spirits,' Eleanor insisted. Her eyes were still closed and her fingertips were still pressed to her forehead. 'They don't wish you any harm. They keep asking you to forgive them. Please, forgive us! But somebody has to find him . . . Somebody has to stop him.'

'*Who*, Eleanor? Who are they, and who's *him*?'

'He has to be found, Jim. It isn't going to be easy. He can hide almost any place at all. But he has to be found, and he has to be killed. Otherwise . . .'

'Otherwise what?'

'Otherwise he'll go on forever, and he'll gather in more and more spirits like a rat-catcher. Innocent spirits, good spirits.'

'For God's sake, Eleanor, *who*?'

Eleanor didn't answer, but began to breathe deeper and deeper, taking in huge lungfuls of air through her nose and exhaling them with a quivering gasp.

'Eleanor. Eleanor! Listen to me! Snap out of it, OK?'

But Eleanor continued to hyperventilate, and her gasps grew more and more desperate, as if she were being gassed, or drowning.

'Eleanor! Listen to me! Eleanor!' Jim grasped her shoulders and shook her. 'Eleanor! Open your eyes! Come on, Eleanor, come back to me! One . . . two . . . three!'

Her eyes remained closed, but her shoulders hunched and her arms and legs started to slacken, as if she were a marionette. It was then that Jim's eye was caught by a flicker of movement on the opposite side of the room. A dark, dancing flicker against the drapes.

There was a pause, and then he saw it again. A tall, attenuated shadow, like the shadow of a man on a winter's day – impossibly stretched-out, and out of proportion. It moved silently across the curtains with a long, giraffe-like lope, even though there was nobody between the table lamp and the window, and the curtains were far too thick for it to have been showing through from outside.

In a few seconds it had vanished, but Jim sat staring at the window bay for nearly half a minute afterward. He had never felt such dread in his life. It was the shadow's way of walking that had frightened him so much – the fluid but wildly uneven gait of somebody who has learned to overcome a terrible disability. Maybe not some*body*, but some*thing* – because it had seemed to Jim to be an assembly of human, animal and insect. It was the shadow of a creature that, seen in the flesh, would lead you straight to madness.

'*Eleanor!*'

Eleanor stopped panting and opened her eyes. She blinked at Jim as if she had never seen him before.

'Are you OK?' he asked her.

'Yes . . . I think so.' She looked around the living room. 'I talked to them. The presences. They were amazing.'

'There was something else here, Eleanor. I saw it.'

'My God, Jim. You're shaking!'

'For God's sake! *There was something else here!* Not just your "presences."'

She looked bewildered. 'What was it? Was it a spirit? What did it look like? Where?'

'A shadow. It walked across the drapes. But it wasn't just a shadow. It was . . .' He couldn't find words to tell her how much it had frightened him. It was everything that comes after you in the middle of the night. Everything that limps and hobbles and hurries through the darkness, and eventually catches up with you, when you're least expecting it.

Eleanor nodded. She looked even more serious than she had before.

'You know what it was?' Jim asked her.

'I think so. I think it was *him*, Jim. The man you have to hunt down.'

Jim sat back. 'Me? Why me? Forget it. Absolutely not.'

'But who else could do it?'

'I don't know, Eleanor, and I truly don't care. I'm not hunting *anybody* down, period. I'm out of this supernatural malarkey, for good and all, you got it? Let me tell you this: whatever it takes to stop me from seeing dead people, and demons, and boogie men and . . . and sinister shadows that hobble across my curtains – if I need therapy – if I need a lobotomy, even – then that's what I'm going to do.'

Eight

Eleanor waited until he had finished. Then, very calmly, she said, 'OK.'

'OK what?'

'OK, if you really don't want to hunt this person down, then nobody can make you – least of all me.'

'That's OK, then,' said Jim. He waited for Eleanor to say something else and when she didn't, he stood up, went back into the kitchen, and took another can of beer out of the fridge. When he returned to the living room, Tibbles followed him in, and jumped up on his chair beside him.

'Look at the state of this cat,' he said. 'She looks like a bomb went off in a toilet brush factory.'

'Yes,' said Eleanor. 'But she's the key to what's happening here.'

'What do you mean?'

'I don't know, exactly . . . but the presences kept trying to make me look at her. Almost as if they were physically trying to turn my head around.'

'So . . . these "presences".' Do they talk to you, or what?'

'No, they don't talk. It's more like I *feel* them. It's like being in a darkened room, with a whole lot of people you've never met before. You can only get to know them by touching them and smelling them. I can't hear any actual words . . . I can only get the gist of what they're trying to tell me.'

'Do you know who they are . . . or who they *were*?'

'No. They didn't live here when they were alive. I'm

89

pretty sure this apartment was familiar to them, but it wasn't their home.'

'Well, Vinnie's uncle lived here for over forty years, almost as long as the building's been standing. And he lived here alone, so far as I know. Well, he probably had his fancy women. Or men. I don't know anything about him, except that he couldn't bear to throw away his shoes.'

Eleanor stood up and paced slowly around the perimeter of the room, her eyes on the floor, as if she were looking for a lost earring. 'They could have been *related* to Vinnie's uncle. They were very passionate, very expressive. Very Latin, if you know what I mean.'

'You don't have *any* idea what their names were?'

Eleanor shook her head. 'The woman may have been called something like Flora or Floretta. She gave me a feeling like lots of little multicolored flowers, but that could have been anything. A favorite dress, maybe. Even an apron. The man . . . I don't know. I get the feeling that he might have had a moustache, that's all.'

'So who's this person who scares them so much?'

'Again, I don't know his name. But the first time they saw him was at somebody's wedding. A close relative, I think, maybe a niece or a nephew. The woman gave me a mental picture of the bride, and the groom, and I could hear accordion music, and people clapping. Then everybody gathered together to have their photograph taken, and it was then that this man appeared. He was all dressed in black, and for some reason the woman felt afraid of him. And I mean, *deeply* afraid.'

'Was he the photographer?'

'I'm not sure. That wasn't very clear.'

'Did you see him yourself?'

'Through *her* eyes, briefly. He was very blurred.'

'Would you know him again, if you saw his face?'

Eleanor stopped by his chair. The hem of her dress was lightly touching his arm, and he could smell that perfume again, as if she had lightly sprayed it on her inner thighs. 'Yes,' she said. 'I think I might.'

He pointed to the painting. 'Do you think it's him? Robert H. Vane?'

She gave him an almost imperceptible nod. 'Either him, or something that's possessed him.'

Jim arrived early the next morning so that he could park his car in the spare space marked Vice-Principal. The previous vice-principal, Dr Friendly, had left West Grove at the end of last semester, and Dr Ehrlichman still hadn't been able to find a suitable successor. As far as Jim was concerned, anybody had to be friendlier than Dr Friendly. Jim had always called him the Grinch.

He climbed out of the Lincoln, caught his foot in the seat belt, and dropped all of his books and files and papers on to the tarmac. Walter the janitor came across the parking lot, trying not to laugh, and helped him to pick them up.

'Goddamn seat belt rewind thing,' Jim complained.

'You want to get that fixed. That's the second day in a row I seen you go ass over apex. My young nephew, he'll do it for you, for cost.'

'Thanks, Walter. It is Walter, isn't it?'

'That's right, sir, Mr Rook.'

'Well, I'll come by your office later today, and you can give me your nephew's phone number. You can also fill me in on all the latest college gossip. I've been away for more than three years, and I'm not sure who's doing the dirty on whom, and why.'

'Mr Rook?'

'Janitors know all the scuttlebutt, don't they? Like, they know which teacher is having an affair with which teacher's wife, and which teacher is trying to undermine which teacher's career prospects. They know which students are pushing naughty salt and which students are snorting it.

They know who's straight and who's acting shady. I like to keep up to speed with all that stuff.'

'I'm not sure I can tell you anything like that, Mr Rook, but I can guarantee you a fine cup of coffee.'

'OK, you're on. That swill they serve in the staffroom – you can only tell it's supposed to be coffee because it doesn't taste like chocolate and it doesn't taste like tea and it can't be piss because it's brown.'

Jim pushed his way through the battered blue double doors into the main corridor. He was just passing Dr Ehrlichman's office when a tall, broad-shouldered student approached him, wearing a West Grove football shirt in purple and yellow stripes. He was one of those young men who are so enormous that they made Jim feel like a squeaky-voiced midget. He knew from experience that most of them were gentle and shy, but he couldn't stop himself from dropping his voice an octave and balancing on his toes.

'Mr Rook, isn't it? I'm Brad Moorcock.'

'Hi, there! How are you doing, Brad? Anything I can help you with?'

Brad nodded. He had tousled blond hair and a wide, bland, movie-handsome face, although it was given some character by the bump on his broken nose. His blue eyes looked so sincere that it was almost laughable.

'Me and Sara Miller . . .' Cough. 'We were, like, an item.'

'I see. You and Sara? I'm sorry.'

'We'd been dating since Hallowe'en last year, but she dumped me the second week of college.'

'I see. Well, I'm sorry.'

'She said I was arrogant and all I cared about was myself and I never respected her.'

'I see. I'm sorry.'

'She said I treated her like I owned her and never considered her feelings, and it was true.' He stopped, and swallowed hard, and there were tears glistening in his eyes.

'How could I have been so selfish, you know? If only I'd known what was going to happen to her.'

Jim dropped one of his books on the floor and had to bend down to pick it up. 'You shouldn't be so hard on yourself, Brad. It wasn't your fault.'

'I guess not.' Brad wiped his eyes with his fingers and gave a loud, snotty sniff. 'It's just that I feel responsible. I mean, I should have been there to protect her.'

'If you had been there, Brad, you'd be clinkers, too. Whoever killed her, there was no way of stopping him, believe me.'

'She didn't suffer, did she? I can't bear to think that she suffered.'

If Brad had been a regular-sized person, Jim would have put his arm around him to comfort him, but it was obvious that he wouldn't be able to reach. Instead, he took hold of Brad's hand, and gripped it tight, and said, 'She didn't suffer, Brad, believe me. It all happened in a flash.'

'Thanks, Mr Rook. I appreciate it. I was going to try to get back with her, you know. I was planning to ask her yesterday morning.'

'I see. I'm sorry.'

'I lost her because I was such a total dork. I was the Duke of Dork. But I saw the light. Bam! Don't ask me how it happened, but I suddenly looked around and saw that I'd been behaving like an asshole. Not just to her, to everybody. My friends, my parents, my teammates. But it was too late, wasn't it? Too late to save Sara, anyhow.'

'Like I say, Brad, don't take it too hard.'

Brad wiped his eyes on his sleeve, and sniffed again. Jim rummaged through his coat for a Kleenex. He felt something soft and papery in his breast pocket and held it out. 'You want to blow your nose?' he asked, but when Brad stared at him he realized that he was holding out a crumpled five-dollar bill.

'Well, ah . . . I guess Mrs Frogg will probably have some tissue.'

Brad nodded. 'You're helping the police, aren't you?' he said. 'I just want you to know that if there's anything I can do to help you – anything at all . . .'

'Thanks, Brad. I really appreciate it.'

'Anything at all, OK? If I can make up for the way I treated Sara . . . even just a little bit.'

'Sure.'

He gave Brad a slap on the back and continued on his way to Special Class II. For some reason, though, he felt as if he had been told something very important. He stopped halfway along the corridor, frowning and thinking, but he couldn't work out what it was.

I saw the light. That's what Brad had told him. *I saw the light.* Just like Saul in the Bible, on his way to Damascus. 'And suddenly a light from heaven flashed around him,' and he was converted to Christianity.

Jim thought of the light that he had seen flashing in his living room. He thought of the naked statue in the hallway of the Benandanti Building – LIGHT SNARETH THE SOUL – and he thought of the picture of Bobby and Sara that had been imprinted on the wall of the beach house, like a photograph. A flash. A photograph. A flash photograph.

He was being told something so loudly that it reminded him of the time that he had gone white-water rafting, with his instructor yelling in his ear. The trouble was – now as then – he still couldn't understand what it all meant, and what he was supposed to do next.

Sue-Marie Cassidy was waiting outside the classroom, wearing the shortest denim skirt Jim had ever seen in his life, with a broad white leather belt and white leather boots. She was even more heavily made-up than usual, and her lips looked as shiny and sweet and red as glacé cherries. She was chewing a massive wad of Doublemint gum.

'Good morning, Mr Rook!' She winked. 'I just *adore* your necktie!'

Jim looked down. He was wearing a bronze-and-silver
affair that he had borrowed from his Greek friend Bill
Babouris after an end-of-semester drinking party, about five
years ago, and never returned. It had pictures of the
Acropolis on it, and the Venus de Milo, and other assorted
Greek marbles.

'You really like it?' he asked.

Sue-Marie took hold of it and lifted it up. 'It's like *you*,
Mr Rook. It's a classic.'

'That's very complimentary of you, Sue-Marie. But the
fact is that I detest this necktie.'

'Oh. Then why did you wear it?'

'Because my favorite necktie, which is based on a painting
by Georges Braque, who exhibited a cubist painting even
before Picasso did, and who was one of the finest of the early
abstract painters, has spaghetti sauce splattered all over it.'

There was a very long pause. Sue-Marie blinked once,
and then again. At last, she asked him, 'Who would know?'

Jim entered the classroom, raising one hand to quell the
usual bustle of basketball-bouncing and hair-spraying and
rap singing. 'OK, settle down now . . . Quieten down. I want
you to know that there will be a joint funeral service for
Bobby and Sara on Wednesday morning at the Rolling Hills
cemetery and all of their classmates are invited to attend. I
have spoken to Dr Ehrlichman and he has agreed to arrange
for a bus so that we can all go to the service together.

'I didn't know Bobby and Sara but I'm very well aware
how popular they both were, and I'm sure you'll all want
to come along. Dress: optional, but respectful. So, Freddy,
I don't want to see you in that T-shirt you wore yesterday.'

'That's a perfectly innocent T-shirt,' Freddy protested.
'All it says is "Beer in the lobby, gambling in the parlor."'

'You think I was born yesterday?' said Jim. 'When I was
at college, that translated as "Liquor in the front, poker in
the rear." I presume it still does.'

'I never realized that,' said Freddy. 'I'm shocked.'

95

'Can I wear white?' asked Ruby. 'White, that's the Chinese color for mourning.'

'What do you want to do that for?' George demanded. 'You're not Chinese, are you?'

'How do you know I don't have Chinese ancestry?'

'Because you're one hundred per cent Puerto Rican. You couldn't even pass for Chinese if you walked around with a wok on your head.'

Jim took off his coat and hung it over the back of his chair. 'Now then, how far did you get with our daguerrotypist, Robert H. Vane? Anybody find out anything interesting?'

Silence. You could almost hear the surf on Malibu Beach, eight miles away.

'You do remember our daguerrotypist, Robert H. Vane?'

Jim waited. The class stared back at him as if he had asked them to remember what they were doing at 3:23 P.M. on August 27, 1996.

'Anybody? No?'

At the very back of the classroom, Philip Genio's cell-phone started to play the theme tune from *Bewitched*. He hurriedly tugged it out of his pocket and switched it off, but not before four or five of his classmates had started singing along.

'Da-*da*! Ta-*ra*! Da-da-da-da *ta-ra*!'

Jim looked down at the floor. 'Don't tell me that out of a class of sixteen, not one single one of you turned up any information whatsoever about Robert H. Vane?'

Special Class II shuffled their feet and frowned and scratched the backs of their necks and pulled a variety of extraordinary faces. Jim paced from one side of the class-room to the other, and then back again,

'If I had never met you guys before – if I had walked into this classroom this morning for the very first time, I would have looked at your faces now and thought that you were right on the verge of opening your mouths and saying something really intelligent.'

He approached Roosevelt, and stood directly in front of his desk, staring at him intently.

'But you're not going to say anything intelligent, are you?' said Jim. 'In fact, you're not even going to say anything stupid. Because not one of you could be bothered. You didn't really understand what I was asking you to do, or *why*, and so you thought, *nyah*, so what? Well, if that's the way you feel, then I don't care either. *Nyah*, so what? I came back here hoping that you might teach me something, and what have you taught me? "Why bother?" That's what you've taught me. "Who gives a damn?" Life's a waste of time and then you die.'

He paused and looked around the classroom. 'Obviously you don't care about yourselves but I had hoped that you might care about me. But, you don't, do you? So my suggestion is that you go back to whatever you were doing – texting your friends, polishing your nails, reading comics, bouncing basketballs – and that's what we'll do every day until you're ready to leave college and go out into the world as fully qualified texters, manicurists, comic-readers and basketball-bouncers, and may the Lord have mercy on your stupid souls.'

Randy slowly put up his hand. 'Please, sir.'

'Yes, Randy. If you want to go to the bathroom and eat two Krispy Kreme donuts on the way there and back, be my guest.'

'I don't need to go to the bathroom, sir.' He frowned at a torn-off sheet of notepaper on the desk in front of him. 'I just wanted to say that Robert Henry Vane was born in Boston, Massachusetts, on August 4th, 1827.'

Jim stared at him. The classroom had fallen utterly silent. At last Jim walked around to his desk and stood close beside him. 'Carry on,' he said quietly.

Randy hesitated for a moment, wiped his nose with the back of his hand, and then continued to read out his notes, gabbling some sentences, stumbling over others.

'Robert Henry Vane's parents were well known and respected in Boston, which led to his birth being recorded in *The Boston News-Letter*. It says in the paper that he was born with a caul on his head. I looked that up, sir – *caul*. It's a piece of membrane which some babies have on their heads when they're born. It's supposed to mean that the baby is always going to have good luck.'

'Where did you get all this?' Jim asked him.

'Right here, sir. In the college library, sir. I never realized how many books they have in there. And I mean they have books about *everything*. Even how porcupines have sex.'

'Did you find out any more?'

'Yes, sir. Although he was born with a lucky caul, young Robert Henry Vane had very little good luck in his formative years. His father was a wealthy maker of gunpowder and fireworks. His mother was Italian, and contemporary portraits show that she was very beautiful. But his father was killed in an explosion at his own factory in 1834 and after that his mother became so ill with grief that she sent young Robert to her parents to be taken care of, and they in turn sent him to an orphanage.'

Randy looked up. He was breathing hard from the effort of reading. 'There's more in the library but my ball pen ran out of ink. I'm sorry.'

'You're sorry? That was *excellent*, Randy. That was exactly the kind of information I was looking for. Why didn't you say anything before?'

Randy's cheeks flushed. 'When nobody else said nothing . . . I thought that maybe I was the only one who had done any work.'

'And you didn't want the rest of the class to accuse you of ass-licking, is that it?'

Randy nodded, and stared down at his desk in embarrassment. But to Jim's surprise, there was no jeering, not even from Shadow. He looked around the class and suddenly realized that almost all of his students were bright-eyed with bottled-up excitement, as if they were all bursting to tell him something.

'So . . . did anybody else look up any facts on Robert H. Vane?' he asked them. 'Sally, what about you?'

Sally was chewing a large mouthful of her own frizzy hair, and she almost choked. It was a habit of hers: she spent most lessons twisting her hair around her fingers or sucking it.

'I found out a little bit,' she said, spitting out hair.

'Even a little bit's better than nothing. Are you going to share it with us?'

She opened her workbook and recited in a sing-song voice. 'Robert H. Vane toured California between 1852 and 1857, from Yosemite in the north to Mission Viejo in the south, taking dagger-type pictures of scenery and pioneer communities and gold diggings. He sent the pictures back to New York in order to encourage people to come settle out west. His most famous dagger-types, however, were those of the indig— indigans?'

Jim looked over her shoulder. 'Indigens . . . it means the people who originally live in a place before anybody else gets there. In this case, rather confusingly, the indigens happened to be the people we used to call Indians. Go on, Sally.'

'That's it,' she said. 'Then my brother came in and said it was his turn to use the computer.'

'OK, Sally,' said Jim. 'That's very good, as far as it goes. And, by the way, it's pronounced da-gair-oh-types. Anybody else?'

Delilah put her hand up. 'I found this old story in *True Crimes* magazine about a man who was arrested in San Diego in October of 1857, for murder. His name was spelled different, Robert V-a-i-n, but he was a photographer, too, so I guessed that he was probably the same guy.'

'That's *very* interesting. Who was he supposed to have killed?'

Delilah read from her computer printout. 'He was accused of murdering John Philip Stebbings, a wealthy department-store owner from Chicago, and Mr Stebbings' wife, Veronica. They were both burned to death when their house caught fire on the night of September 9th, 1857. Actually, they were almost cremated, because there was nothing left of them except their bones and their engraved wedding rings.'

'Go on,' said Jim.

He thought *this sounds horribly like the way that Bobby and Sara were killed*, but he didn't say anything. It could be nothing more than coincidence, and in any case the class didn't yet know the full grisly details of Bobby and Sara's incineration. Hardly anybody knew, because they hadn't been released to the media.

Delilah momentarily lost her place, but then she found it again. 'Oh, yes! Mr Vain was arrested and charged because two stable hands said they had seen him running away from the scene of the fire. Then one of the Stebbings' chamber-maids came forward to say that Mr Vain had been "paying calls" on Mrs Stebbings during the summer of 1857, while Mr Stebbings was away on business in Chicago. I guess "paying calls" is 1857-speak for having an affair.'

Jim nodded. 'They might have been having an affair, yes. But even if they weren't actually going to bed together, it wasn't considered proper in those days for a married woman to receive gentleman callers, not on her own, anyhow.'

'You hear that, Shadow?' called out Vanilla. 'So don't you go calling me on my cellphone no more, it ain't proper.'

Delilah hesitated, but then she went back to her reading. 'The chambermaid said that Mr Stebbings had found out about his wife's friendship with Mr Vain and ordered her to stop seeing him. Mr Vain was very angry about this, and the chambermaid thought that he might have burned the house down, with Mr and Mrs Stebbings in it, out of revenge.'

'Was Vain ever tried?'

Delilah shook her head. 'He had witnesses who swore that at the time the fire was started he was playing cards at the home of A. T. Peebles, the hardware millionaire, and two other men. The sheriff decided that because the stable hands were Mexican their evidence was probably unreliable, and that the Stebbings' house had more than likely been struck by a freak bolt of lightning. Their deaths were officially entered in the county records as an act of God.'

'That's wonderful,' said Jim. 'That's first-class historical research. We'll have to check if "Mr Vain" was *our* Mr Vane, won't we? but it sounds very likely.' Especially since the Stebbings had been burned to death by 'a freak bolt of lightning', he thought.

He circled the classroom again. 'Anybody else have anything?'

David had been jabbing his hand up in the air for the past five minutes. 'These, sir. Look, sir. Printouts of some of Robert H. Vane's pictures, from the Internet.'

'Now these I have to see,' said Jim. David handed him four sheets of paper and he held them up in front of the class, so that everybody could see them. '*A view of Lake Berryessa, 1851*. Looks mountainous, doesn't it, and bleak? But there are two figures in the foreground here, both of them wearing hoods over their heads, and hats, so they look like a couple of bee-keepers. Any ideas who they could be, anybody? *A portrait of Two Noses, the Dagueno chief, with the skull of his dead grandfather, 1852*. You can see why they call him Two Noses, can't you? But he doesn't look too happy, does he? And what's this? *Funeral at Placerville, 1854, of the gold-prospector John Keating*, complete with horse and carriage and brass band. And look at this! A self-portrait, taken in 1856, in his own studio in Los Muertes.'

Now, for the first time, Jim saw the face of the man whose portrait was hanging over his fireplace. Robert H.

Vane was standing in the oddly angled corner of a wooden building, with a calico shade drawn halfway down. He was wearing a black frock coat with a long watch chain and his arms were folded. He was thin-faced, almost cadaverous, with eyes that were so deep-set they appeared to be nothing but black holes. He was staring directly at the camera lens as if he were trying to intimidate anybody who ever had the impertinence to look at him, or to wonder who he was, and what he had done.

'That is one seriously creepy dude,' said George.

And Jim thought: *if ever I saw a man who looked capable of burning people to ashes, this has to be him.*

Nine

Most of the rest of the class had found out odd bits and pieces about Robert H. Vane, but the more Jim learned about him, the more shadowy Robert H. Vane seemed to become, because no two descriptions of his life and his behavior seemed to tally. Several different accounts had spoken of a 'chilly demeanored, black-dressed figure, like a mortician' and many people who had met him seemed to have been deeply frightened of him, for no accountable reason. One woman said that 'the night after meeting him, I had a nightmare in which my mouth was filled with crawling cockroaches.'

He had traveled from one settlement to another, taking pictures of families and weddings and scenery, and any other oddity that took his eye. There were several hints that he might have had a way with women, although he had never taken more than two or three pictures of any one woman in particular, and he always appeared to have traveled alone.

But for all those who found him 'disturbing' and 'sinister' there were almost as many who thought he was a shining inspiration. Father Juan Perez, of the Santa Juanita mission near San Diego, had written in his diary that Robert H. Vane seemed to 'carry with him the power of divine conversion.'

Mr Vane visited and made daguerrotypes of many of our local families and settlers, and I observed that after his visits those who had posed for his pictures seemed

103

to be almost saintly in their goodness and their generosity, and that many remarked how greatly their temperament had improved, as if all the badness had been taken out of them.

Pinky, of all people, had found out about the Dagueno Tragedy. 'It's in this website I found on the Internet called *The Native Peoples of Southern California In Pictures*, and it's got, like, photographs of all the Indian tribes that died out. Some of them got extinct even before anybody got the chance to get to know them, because the first explorers were carrying all kinds of diseases that the Indians never had before, like the flu and stuff, and the Indians didn't have no immunity to them. So they died, like, you know, *flies*.

'Anyhow, this website has pictures of the Dagueno Indians that Robert H. Vane took. It says that the Daguenos were really hostile before he went to visit them, but that afterwards they became one of the friendliest tribes out of all of them. But about a month later they attacked the nearest white settlement by surprise and they killed everybody – sixty-five men, women and children – and cut their ears off and pulled out their intestines and everything. So the white settlers got up a posse and went to the Dagueno village and wiped out the whole tribe. It says the Daguenos didn't even try to fight back, which was weird, wasn't it?'

Jim said, 'Yes it was. Very weird.'

Even weirder – why had Robert H. Vane covered his head in a black cloth, in mourning for the Daguenos? Had he somehow felt responsible for what had happened to them? And what exactly *had* happened to them? Why hadn't they fought back?

Mysteriouser and mysteriouser, as Alice might have said.

Philip had found out what sort of camera Robert H. Vane had used – two wooden boxes with one sliding inside of the other – but of course it was Edward who had researched all the technical details about daguerrotypes.

'It was 1833,' he announced dramatically. 'It was in France.'

'OK,' said Jim. 'It was 1833, and it was in France.'

'I was just setting the scene,' Edward explained. 'There, in 1833, in France, in his shabby studio, the highly-talented, little-known artist Louis Daguerre made a discovery that was going to change the world.'

'Who are you?' Shadow complained. 'His publicist?'

Edward ignored him. 'Louis Daguerre discovered that if he coated a copper plate with silver, and then exposed the silver surface to iodine vapor, it became sensitive to light. So he put the plate inside a totally dark box, right, and then he let the sunlight shine into the box for a few minutes, through a tiny hole. After that, he fumed the plate with mercury vapor, so that the mercury amalgamated with the silver, and what do you think he had managed to do?'

'Choke himself?' Randy suggested.

'No . . . he had made himself a visible picture. A photograph! All he had to do then was stop the picture from fading away by fixing it with a strong salt solution. In a very short time, this method of taking pictures swept the world, and photographers were still taking daguerrotypes until 1885 when George Eastman invented the roll film and the Kodak camera.'

Brenda said, 'I didn't understand any of that.'

'Well, it isn't all that difficult,' Jim put in. 'Imagine a mirror inside a closed box, but then you make a small hole in the box so that the light can shine in. The mirror would show you a reflection of what was outside, wouldn't it? Louis Daguerre simply found a way of fixing the reflection on to the silver so that it stayed there. In fact, in the early days, cameras were called "mirrors with memory."'

'That's why a lot of people didn't like having their pictures taken,' said Edward.

'How's that?' Jim asked him.

'I looked up all this cool occult stuff about daguerrotypes.

Some superstitious people refused to have their pictures taken because daguerrotype plates were coated with silver, and silver is so pure that it reflects all of the evil inside of you.'

'Evil, man?' said Roosevelt. 'Speak for yourself. I am so damn good I have a different halo for every day of the week.'

'*Everybody* has evil inside of them,' Edward insisted. 'Otherwise, we wouldn't know the difference between good and bad, would we? Every time you look in a mirror or a shiny silver tray, you can see your evil self looking back at you. The thing is, though, once you stop looking in a mirror or a shiny silver tray, your evil self vanishes back inside your good self. Now you see it, now you don't. But if your evil image got *fixed*, like it does in a daguerrotype, all of your badness would stay trapped in the silver, for ever.'

'Why wouldn't people want that to happen to them?' asked Brenda. 'I mean, it would be good, wouldn't it, to have all the evil taken out of you?'

Edward shook his head. 'You wouldn't survive for five minutes, would you, without some evil in you? If somebody mugged you, you'd never fight back, in case you hurt them. Or if somebody killed your kid brother, you'd forgive them, and nobody would ever get punished.'

He looked around at the class, and he sounded almost evangelical. 'Silver is so pure that it can capture the blackest part of your soul ... like, Judas betrayed Jesus for thirty pieces of silver. And werewolves can be killed with silver bullets, because the bullet absorbs all the hairy evil in them, and just leaves the good, non-hairy bit.'

Jim looked at him with one eyebrow raised. 'And where, exactly, did you find out all of that baloney?'

'*The Twilight Zone*,' said Edward, unabashed. 'It was an episode called *Silver Lining*.'

'And you think that *The Twilight Zone* is a reliable source of mythological information?'

'I don't know, sir. But all myths are made up, aren't they?'

'OK, good point,' Jim agreed. 'It's just that a myth made up by a 1960s TV writer doesn't have the same sociological resonance as a myth that's been passed down by word of mouth since biblical times.'

'I think Edward's myth about silver is true,' said Pinky. 'Like, there's so many Indians in those pictures who are covering up their faces or looking away. I mean, why did they do that? Did they know something we've forgotten about?'

Jim was leaving the classroom at the end of the second lesson when Walter the janitor came past, carrying four stacking chairs.

'Mr Rook . . . I was just about to brew up a pot of coffee. You want to join me?'

'I . . . ah . . . sure. Let me help you with these chairs.'

They walked out of the main building and across to the college gymnasium. Walter's 'office' was a lean-to building up against the gymnasium wall, and it was crowded with cleaning materials and brushes and vacuum cleaners and odd pieces of shelving and broken desks. In the center of this disorder was a battered old desk, a swivel chair and a big brown leather couch with half of its orange foam stuffing bulging out.

Walter put down his chairs and Jim stacked his on top of them. 'Thanks for that,' said Walter. 'I'm not getting any younger, and I can't tote stuff around the way I used to.'

'You and me both,' said Jim.

'You – there's plenty of years in you yet, Mr Rook.'

'I know. It's not the years I'm worried about, it's the way I'm going to live them.'

Walter opened a blue ceramic coffee jar and spooned three generous helpings of ground coffee into a glass cafetière. 'I don't believe in no percolation,' he said. 'Ruins the taste.'

Jim sat on the couch. It made a loud farting noise and he sank down almost two feet.

Walter said, 'You've been through some difficult times, Mr Rook, from what I hear.'

'Difficult, yes. Huh! You could call them that.'

'So how are you making out?'

'I don't know. Not very well. I get up, I come to college, I go home. I feel like a broken jug, if you want to know the truth. I need some Crazy Glue for the soul.'

Walter poured boiling water into the cafetière. His office was soon filled with the strong aroma of arabica. 'What you need is other people.'

'Maybe. The question is, do other people need me? I don't really think I'm such good company, just at the moment.'

Walter opened the top drawer of his desk, and took out a well-creased envelope. 'You take a look at these, Mr Rook. This is a party that my family held for me, after my Gloria's funeral. You wouldn't think that I'd just buried my wife, the only woman who ever meant anything to me, my life companion. Everybody laughing and singing and having a good time. And the reason for that is, life is a happy thing, despite all its painfulness, and all its losses, and you might as well celebrate what you got, and forget about what you ain't.'

Jim took the photographs and looked through them. Walter was right. It looked more like a birthday party than a wake. A birthday party. An end, but a new beginning.

'They're good,' he said. 'They're very . . . cheerful.'

He was handing the envelope back to Walter when it fell open and a shower of negatives fell out on to the floor. 'I'm sorry . . . here, don't worry, I've got them.'

He picked them up and tidied them. He held one of them up to the light, to make sure he had it the right way round. It was a picture of Walter with his arm around one of his sisters. Walter, with a white face and black hair.

He slid the negatives back into the envelope. White face. Black hair. Just like the person who had been seen at the Tubbs' beach house, on the night that Bobby and Sara had been burned to death, except the other way around. Black face. White hair.

'Are you OK, Mr Rook?' asked Walter. 'How about a chocolate-chip cookie?'

'No thanks, Walter. Just the coffee.'

'You mind what I told you, Mr Rook. Celebrate what you got. Forget what you ain't got. Otherwise, you going to be miserable for the rest of your days.'

It was almost seven thirty in the evening by the time Jim had finished marking work and planning for the next day's lessons. The sky was cloudless and clear except for a pink vapor trail in the shape of a question mark, and a warm wind was blowing from the south-west. He was halfway across the parking lot when a voice called out, 'Jim!'

He stopped and turned, shielding his eyes against the sun. Karen came toward him, carrying her books in her arms. She was wearing a flowery blouse and a trim blue skirt and she looked the same as she did all those years ago, when he had first realized he was in love with her.

'You've been avoiding me.' She smiled.

'Of course not. I've had so much catching-up to do, that's all.'

'Sure,' she said sarcastically. 'So, tell me . . . is it good to be back?'

He pulled a face to show her that he hadn't really decided yet. She kept her eyes on him, still smiling.

'Vinnie tells me that you're living in his uncle's apartment.'

'That's right. The Benandanti Building, in Venice. Jesus – it's like something out of Edgar Allan Poe. *The Fall of the House of Usher*, only spookier. You must call by and pay me a visit sometime.'

'And Tibbles? You still have Tibbles?'

'Yes, I still have Tibbles. "That darned cat."'

There was a lengthy silence. Jim realized he was tugging

at his left earlobe, which was always a sign that he was tense. He stopped doing it immediately, and flapped his arm as if to say, oh well, that's life, what can you do?

Karen said, 'I heard what happened in Washington. Well, some of it.'

'Yes. It was . . . tragic.' He didn't want to say any more. Sometimes it was better to leave things alone for a while, let them settle. In his mind, he heard a split-second blurt of screaming, and saw blood spraying like an action painting.

'You're coming to the funeral?' Karen asked him. 'Bobby Tubbs and Sara Miller?'

He nodded.

'Maybe we could go together, if that's OK with you.'

'That would be good. Are you . . . what about Perry?'

'Perry?' She looked genuinely bewildered. 'You mean Perry Ritts? What about him?'

'You're not . . . seeing him or anything?'

Karen laughed, that bright, sharp laugh like a window pane breaking. 'I hope you think I have better taste than that!'

'Oh, well, sure. Of course I did. I was only kidding. I saw you together yesterday, you know, and he looked kind of bright-eyed and bushy-tailed, so I just thought . . .'

Karen brushed her hair away from her face. 'I know what you thought, Jim. You don't have to find the words for it.'

He stayed where he was, his hand still raised against the sun. LIGHT SNARETH THE SOUL. Karen came up to him, stood on tippy-toe, and kissed him on the cheek.

'What was that poem you were always quoting me?' she asked him.

He knew which poem she meant, but he didn't say anything. He wanted to see if she could remember it.

'"O who can be, both moth and flame?"' she whispered.

'"Whom can we love?"' Jim continued. '"I thought I knew the truth. Of grief I died, but no one knew my death."'

Karen looked at him seriously. 'You're not dead yet, Jim. Of grief, or anything else. And sometimes there's no shame in coming back. Sometimes we need to come back, to remember who we are, and why people loved us.'

He made himself spaghetti Bolognese for supper. He considered himself to be an expert at spaghetti Bolognese – he always splashed in plenty of Worcestershire sauce and Tabasco sauce and stirred in spoonfuls of mixed herbs and fifty-five grindings of fresh black pepper, before simmering it for forty-five minutes with two glasses of strong red Italian wine. Apart from hating garlic, Tibbles didn't think much of Tabasco sauce, either, so he gave her a bowlful of raw ground beef with cat biscuits mixed into it. She was already starting to sprout some bristly patches of fur, but they made her look scruffier than ever.

When he had finished eating he went into the living room and switched on the television. He didn't feel like watching *CSI* or *Law and Order* or *The Dead Zone*, and in the end he found himself looking at an old Discovery program about a man who had traveled across America in the 1900s, visiting fairgrounds, and compiling a catalog of all the freaks he had could find.

'He found Hairy Mary the Baboon Woman, and Kaliban the Human Toad, as well as the Boy With No Brain, who could shine a strong light through his skull and show that his head was empty. One of the strangest was the Negative Man, who was touring with Forepaugh and Sells through Illinois and Idaho and other mid-Western states. The Negative Man had to keep his head covered with a cloth during the day, because he was so sensitive to sunlight; and his show tent was lit only by a red lamp, like a photographer's darkroom. When he removed the cloth from his head, which he would do for the entrance fee of two bits, his face appeared utterly black, while his eyes were white, like a photographic negative. The Negative Man was arrested in 1909 after a series of arson attacks in Indiana, in which seven people died. He escaped from custody in

Crawfordsville and was never seen or heard of again.'

Jim looked up at the painting of Robert H. Vane. Maybe, after all, he wasn't in mourning. Maybe he was hiding his face, for one reason or another. Maybe he hadn't been able to show it in daylight.

He switched off the television. He had made his mind up: he would take the painting down again, first thing tomorrow morning, and drive it to the auction house. If it had belonged to him, he would have carted it out to the nearest patch of waste ground and burned it.

How could Bobby's and Sara's deaths have had any connection with his moving into the Benandanti Building? Yet the prime suspect in Bobby and Sara's killing was a man with a black face and white hair, like a living negative. And here in this apartment was a painting of Robert H. Vane, who had spent his life working with negatives, and who had once been accused of burning people to ashes, just like Bobby and Sara had been burned to ashes.

And what about the brilliant flash of light, and the photographic image of Bobby and Sara on the wall, and the way that Tibbles had been burned? What about the daguerrotypes that Robert H. Vane had taken, and the Dagueno tribe, and the Negative Man? What about the misshapen shadow that had lurched across his curtains?

There didn't seem to be any logical reason why any of these occurrences should be related. Robert H. Vane had lived more than a hundred and fifty years ago, and so he was long dead. The Negative Man had escaped justice, but that was nearly a hundred years ago, and so he was long gone, too.

Half of what Jim had discovered was history, and half of it was psychic claptrap, and all of it seemed like coincidence. Yet he couldn't help feeling that it all fitted. It was like sitting in a darkened room, with somebody handing him the pieces of a broken vase, one by one, and expecting him to stick them all back together. The question was: who was giving them to him, and why? And why *him*?

* * *

He showered and put on a pair of shorts with a faded sepia T-shirt that had a picture of Charles Dickens on it, which Karen had given him more years ago than he cared to recall. Wearing it tonight, after meeting her again, seemed especially appropriate.

He sat up in bed and read for a while – a travel book about North Africa. He had never managed to get beyond the second chapter, because the writing was so soothing and hypnotic, but that was part of the reason he read it. Under the dark blue skies of the Sudan he could forget all about Special Class II, and what had happened to him in Washington, and the painting of Robert H. Vane.

> Far, far to the south lie the broad savannahs, the shimmering grasslands where naked black men of infinite beauty and dignity herd their lyre-horned cattle. Beyond begins the bush and the forest throbbing with drums; the jungle through which broad, calm, dangerous rivers can float you right out to the sea.

He began to doze, and the book gradually slipped from his hand. After less than ten minutes, however, something woke him up. He looked around, blinking. Tibbles had settled herself close beside him, and she was rattling loudly. The clock on his nightstand said 12:03 A.M.

He lay back and listened for a few minutes, but all he could hear was the soft teeth-chattering of the air-conditioning unit, and the low thunder of planes taking off from LAX. A woman was shouting in the street. 'You're crazy, do you know that? You're out of your mind!'

He switched off his bedside light and closed his eyes. The shimmering grasslands whispered all around him, and the wind blew south toward the forest. He could almost hear the cattle as they tore at the grass all around him.

Suddenly he was jerked awake again. He heard a noise

113

in the living room, a heavy thump, and then a clatter. There was silence for a moment, but then he heard a tapping noise, like somebody trying to negotiate their way around the room with walking sticks.

He sat up. The tapping continued, but then it was accompanied by a clicking sound, and then a complicated bumping.

'OK!' Jim called out, switching on his bedside lamp. 'Whoever you are, you'd better get the hell out of here, quick!'

He swung his legs out from under the covers and scrabbled under the bed for his baseball bat. He just hoped his intruder didn't have a gun. He didn't want to be too confrontational. After all, nothing in this apartment was his, and a few pieces of somebody else's second-hand china weren't worth getting himself killed for.

He stood up, slapping the baseball bat into the palm of his hand. But as he walked around the bed, the bedroom door slammed open, so violently that it shuddered on its hinges. Into the room stalked a creature like nothing else Jim had ever seen or imagined, and he let out a shriek of terror.

The creature was so tall that it almost touched the ceiling. A construction like a huge spider, long-legged and awkward, except that its legs were the legs of a photographic tripod, made out of polished mahogany, and its body was the black, hunched body of a badly deformed man, with a black cloth folded over his head. Its shadow on the walls was equally terrifying, a nightmare assembly of stilts and crutches and tattered black fabric.

Jim stumbled back, colliding with his nightstand so that his clock tumbled on to the floor. The tripod spider took another lurching step into the room, almost overbalancing, and then another. It uttered a harsh metallic noise. *Ker-chikkk!* And then *Ker-chiikkk!*

Tibbles suddenly woke up and screamed like a horrified child.

Ten

Jim backed up against the wall. He couldn't believe what he was looking at, but the camera creature was there, hanging right over him, its feet sliding on the polished wood floor like a horse trying to find its footing on an icy road. Its black bulk was unsteadily swaying from side to side, as if it could all collapse on top of him at any second. It reeked of chemicals, so that Jim's eyes were crowded with tears and his sinuses were stung raw.

He edged back toward the window. He had almost reached it when the creature started to walk toward him, its joints creaking. Jim hefted his baseball bat. He didn't know if hitting this apparition would do anything to deter it, but he could try. Its legs looked precarious enough, and it didn't seem to be able to keep its balance.

He wrenched back the dusty velvet drapes and retreated into the window bay. The creature took another clattering step nearer, and then it stopped. He could hear it breathing, high and harsh, like a very old man struggling for air; and its breathing was punctuated every now and then by slow, mechanical *ker-chikk.*

As far as Jim could see, there was only one way for him to escape, and that was to dodge between the creature's legs and try to reach the door. Tibbles would have to fend for herself. He could see her cowering underneath the bed and he reckoned that was probably the safest place for her to be.

He edged cautiously out of the window bay, weighing

115

his baseball bat in both hands. 'OK, whatever you are. Let's see what you're made of, shall we?'

He brandished his bat as if he were going to strike the creature on one of its jointed knees. He glanced up at it, to see if it was going to react, but all he could see on top of its tripod legs was a ragged black coat, and that black, all-covering cloth. Underneath the cloth, it looked blacker still. As black as a coal cellar. As black as your very worst nightmare.

Jim could hear his blood thumping in his ears. He took another step forward, and raised the baseball bat higher still. 'You hear me?' he screamed. 'I'm walking out of here, and there's nothing you can do to stop me!'

The creature hesitated, and then took one defensive step backward. Jim immediately jinked sideways, to the right, and then rolled on to the floor, commando style.

He rolled again, and again, gasping with fear and exertion. As he rolled over the third time, his left ankle became entangled with the table lamp wire, and as he rolled over yet again, he pulled the plug out of the wall, and the bedroom went totally black.

He struggled up on to his feet. With his arms thrashing in the darkness, and the table lamp still bouncing along the floor behind him, he blundered his way toward the door.

Just as he reached it there was a dazzling flash – so bright he felt as if the world had been turned inside-out. For a split second he saw the creature standing at the end of the bed, its cloth half-lifted in its arms, and he thought that he could see its face, although it might have been nothing more than shadows and distorted fabric. A cadaverous face, as white as death, with a huge single eye. A face that was beyond evil, beyond any feeling, like a poisonous spider. Robert H. Vane.

Without warning, there was a second flash, even more intense than the first. A blast of heat scorched his cheek and blistered the paint on the door beside him. The bed caught fire, instantly and ferociously, as if it had been doused in gasoline, and the bedroom was filled with flames and sparks and choking smoke. Jim could hardly see anything but after-images, orange and green blotches, but he saw Tibbles scampering out from under the bed as if all the demons in hell were after her, and rushing into the living room.

By the dancing, lurid light of his burning bed, he saw the camera creature walking unsteadily across the room toward him. He froze for a moment, uncertain if he ought to attack it or run away. But then the creature clumsily started to lift up its cloth again, and he went after Tibbles, slamming the bedroom door behind him.

'Come on, let's get the hell out of here,' he told her, and they stumbled over Vinnie's uncle's shoes, and out through the front door into the corridor.

Tibbles went scampering off toward the elevators. But Jim said, 'Wait up! I'd better call nine-one-one before the whole damn building burns down!'

He turned to go back into his apartment, but just before he could reach it the front door slowly clicked shut, locking him out. 'Shit! Tibbles, will you wait up a minute? I can't just leave my apartment on fire!'

He went across the corridor and jabbed Eleanor's doorbell, again and again. She didn't answer, so he hammered on the door with his fist. 'Eleanor! I need to use your phone! Eleanor! My apartment's on fire!'

He heard locks being unlocked and chains being drawn back and bolts being unbolted. At last Eleanor stood, blinking, in front of him. She was wearing a black headscarf, a shiny black satin negligee, and her face was utterly white with face cream.

'I'm so sorry, I have to use your phone. My bed caught fire.'

She opened the door wider and pointed to the antique-style telephone on the hall table. 'Your *bed* caught fire? You know that smoking isn't allowed in this building.'

'I wasn't smoking.' He picked up the receiver and dialed

911. 'Something came into my room – a thing, a creature. It was like Robert H. Vane all mixed up with a tripod.'

'What? What are you talking about?'

'Hallo, emergency? I need the fire department. The Benandanti Building, fifth floor. My apartment's on fire. I don't know. The door's locked and I can't get back in.'

He gave his name and his telephone number and then he put the phone down. Eleanor said, 'I have a key. Mr Boschetto left it with me, in case I needed to let anybody into his apartment when he was away on vacation.'

'That's great. Look, there's a fire extinguisher down the end of the corridor. Maybe I can put out the fire with that.'

He hurried down to get the fire extinguisher, while Eleanor went in search of the key. By the time he got back, she was already inserting it into the lock. Smoke was pouring out from the under the door, and there was a strong smell of burning in the air.

'Careful,' he warned her. 'That thing's still in there.'

She looked at him out of her white face mask. 'Do you know what it was?'

'A *thing*, that's all I can tell you. It looked like a man walking on stilts, only he was all bent over. There was a flash, a really bright flash, but I think I saw his face. One of my students managed to find a picture of Robert H. Vane, and brought it into class today, and that was exactly what he looked like.'

'He's come looking for you, then,' said Eleanor. 'He's come looking for you, before you can go looking for him.'

'You believe me?'

'Of course I believe you. What do you think the presences were warning me about?'

Jim pulled the safety pin out of the fire extinguisher and then quickly touched the door handle with his fingertips to test if it was hot. It was quite cool, but he pressed his hand flat against the door panel, just to make sure. He had seen too many movies in which unsuspecting people flung open doors in blazing buildings and *whoosh!* they got themselves incinerated on the spot.

He eased the door open. The apartment was foggy with smoke, but there was no sign of flames, and there was no sign of the camera creature either. He went through to the living room. The painting of Robert H. Vane was still hanging over the fireplace, although he could have sworn it was slightly tilted, which it hadn't been before. Eleanor, who was close behind him, said, 'I told you, didn't I? He's right inside it. And tonight, he came out.'

Jim thought of the thumping that he had heard, and the clatter that had sounded like walking sticks. It was impossible, right? People didn't climb out of paintings. *People didn't climb out of paintings.* So what was it that had entered his bedroom? What was it that had set fire to his bed?

He switched on the light in the small hallway between the living room and the bedroom. The bedroom door was still closed, so maybe the camera creature was still in there, waiting for him. He looked quickly at Eleanor but she said, 'It's up to you, Jim. You can wait for the fire department, or you can face it yourself.'

'So what are you telling me? I have to hunt this thing down, whether I want to or not? I don't have any choice in the matter?'

'I don't think you do – do you? Once your quarry starts to come after you, the decision is taken out of your hands. It's kill or be killed, isn't it?'

Jim gingerly touched the door handle. It was hot, but not hot enough to burn him. He listened, and he thought he could hear a faint crackling sound, but that was all.

'All right,' he said, and pushed the door open.

The bedroom was thick with dark brown smoke, so that he could barely see. The flames had died down, but the mattress was burned to the springs, and the wooden headboard was charred. The pale green wallpaper was covered with a thin film of greasy soot, and the spiderwebs around the chandelier were fluttering like long black flags.

The camera creature had gone. Jim went over to the window, but it was still locked closed, and there was nothing hiding behind the curtains. He looked under the bed, but there was nothing there either.

'Well, I don't know where it came from, and I don't know where it's gone, but it's certainly not here any longer.'

'If it came from the painting, maybe it went back to the painting.'

'You really believe that?'

'If you're telling me the truth, and you really did see a creature like you say, what else am I supposed to believe?'

'I don't know. I can't understand any of this. Everywhere I look, there are clues about photographs and negatives and people being burned. I turn on the TV and there's a program about the Negative Man, whose face was black and whose hair was white, and who was supposed to have burned people alive. And all of these clues come from different times, and different places, and different sources, and there's no reason for them to fit together, yet they all . . .' He interlocked his fingers, like cogs.

Two firefighters appeared in the doorway, their waterproofs rustling and their rubber boots wobbling, carrying axes. They were closely followed by Mr Mariti, the super, with his shiny black hair and his neatly clipped moustache, wearing a maroon satin robe.

'Mr Cook? You called nine-one-one?'

'It's Rook, not Cook. My . . . uh . . . my mattress caught fire. It's OK now, it's pretty much out.'

The firefighters inspected the ruined mattress, prodding it with their axes. 'You sure cooked it good, Mr Rook. We'll just heave it out of here and dump it for you. What were you doing? Smoking in bed?'

'I . . . ah . . . no.'

'We have to report a cause, sir. In case any building

regulations were being ignored – you know, like wiring or ventilation or something.'

'This building is one hundred per cent,' put in Mr Mariti. 'No – two hundred per cent!'

Jim said, 'I lit a candle. I guess it must have fallen over. I went into the kitchen and when I came back the bed was alight.'

'You lit a candle?'

'A votive candle. To St Agnes.'

'Who's she?' asked one of the firefighters. 'The patron saint of arsonists?'

'Assholes, more like,' muttered the other.

Once the firefighters had gone, Jim opened all of the windows, to let out the smoke. Mr Mariti said, 'I have to report this, you know, sir, for the fire insurance.'

'Listen, Mr Mariti, it was an accident, it won't happen again.'

'Well, I don't know.'

'I'll see you in the morning, OK? I'm sure we can sort something out.'

Mr Mariti understood at once what Jim was suggesting. 'I suppose so. It's only a little smoke damage, after all. A hundred should cover it.'

Jim saw him to the door and closed it behind him. 'Bloodsucker,' he muttered.

'What are you going to do now?' Eleanor asked him.

'Get rid of that painting, for starters. I was lucky tonight. Tomorrow night, I could end up barbecued.'

'I don't know if that will do it. Even if you burn it – well, Vane's spirit could find someplace else to hide. Some other picture, maybe.'

'That's a risk I'll have to take, isn't it?'

Eleanor came up to him, very close. She licked the tip of her finger and wiped a smudge of smoke from his cheek. It was a startlingly intimate gesture, the kind of thing that mothers do for their children, or women do for their lovers.

'You're the only one,' she breathed. 'You're the hero, you're the knight errant who has to slay the dragon. Nobody else can do it.'

'I still don't understand.'

'You will, I promise you.'

She kissed him on the lips, very lightly, and then went back to her apartment. As she walked away, he couldn't help noticing the way her silky black robe slid over her buttocks. He stared very hard at a bronze statuette of Pan, who was dancing on one of the side tables, playing his pipes.

'What do you think about that, Pan? Was that a come-on, or what?'

Tibbles came back in and stared at him jealously.

Jim left the windows wide open for the rest of the night. By the time the sun came up, and gilded all the dust on the living-room drapes, the smell of smoke had almost completely faded away. He sat up straight, stretched, and groaned. He had stayed all night in his throne-like chair, right in front of the fireplace, and he felt as if his neck and knees had been held in clamps. He could have slept in the second bedroom, but the big pink comforter was damp and smelled funny. Not only that, he had wanted to keep guard on the painting of Robert H. Vane.

He shuffled through to the bathroom and stared at himself in the mirror. The greenish light in the bathroom was less than flattering at the best of times, but today he looked as if he had been floating in a pond for a week. He splashed cold water on his face and wet his hair so that he could brush it into a casually messed-up kind of look.

'You're the knight errant,' he said. 'You're the hero. Only you can slay the dragon – or, in this case, something halfway between a camera tripod and a human being.'

His reflection looked back at him, and said, 'You're losing it, dude.'

'Oh, yes?' he retorted. 'Look at your bed. You're trying to tell me that didn't happen?'

'No. But that doesn't mean that you have to get yourself involved, does it? If I were you, I'd look for someplace else to live, and do it today.'

'But I like this apartment. It's cool. And it's enormous. And it's *cheap.*'

He left the bathroom and went into the kitchen. He opened the fridge and took out a giant-size Minute Maid orange juice. He gulped it straight from the carton, and managed to pour half of it down his chest. 'Sorry, Mr Dickens,' he said, mopping his T-shirt with a wet cloth.

'You're apologizing to your T-shirt?'

'Karen gave it to me.'

'I see. Is that why you couldn't keep your eyes off Eleanor's ass?'

'Eleanor's attractive. So what?'

'So why is she maneuvering you into this knight errant business? Like, what's really going on here? Do you really think you ended up in this apartment by chance?'

'What are you talking about? Vinnie's uncle died and Vinnie wanted somebody to take it over, that's all. He couldn't have planned it, could he?'

'But Bobby and Sara . . . the way they died, cremated in their bed? And your bed, last night? You would have been cremated, too, if you hadn't woken up. Come on, Jim, wake up!'

He switched on the kettle to make himself some coffee. He was right. He needed to find out what was really happening here. He would take the painting down to Julia Fox at the auction house, and then he would go talk to Vinnie – and Lieutenant Harris, too. It was time to find out what kind of a vase he was supposed to be re-assembling, and who was giving him the pieces, and why.

He rang Mr Mariti's doorbell, down in the basement. There

was no reply, but he could hear classical music playing somewhere inside his apartment – *Ruslan and Ludmila*, by Mikhail Glinka. Good to know he has taste, thought Jim, but I wish he'd answer his goddamned doorbell. He rang it again, and shouted, 'Mr Mariti!'

The door opened almost immediately and Mr Mariti appeared. He was wearing a pale-green shirt, a dark-green necktie, socks, but no pants. His pants were folded neatly over his arm.

'Sir? Your apartment isn't on fire again?' Jim looked down at his legs and then he looked down at his legs, too. 'Oh. *Scusi*. I press my pants.'

'I just want to say sorry for all the disturbance last night,' said Jim. He handed Mr Mariti two fifty-dollar bills. 'I hope that should cover any damage.'

The bills disappeared like a conjuring trick. 'No problem, sir. If there is anything else . . .'

'As a matter of fact, yes, there is. I was wondering if you could help me to carry a painting downstairs. It's a little too heavy for me to manage on my own.'

'Of course, sir. Give me two minutes.'

When he saw the painting, however, Mr Mariti looked very dubious. 'Mr Boschetto say this painting must always hang here,' he said.

'Mr Boschetto is no longer with us.'

'Of course, but he was very insistent. He ask me one time: "Guido, what do you think of this painting?" and I say to him, "Mr Boschetto, you want my frank opinion, it gives me the willies."'

'That's the reason I want to get rid of it. It gives me the willies, too.'

'But Mr Boschetto, he say, this painting must always hang here, so that whoever lives in this apartment can watch it.'

'He said "watch it" – not "look at it"?'

124

Mr Mariti nodded emphatically. 'He say "watch it".'

Jim thought about that for a moment. Then he said, 'Mr Mariti, do you want to know what *really* happened here last night?'

Mr Mariti took off his coat and rolled up his sleeves. 'No, sir.'

'Right, then. Let's just get this damn thing down, shall we? I'll be glad to see the back of it.'

Julia Fox wasn't very impressed by the painting, either. When two of her assistants lifted it out of Jim's car and carried it into her shiny, brightly lit display room on Rodeo Drive, she stood back and made seven different expressions of bewilderment.

'I don't have any doubt at all that this was painted by Gordon Welkin,' she said. 'Look in the corner – you can see his initials G.S.W. Gordon Shelby Welkin.'

'Is that good?'

'It's good as far as it goes. Welkin was one of the finest West Coast portrait painters of the mid-nineteenth century. But I ask myself why.'

Jim stood very close to her, trying to see the painting the way she saw it. She was very tall, nearly six feet, with her blonde hair swept into a French pleat, and she wore a classic light-gray suit and very high heels. Jim's nose only came up to her shoulder pad.

'You ask yourself why,' he said after a while. 'Do you mind if I ask you *why* you ask yourself why?'

'Why should a portrait painter want to paint a man with a black cloth covering his head?'

'Well, it says on the label that Robert H. Vane was in mourning for the Dagueno tribe, after they were all massacred in . . . what was it? 1853.'

'All the same, it's so strange, quite unlike Welkin. He would have wanted to show the man's grief in his face. His fellow artists said that he could capture a person's soul.'

'Maybe he *did* capture his soul. But maybe he didn't like the way it looked.'

Julia stepped closer. 'I can't understand it. The painting tells us nothing at all. It's like a closed book. Yet look at the way he's handled the drapery! Look at the man's hand! You can almost see him breathing, under his cloth.'

'Yes,' said Jim, uneasily. 'I felt that, too.'

'I can auction it for you,' said Julia. 'However, I doubt if it will raise as much as a conventional Gordon Welkin. A local gallery may be interested, for its historical value. But this is not really the kind of picture that anybody would want to hang over their fireplace, is it?'

'You don't know how right you are, Julia. Please, just take it off my hands. If you get a hundred for it, I'll be happy. At least I won't be out of pocket.'

When he arrived at college, he found that a lime-green Volkswagen Beetle was parked in the vice-principal's space, so in the end he had to leave his Lincoln right around the back, next to the overflowing dumpsters. Walking back to the main building, he came across Walter, carrying his box of tools.

'Some usurper has parked in my space,' he complained.

'The new vice-principal,' said Walter. 'She started this morning.'

'She?'

'Dr Washington. You'll *like* her.'

Jim stopped, and turned around. 'Do I detect just the teensiest hint of sarcasm, Walter?'

'Sarcasm, Mr Rook? I think you got the wrong man. I haven't been sarcastic since Dr Ehrlichman wanted me to paint blue dolphins on the bottom of the pool.'

Jim went to the staffroom first. He needed to tell Vinnie about the fire, and that he had taken the painting of Robert H. Vane down to the auction room.

He couldn't decide if he ought to tell Vinnie about the

126

camera creature. It would probably be better if he didn't –
not yet, anyhow. Vinnie would probably think he was
drinking too much, or having a breakdown, and ask him to
find someplace else to live. In spite of what had happened
last night, he didn't want to start looking for a new apartment, especially now that the painting had gone. Where
would he find anywhere so grand, and so inexpensive? If
Eleanor was right, and the painting *really* contained the
soul of Robert H. Vane, then presumably the apartment had
now been exorcized, and there would be no more flashes
of light or spontaneous fires or tripod-legged beasts crawling
into his bedroom.

He found Karen in the staffroom, trying to force too many
books into her embroidered denim shoulder bag, but there
was no sign of Vinnie.

'Hi,' he said. 'How about a coffee?'

'Sorry, I don't have time, and neither do you. You can
probably hear Special Class II from half a mile away. But
later, maybe.'

'You seen Vinnie?'

'Vinnie? He's away at a three-day history seminar.
Portland, I think.'

'Oh, OK. He didn't say anything to me.'

'Everything all right? You look a little . . . flushed. Have
you been overdoing the sunbed?'

He touched his cheek, where the flash had scorched it.
'No. I was making cheese on toast and I stood too close to
the grill, that's all.'

She looked at him narrowly. 'You're lying to me, aren't
you?'

'How do you know?'

'I can always tell when you're lying to me, but the funny
thing is that I can never tell why. Cheese on toast, I ask
you!'

'I guess I don't want to over-complicate things, that's
all.'

127

She slung her bag over her shoulder. 'I'm not one of your students, Jim. I found out a long time ago how complicated life can be, and how inexplicable, and why lying isn't worth it.'

She walked out of the staffroom and left him standing there. She always made him feel as if he were trying to patronize her, and that he underestimated her intelligence. But how could he tell her that his face had been scorched by a hunched half-human creature on stilted legs? She would think he was ready for a straitjacket; and maybe she'd be right.

Eleven

On his way to Special Class II, he stopped by the lockers and called Lieutenant Harris on his cellphone.

Lieutenant Harris sounded harassed. 'Before you ask, Mr Rook, we haven't yet identified our suspect. Between you and me, we're trying to find a more credible witness than Mr Hayward Mitchell. Somebody who wasn't so inebriated.'

'That's why I called you, Lieutenant. Something occurred to me. Call it intuition, if you like.'

'Fire away. That's what I want from you, intuition.'

'Well . . . it's about your computer image. Why don't you try reversing it, so that the suspect's face is white and his hair is black?'

There was short pause. Then Lieutenant Harris said, 'Are you trying to be politically correct or something?'

'No, of course not. It's just a hunch.'

'Mitchell was pretty damn sure that the suspect was Afro-American.'

'I know. But just try it.'

'OK, why not? I'll get back to you.'

Special Class II were in their usual state of exuberance when he walked in the door. Ruby, Vanilla and Sue-Marie were standing together on top of Sue-Marie's desk, singing 'The First Cut is the Deepest' in close harmony, while Shadow was practicing one-handed press-ups and Randy was tossing caramel popcorn at Edward so that it stuck in his hair.

129

Jim hung up his coat. Then he went to the chalkboard and wrote LIES.

Almost at once, the class quietened down. Ruby, Vanilla and Sue-Marie wound up their singing with a high-pitched caterwauling of '*oh yeeaaahhhh!*' and clambered down from their stage; while Brenda took out her earphones, Delilah put away her copy of *Cosmo* and George quickly thumbed out one last text message on his cellphone. They didn't exactly show Jim that they were paying attention. That wouldn't have been cool. But even though they were all lolling around, they were at least lolling at their own desks, and when they talked to each other, they kept their voices reasonably low, and there was hardly any of that hyena-like laughing, or swearing, or the endless banter that was only one step away from being out-and-out aggression.

'You so ugly, every time you get in the bath, the water jump out.'

'That's nothing. You so ugly, when you was born, the midwife slap your mother.'

'Today,' said Jim, as the hubbub died down, 'today, I want you to teach me how to tell lies.'

'That's crazy,' said Shadow. 'You come to college to find out what's true, don't you?'

'Maybe you do. But how do you know for sure if something's true?'

'You don't,' said Sue-Marie. 'You just have to trust people.'

Jim nodded, and then walked slowly up the aisle. 'So you believe, for instance, that men have walked on the moon? Just because NASA tells you so?'

'I guess so.'

'Oh, come on,' said Edward. 'All of that moon-landing stuff was done at Universal Studios. A friend of mine knows a guy who knows a guy who made all the moon rocks.'

'So you think it was a lie?'

'Of course it was. We didn't even have the technology to go to the moon back then.'

'But you can't *prove* that it was a lie, any more than Sue-Marie can prove that it was the truth.'

'That's not the point, is it? Sue-Marie thinks it's true; I think it was all a hoax. But it really doesn't matter if it was true or not, just so long as people wanted to believe it.'

'What are you talking about, man?' asked Roosevelt. 'You talking in complete riddles.'

'Think about it, dummy! We made the Russians believe that we won the space race, didn't we, even though we didn't go no further than Pasadena! We saved ourselves a shitload of money, and nobody had to risk getting killed. In fact, I respect the government a whole lot more for making it up, instead of being dumb enough to try it for real. I mean, what was the point of going to the moon, anyhow? Who gives a shit what it's made of?'

Jim smiled. 'So, when we say something – even if it isn't true – all that really matters is the effect that it has on other people? And if the effect is generally good, that makes it justifiable?'

'Huh?'

'What I'm asking you is this: can there be good lies, as well as bad ones?'

'Oh,' said Edward. 'Absolutely. I mean, what's the point of telling the truth if it just gives people grief?'

'OK, then,' said Jim. 'I want you all to write down three good lies – and I want you to be able to tell me *why* they're good.'

Roosevelt put up his hand. 'I'd really like to do that, sir, but I'm suffering from repetitive strain disorder and I can't write.'

'You've been spanking the monkey too much, that's your trouble,' put in Philip.

'Roosevelt, you're telling me a lie,' Jim told him. 'Not only that, it's a bad lie, not a good one.'

'It's a good lie for me, sir, if I don't have to write nothing.'

'I don't think so. If I believed for one moment that you were genuinely suffering from repetitive strain disorder – which I don't – I'd send you out to find Walter the janitor so that you could do something useful instead. I understand he's on his way to unblock the toilets in the girls' changing rooms. By thrusting his entire arm down the U-bend.'

Roosevelt waved his right hand, flapping it one way, and then the other. 'It's cured! Would you believe that? It's cured! It's a miracle!'

While the class frowned at their notebooks, and then at the ceiling, and then at each other, trying to think of three good lies, Jim looked out of the window at Tom Mix's cedar tree. Supposing we hadn't been to the moon, would it have made any difference? Would we be any less super-stitious? Would we be any worse off? Maybe we should have explored our souls, he thought, instead of space.

At lunchtime, Jim sat on the shady knoll overlooking the tennis courts, so that he could eat his salami-and-tomato sandwiches and read a book. Making sandwiches that stuck together had never been one of his greatest talents, and slices of tomato kept dropping out on to the grass. Two California quail bobbed around nearby, obviously hoping that he was going to leave them there.

He had been sitting there for less than ten minutes when he saw Lieutenant Harris's car speeding up the driveway between the trees, followed closely by a black-and-white squad car. Lieutenant Harris caught sight of him and pulled into the curb. He came hurrying over in his shiny bronze suit, holding up a large Manila envelope.

'Mr Rook, I don't know what kind of a hunch that was, but I sure wish that I could have hunches like that.'

Jim put down his book, wiped his hands, and opened the envelope. Inside was a 10 x 8 picture of the suspect Hayward Mitchell had seen entering the Tubbs' beach-house. Now, however, the suspect had a white face and dark hair, and

Jim was startled to see who it was. The artist's impression was slightly too long in the face, and his eyebrows were too heavy, but there was no doubt at all that it was Brad Moorcock.

'Unbelievable, isn't it?' said Lieutenant Harris. He popped his fingers. 'I recognized him just like that.'

Jim handed the picture back. He was surprised, and more than a little sorry. From what he had seen of Brad, he had seemed like a regular, decent young man. 'Brad came up to me in the corridor only yesterday to tell me how regretful he was.'

'Well, now you know why, don't you?'

Jim stood up and brushed the crumbs off his pants. 'What are you going to do now? Arrest him?'

'I don't have any choice.'

'I'll come with you,' Jim told him.

Lieutenant Harris beckoned to the two officers in the squad car, and together they walked toward the college entrance. Lieutenant Harris said, 'I still can't work out how you knew this picture was the wrong way round. Black instead of white.'

Jim couldn't tell him about Robert H. Vane. Instead, he said, 'Reverse thinking, Lieutenant. Sometimes, if you can look at a problem the other way around, the answer is staring you right in the face.'

First they went to see Dr Ehrlichman. Even before she knew what they wanted, Mrs Frogg stood up and said, 'I'm sorry, gentlemen. The principal is very tied up.'

'In that case, you'll have to untie him,' said Lieutenant Harris. 'We've come to arrest one of your students on suspicion of first-degree murder. Brad Moorcock.'

Mrs Frogg's eyes bulged. She hurried into Dr Ehrlichman's office, and almost immediately Dr Ehrlichman emerged, flustered and obviously shocked. 'There must be some mistake, Lieutenant. Brad Moorcock is captain of our football team.'

'I'm sorry, sir. Just because a student excels at sport, that doesn't give him carte blanche to kill people.'

Dr Ehrlichman accompanied them to the gym, tutting and shaking his head and making little puffing noises. Brad Moorcock was there with five of his friends, practicing basketball passes. The gym resounded with squeaky echoes, and shouts of 'Give me the ball, you moron!'

Lieutenant Harris walked directly up to Brad and said, 'Brad Moorcock, I'm arresting you on suspicion of murdering Bobby Tubbs and Sara Miller.'

The gym immediately fell silent. Brad stared at Lieutenant Harris in disbelief. 'What?'

'You heard me, son. You have the right to remain silent, but anything you do say—'

'I didn't kill anybody! This is crazy!'

Jim went up to him. 'Somebody saw you down at the beach, Brad.'

'How could anybody see me? I wasn't there! I was at home that night!'

'If you can prove it, fine,' said Lieutenant Harris. 'Meanwhile, you need to come down to headquarters.'

'I wasn't there! And why would I kill them?'

'Maybe you were sore because Sara dumped you. Maybe you didn't like the idea of her dating anybody else.'

Brad turned to Jim in desperation. 'OK, I treated her bad. But I admitted it, didn't I? I took advantage of her. But I never would have hurt her. Never. I wouldn't hurt anybody.'

'Save it,' said Lieutenant Harris. He jerked his thumb in the direction of the gymnasium doors, and the two officers escorted Brad away.

'This is *very* distressing,' said Dr Ehrlichman. He gave Jim a meaningful look and loudly blew his nose. 'I had hoped that West Grove had finally refurbished its reputation.'

'You're not suggesting that this has anything to do with me?' Jim asked him.

'Of course not, Mr Rook. However . . . it does seem as if you're dogged by unusually persistent ill luck.'

Lieutenant Harris laid his hand on Jim's shoulder. 'Believe me, Principal. I see it every day, every place I look, twenty-four seven. The whole world is dogged by unusually persistent ill luck.'

When Lieutenant Harris and Dr Ehrlichman had left, Jim turned to Brad Moorcock's friends. 'That's it,' he said. 'There's nothing we can do but wait and see.'

'Did he really kill Bobby and Sara?' asked a tall black boy with a lightning flash shaved into his hair.

'I don't know,' said Jim. 'Some wino on the beach saw a young man entering the beach house just before Bobby and Sara got burned – and judging by his description it could have been Brad. But what happened that night . . . it was all very outré.'

'Outré?'

'That means weird. But I'm not supposed to tell you anything more. I'm sorry.'

'I'll tell you what's outré,' said a stocky boy with ginger hair. 'It's the way that Brad's been acting for the past three weeks.'

'Oh, yes? What makes you say that?'

'He hasn't been normal, that's all.'

All five boys nodded in agreement. The ginger-haired boy said, 'Don't get me wrong or nothing. Brad can be a great guy, and he's a terrific captain of football. But he was always throwing his weight around and making sure that everybody knew what an all-round amazing dude he is, especially when it came to girls.'

'So, what's changed?'

'He's kept his yap shut for a change. He's been *modest*, even. He's stopped flicking people on the ass with a wet sports towel and generally acting like a dork. You wouldn't have thought he was the same guy. Like today – he always used to hog the ball when he played basketball, and slam people right in the face with it, and think that was hilarious. But not any more.'

'And he's been like this for how long? Three weeks?'

'That's right. We met him on the beach, three Saturdays back, and he was horsing around the way he always does, kicking sand and pulling people's shorts down and half-drowning them in the ocean. But when he came to college on Monday, he was totally changed.'

A boy with a black buzzcut and a hoarse, adenoidal voice said, 'We first noticed it when Ollerkin got into trouble in the pool.'

'Ollerkin?'

'If you'd met Ollerkin, sir, you wouldn't need to ask. Like, if somebody from another planet wanted to know what a dweeb was, you'd only have to point to Ollerkin.'

'So what happened?'

'We were walking past the pool and Ollerkin was coughing and spluttering in the water and waving his arms and calling out "help!" Brad dived in, fully dressed, with his sneakers on and everything. At first I thought he was going to push Ollerkin under the water. That's the kind of thing he would have done before. But he supported the guy's head, and he swam with him right to the side of the pool and helped him out. We just stared at each other, like, *duh*.'

'And he's been like that ever since?'

The five boys nodded.

'The trouble was, we didn't like to make fun of him in case he was kidding us along. Believe me, Brad's the kind of guy who wouldn't hesitate to empty a whole can of wood preservative over your head, or crap in your lunchbox. Well, he *used* to be. But for three weeks he's been acting like a pussy.'

Jim took off his glasses. 'Do any of you know if anything happened to him that particular weekend? Anything out of the ordinary?'

'What, like God spoke in his ear and told him to get his shit together, or he'd never get to heaven?'

'Exactly that.'

They looked at each other, but they all shook their heads. Jim said, 'All right. Thanks. You're all coming to the funeral tomorrow, I expect?'

He was cleaning the chalkboard at the end of the day when a short black woman in a bright-pink pants suit came into the classroom on clicky-heeled shoes. She had a flat face but a very bouffant wig, like a bronze chrysanthemum.

'So this is pandemonium,' she said, in a voice as dry as crushed crackers.

'Excuse me?'

'This is the class that all of the decibels come from.'

'Oh, yes. Special Class II. They can be a little exuberant, but they're pretty well behaved, considering their various difficulties.'

The woman came forward and held out her hand. Her nails were like bronze claws, to match her wig. 'Raananah Washington. Your new vice-principal.'

'Jim Rook. That's an interesting name, Raananah.'

'It's biblical, Jim. It means "unspoiled".'

'Unspoiled. I'll remember that.'

Raananah Washington looked at the chalkboard, where Jim had rubbed off everything except the word *phantoms*.

'So, today you've been teaching your special students about ghosts?'

'No. We've been discussing what makes human beings human. That's from a poem by Robinson Jeffers: "They have hunted the phantoms and missed the house. It is not good to forget over what gulfs the spirit of the beauty of humanity, the petal of a lost flower blown seaward by the night-wind, floats to its quietness."'

'And they understand that, your special students?'

'They understand about being human, yes.'

'Good. Because it's my personal feeling that special classes like this are not the way to draw disadvantaged students into the educational community.'

Jim had been just about to erase *phantoms*, but now he hesitated. 'Um . . . what exactly do you mean by that?' he asked her.

She circled around the classroom in her clicky shoes, like an over-trained circus pony. 'My personal feeling is that special students should intermingle with the rest of the college. Special classes such as these are educationally segregationist, socially demeaning and have a negative effect on young people with learning difficulties.'

Jim left *phantoms* and lowered his eraser. 'I'll tell you what *does* have a negative effect on young people with learning difficulties, Raananah – sitting in a class with other students who can read and write ten times better than they can. In my experience they very quickly give up trying to compete, because they feel humiliated, and then they're lost to us forever.'

'I'm sorry, Jim. I think that remedial classes are patronizing and outdated. And what are you teaching them? Robinson Jeffers? A white male poet who died in 1948?'

'Shakespeare was a white male poet who died in 1616. I teach him, too.'

'There's no need for sarcasm, Jim. I just want to put you on notice that I plan to close down all of West Grove's remedial classes and welcome their students into the educational mainstream.'

'Well, thanks for the warning, Raananah. Maybe I can put *you* on notice that if you do that, all of my students will still be semi-illiterate when they leave college. Because of that, they will justifiably feel cheated by the education system and ostracized by society as a whole. They will become anti-social, welfare-dependent, and a high percentage of them will turn to drugs and crime as the only way they can make a living. Not only that, they will bring up the next generation of children the same way.'

'They warned me that you had a tendency to over-dram-
atize, Jim.'

Jim rubbed out *phantoms*.

When he arrived home that night, Tibbles was waiting for
him, sitting on Vinnie's uncle's shoes. Her eyes reflected
yellow in the darkness.

'Hi, TT. How was your day? I'll bet you didn't have
some pompous vice-principal in a Jessica Fletcher wig
telling you that you were outdated and socially demeaning.
Damn these goddamn shoes, I have to throw them away!
And damn all these goddamn hats!'

Tibbles mewed and clung around his ankles. 'What?
You're not hungry? Come on, I left you plenty. You're
thirsty? Well, you're not the only one.'

He walked directly through to the kitchen. He took the
milk carton out of the fridge and filled up Tibbles's bowl.
Then he opened a can of beer and went back into the living
room. 'You should see this woman. Raananah Washington.
She looks like Aretha Franklin and talks like Fidel Castro.'

He switched on the table lamps one by one. He was just
about to take a swig of beer when he looked up and saw
the painting of Robert H. Vane hanging over the fireplace.

He felt as if a cold eel had slithered all the way down his
back, inside his shirt, and then down between his legs. He
stood in front of the painting, staring at it, in the same way
that Tibbles had stared at it. Shocked, numb, unable to think.

Slowly he approached it. It was the same painting, no
question about it. There was the same chip on the right-hand
side of the frame, and the initials G.S.W. in the corner. But
this time there was no feasible way to explain how it might
have returned to its place on the wall. Julia wouldn't have
brought it all the way back from the auction house without
calling him first. Even if she *had*, and even if Mr Mariti
had let her into his apartment, which he wouldn't have done,
she certainly wouldn't have bothered to re-hang it.

He eased himself down on his shabby throne. Tibbles climbed up on to his lap and sniffed at his necktie. She could probably smell years of moussaka. He stroked her, and tugged at her patchy fur.

Up above the fireplace, Robert H. Vane stood with his head still covered by his black cloth, his skull-like ring gleaming on his finger. Jim could only imagine what his face looked like underneath his cloth. Triumphant? Sneering? Or did he look as stony-eyed as his self-portrait; a man who observed human life but never joined in?

The doorbell buzzed. He lowered Tibbles on to the floor and went to answer it. Eleanor was standing outside, wearing a long black roll-neck sweater and black pointy boots.

'Jim ... I hope I'm not disturbing you. I just had to check.'

'Check? Check what?'

She looked around the room. 'I heard some terrible bumping and banging in your apartment. I thought you were moving some furniture or something. I rang your doorbell but I couldn't get an answer. I was going to let myself in, but then the banging stopped. I watched your door for a while, in case it was burglars, but nobody came out.'

Jim said, 'What time was this?'

'I don't know. Three o'clock this afternoon, round about then.'

He nodded toward the painting. 'It was Mr Vane, I expect. Hanging himself back on the wall.'

'Oh my God,' said Eleanor.

'I took it down to the auction house on Rodeo Drive this morning. My friend Julia Fox took a look at it, and told me that she could probably sell it for me. I walked away and left it. But here it is, back again.'

Eleanor approached the painting, her hand pressed against her mouth.

'Still,' said Jim. 'Rodeo Drive is only about seven miles

from here. Some cats and dogs walk hundreds of miles to get back to their owners. Seven miles is nothing.'

'This is nothing to laugh about,' said Eleanor.

'Who's laughing? I can't get rid of the damned thing, can I?'

'You won't be able to.'

'Oh, no? I'm going to take it straight down to the basement, break it up, and shove it in the boiler. Let's see if it can hang itself back up again after that.'

'Jim, seriously, I wouldn't advise you to try. He almost killed you last night, didn't he?'

'It's not a "he," Eleanor! It's nothing but a goddamned painting!'

'You don't understand,' said Eleanor. But Jim stalked through to the kitchen, took a carving knife out of the wood block next to the sink, and stalked back in again.

'Jim, please, this is only going to make things worse!'

'It's a painting, Eleanor, that's all!'

'You know that's not true! You've seen it for yourself! It's a painting with a man's soul in it!'

Jim dragged his chair over to the fireplace, balanced on it, and raised the carving knife so that the point was directly over the black cloth that covered Robert H. Vane's head.

'Jim! *Don't!*'

Jim plunged the knife into the painting. At that instant he was blinded by a devastating flash of blue-white light. A blast of heat hurled him backward off the chair, so that he toppled against the couch and collided with one of the side tables, sending a lamp crashing on to the floor.

He lay on his back, scorched and winded and unable to see. Eleanor knelt down beside him and lifted his head up.

'Jim, are you OK?'

'Can't see,' he whispered. His lips felt puffed-up to three times their normal size. 'Can't breathe.'

Thirteen

Eleanor helped Jim to climb back on to his feet. He had jarred his back against the arm of the couch, and bruised his left shoulder against the floor. His face felt burning hot, and he could smell smoldering hair. Eleanor guided him over to one of the basketwork chairs so that he could sit down. All he could see was a dancing after-image of the cloth that covered Robert H. Vane's head, in lurid orange.

'You want a drink?' Eleanor asked him.

He nodded, and she placed the can of beer into his hand. He took three icy-cold swallows, and then he had to stop because it made his palate ache.

'Can you see anything yet?'

He coughed and shook his head. He couldn't help thinking of the poem '"Butch" Weldy' by Edgar Lee Masters, about a man who had been caught in a gasoline explosion, and whose eyes were 'burned crisp as a couple of eggs.'

'Your eyebrows,' said Eleanor, gently stroking his forehead.

'What about them?'

'Gone, I'm afraid. The front of your hair's looking a little spiky, too.'

'Jesus.' He stretched the sides of his eyes with his fingertips. Gradually, to his relief, his peripheral vision began to edge back. Off to his extreme left he could see part of the couch, and one of the cushions, and off to his extreme right he could see the door frame, and Eleanor's hair.

'I did warn you,' said Eleanor. 'This is a *very* powerful spirit we're dealing with here. A totally evil one, too.'

Jim felt his eyebrows. Eleanor was right: there was nothing left of them but prickly stubble. He turned toward her and blinked, and then he blinked again, and at last he could dimly see her face.

'My sight's coming back, thank God.'

'You didn't get the full flash. Vane couldn't lift up the cloth over his head, because you stuck your knife into it. That's what saved you.'

'What do you mean he couldn't lift it up? Eleanor, that isn't a real man, and that isn't a real cloth. That's a *painting*.'

'Well, it is and it isn't.'

She was silent for a while, as if she were trying to decide what to say to him. In the end, Jim said, 'You know a whole lot more about this than you're telling me, don't you?'

'I only know what Raymond Boschetto told me.'

'You mean Vinnie Boschetto's uncle? I thought you hardly ever spoke to him.'

Eleanor drew back her hair with her hand. 'I didn't. But the only reason I'm living in this building is because they wanted me close at hand, if Raymond ever needed my help. You don't think that I could possibly afford to live here if they hadn't?'

'Who are "they"?'

'The Benandanti. The people who own this building.'

'So why would Raymond Boschetto have needed your help?'

'Because I'm a sensitive. Because I can communicate with presences.'

'Any presence in particular?'

'Of course. Robert H. Vane. Raymond Boschetto was trying to find a way to do what you've been trying to do.' She nodded her head toward the painting. 'Get rid of *that*.'

'I see. Obviously he didn't succeed.'

'No,' said Eleanor. 'Raymond tried to dispose of the

painting dozens of times. He told me that he took it on the *Mauretania* once and threw it into the ocean, mid-Atlantic. Another time he drove it out to Death Valley. But it always came back. However, he *did* discover how to keep Vane's spirit trapped inside it, so that Vane couldn't get out.'

'How did he do that?'

'He wouldn't tell me. He couldn't trust anybody, even me. He thought that if I knew, Vane's spirit might enter my mind and persuade me to set him free. Before he found out how to keep him trapped, Vane's spirit was always climbing out of the painting, especially at night – the way he climbed out last night and set fire to your bed.'

'Why didn't you tell me this before? For Christ's sake, I could have been cremated in my sleep! I could have been nothing but ashes and bones and –' he held up his right hand – 'my old fraternity ring!'

'I'm sorry,' said Eleanor. 'We knew that your ability to sense the presence of evil spirits was very highly developed. We guessed, rightly, that the painting would disturb you, and that you would want to get rid of it as soon as you could. But wrongly, we guessed that you might have the strength to dispose of it forever. You can understand that we didn't want to tell you any more than we had to, in case you came under Robert H. Vane's influence, and decided to help him.'

'Help him? Help him to do what?'

Eleanor didn't answer. Jim closed his eyes and pressed his fingertips against his eyelids. He could still see orange blodges, as well as a dancing pattern of green diamonds.

'Are you all right?' Eleanor asked him.

'Sure. I think so. Half-barbecued and half-blind, but I'll survive.'

'Jim, I can't tell you very much more. I don't *know* very much more.'

'All right – but how come Vane can still be trapped inside this painting, after all these years? He should be long dead.'

144

'Dead, yes. Of course he's dead. But he's not at rest.'

'I don't get it.'

'Oh, come on. You must have seen hundreds of wandering souls – people who still have unfinished business in the real world, or who can't believe that they're really dead. How many religions believe that you can't pass over to the other side unless your entire body has been buried or cremated? That's why some Native American tribes used to cut off their victims' heads and take them away, isn't it? So that they could never go to the happy hunting ground.'

'Robert H. Vane didn't have his head cut off.'

'I know. But if you want to find peace when you die, your soul has to be complete, as well as your body. The good side of your soul, and the evil side, too, they have to be together. That's why Robert H. Vane has never been able to rest. His good side is lying in a cemetery some-place, although we don't know where. But his *dark* side is still trapped inside this painting. He carries on doing what he was charged to do, when he was alive, and he won't hesitate to kill anybody who tries to stop him. He believes that he's on a divine mission.'

Jim looked up at the painting. His carving knife was still sticking out of Robert H. Vane's head and casting a trian-gular shadow, like the pointer on a sundial. 'So what is this divine mission?'

'To capture the evil side of people's souls, so that the world will be a better place.'

'And who told him to do this?'

'The Benandanti.'

'But those are the same people who want him dead.'

Eleanor nodded. 'They didn't realize that Vane's mission would go so disastrously wrong, and that capturing the evil side of people's souls would cause such death and calamity. They're desperate to have him destroyed. They've been desperate for over a hundred and fifty years.'

Jim picked up his can of beer and took another swallow.

He couldn't take his eyes off the painting. He had found it unsettling from the moment that he had first seen it, but now he found it totally frightening, as if it were a bomb that could explode at any moment.

'So who *are* the Benandanti?' he asked.

'They're a secret society. They started off in northern Italy in the fifteenth century, as a fertility cult, worshiping the goddess Diana. Their name means "those who go well" or "good walkers." What we would call do-gooders. They were always incredibly secretive, and what little we know about them comes from the Inquisition, who tortured the Benandanti because they believed that they were witches.

'The Inquisition were right, in a way. The Benandanti do use magic. But it's white magic, and they are sworn to root out evil, no matter where it appears. They wage a never-ending war against the forces of darkness – night after night, week after week, year after year.'

'I'm amazed I've never heard of them before.'

'They're a secret society, that's why, and they don't exactly advertise themselves. All the same, Jim, they're the only true guardians of the spirit plane. They make sure that all of us are healthy, and fertile, and prosperous.'

'All of us? I don't think so. You're talking to somebody who suffers from chronic hay fever, has no children, and is practically flat broke.'

Eleanor smiled. 'You don't know how bad things could be if the Benandanti weren't fighting on our side.'

'So who's fighting on the *other* side?'

'The legions of evil. The Benandanti call them the Malandanti.'

'And how do the Benandanti fight them? And where?'

'Usually by leaving their bodies, using astral projection, and hunting down the Malandanti in the shadow planes. The Benandanti can also leave their bodies to have secret meetings, anywhere in the world.'

Jim said, 'Yes . . . I've done some of that leaving-your-body stuff. Not recommended for anybody who has to get up for work the next morning.'

Eleanor stood up, and came close to him, looking up at the painting. 'When photography was invented, the Benandanti thought that they found a scientific way to banish evil forever. They would send photographers like Robert H. Vane all around the world, like missionaries, taking pictures of as many people as they possibly could. The silver in the photographic plates would not only *reflect* whatever evil people had inside them, but once the plate was fixed, the evil would *stay* there.'

'And it worked?'

'Oh, yes,' said Eleanor. 'It worked all right. But the Benandanti hadn't understood that when people have been purged of all of their evil, they become weak and vulnerable, and they're no longer willing to protect themselves. All of those Native Americans that Robert H. Vane took pictures of . . . they died in their thousands, either of sickness, or because they put up absolutely no resistance to rapacious white settlers, or any of their enemies.'

'The Daguenos, for instance,' said Jim. 'For whom Robert H. Vane is still in mourning.'

'That's right.'

'But wait a minute – didn't the Daguenos attack a white settlement, and murder everybody, and pull their guts out? *That* wasn't a very weak and vulnerable thing to do, was it?'

'That was the other face of the disaster. Yes, everybody who was photographed had the evil taken out of them, and caught on a silver plate. But every image has a life of its own, as you know. Every portrait can see, and think. Some portraits, under some circumstances, can move – especially at night, when those who knew the people in the portraits are dreaming about them.'

Jim sat down again. He had seen photographs moving for himself. Once he had even heard one speak – a single, anguished appeal: '*Mother!*' He had seen portraits cry, out of sadness, or frustration. It wasn't hard to imagine what had happened to the portraits on Robert H. Vane's daguerrotype plates. As darkness fell, they had walked abroad, images of pure evil, but reversed, like negatives. White men with black faces and white eyes, looking to murder, and to burn, and to wreak any kind of havoc they could.

'What happened to Vane?' he asked Eleanor.

'As soon as the Benandanti discovered what was happening, they found him and ordered him to stop taking pictures, which of course he did, although they never told him why. But they didn't realize that he had taken a self-portrait, and that his own evil image was stored on a daguerrotype plate in his studio, along with all the rest.

'His good self stopped taking pictures, but every night the evil part of his spirit emerged from his self-portrait, and went out to take more. The more he took, the more he mutated, until he became the creature you saw last night, half-camera and half-man. In those days, in Southern California, people were afraid to go out at night, because there were so many murders and terrible acts of rape and mutilation. What they didn't realize was that they were being plagued by themselves – their own evil images, from Robert H. Vane's plates. And, of course, being so good, they were defenseless.

'At last one senior Benandanti missionary realized what was happening, and the Benandanti sent their agents to hunt for Vane's evil spirit. They found several of his secret studios and storehouses, and they smashed hundreds of daguerrotypes. But Vane took out insurance against his own daguerrotype being broken. He went to the best artist he could find – Gordon Shelby Welkin – and paid him a fortune to paint this portrait. On a thin sheet of silver-plated copper, which is why this painting is so heavy.

'In his diary, Welkin wrote that he was ordered by Vane to grind up the dried caul that Vane had been born with, and mix it into his oils.'

'His caul?'

'Yes – the Benandanti set great store by the magical powers of a baby's caul. Most of them carry their cauls around their necks, in a hollow tube, for the rest of their lives. I don't know if I believe it myself, but I can't think what else might account for this painting being indestructible, and un-sellable, and why it always comes back to this apartment.'

Jim was so angry he could hardly breathe. 'Vinnie must have known about this.'

'Yes,' said Eleanor. 'I suppose he must have done. But I never knew anything about Raymond's family. The Benandanti never tell you more than you need to know, and most of the time they tell you very much less.'

'Goddamn it, no wonder Vinnie let me rent the place so goddamned cheap! And no wonder he asked me if I was managing to sleep OK. "Haven't been disturbed by any hunchbacks, have you, Jim, with legs like tripods? No-o-o? That's a relief!"'

Eleanor caught hold of his sleeve. 'I swear to you, Jim, all I know is that the day after Raymond died, I had a phone call from the Benandanti telling me that they were urgently looking for somebody to take his place, but meanwhile I should be extra watchful.'

'I see. They were looking for somebody to take his place, were they? Somebody with psychic abilities, who could take on Robert H. Vane and stop him from turning the world into negative hell, but somebody that no one would miss if anything went badly wrong? Who better than good old Jim Rook?'

'Jim, when they told me you were moving in, you've no idea how relieved they were. People of your abilities – well, they're one in ten million.'

Jim didn't know what to say. What had seemed to be a bargain had turned out instead to be a death trap; and the people who had pretended to be friends had turned out to be vipers. He could have been incinerated last night. He might have been incinerated only a few minutes ago, if he hadn't been lucky enough to pin down the cloth that covered Robert H. Vane's head. He could be lying here now, on the rug, nothing more than a heap of gray ashes, a ribcage, and a skull.

'I think you'd better leave,' he told Eleanor.

'Jim . . . I promise you . . . I know the Benandanti – I trust them. If they could have thought of any other way . . .'

'They didn't even *ask* me! They didn't even call me up and say, "oh, excuse us, we're the Benandanti and we happen to have an oil painting which can reduce a human being to cigar ash in five seconds flat, and would you mind keeping an eye on it for us?"'

'You would have refused, that's why.'

'Too damn right I would have refused!'

'Even if you knew what Vane is capable of doing whenever he gets out? Jim, he goes around capturing the evil in people's souls, anybody he can find, and he stores them up in their hundreds, on his silver plates, so that one day you won't be safe anywhere, day or night, because the world will be overrun with the negative images of people's spirits, their evil selves, and their good selves will be far too weak to stop them.'

Jim ran his hand through his prickly hair. 'I'm sorry, Eleanor. I like you, and I can understand what you're saying, but no, this isn't a job for me. I've had enough bad experiences with evil spirits for one lifetime, believe me, and after what happened to me in DC . . .'

An appalling thought occurred to him. Supposing the Benandanti had heard about his psychic abilities while he was still in Washington, working for the federal department of education? How would they have made sure that he return to Los Angeles, and to West Grove Community College? Only two days after that terrible incident in Washington, while he was still in shock, his phone had rung and it was

Seymour Wallis from the West Grove board of governors. Seymour Wallis – white-bearded, avuncular, reassuring. 'We don't know how you're making out in DC, Jim, but your old job with Special Class II just became vacant . . . is there a small chance that you might be interested?'

He said to Eleanor, 'I'll be staying someplace else tonight, and tomorrow morning I'll be packing up my stuff and leaving.'

She took hold of both of his hands, her silver rings digging into his fingers. 'Jim, I'm so sorry. Please don't go. I don't know what's going to happen if you do. It won't be like *The Night of the Living Dead* – it'll be far worse than that. The negative people are absolute evil . . . they're worse than vampires, and they multiply as fast as Vane can take their pictures. Crowd scenes, hundreds at a time.'

The phone rang. Jim pulled himself free from Eleanor and went over to pick it up.

'Jim? It's Julia Fox. Listen, I have something terribly embarrassing to tell you. We have such high security at the auction house. We've had Rembrandts here without any incident. But somehow your Welkin has gone AWOL.'

'Don't worry about it, Julia. Like you said, you probably couldn't have knocked it down for very much.'

'All the same, we've informed the police, and they'll probably want to come talk to you.'

'OK, Julia, thanks.' He hung up. Eleanor was standing with her arms by her sides, watching him.

'The auction house,' he said. 'They think that somebody's stolen my painting.'

'Jim,' Eleanor pleaded.

'No. I wouldn't have moved here if Vinnie hadn't lied to me, and I wouldn't have stayed here if you hadn't compounded that lie. "I sense two presences." Do me a favor.'

'Oh, those two presences are here all right. They're Raymond's mother and father.'

'Really? Thanks for telling me.'

'Please, listen. Raymond's mother and father were attending a family wedding – one of Raymond's cousins – when Robert H. Vane appeared and took their pictures. After that their evil selves used to come here night after night, beating at the door, until one day Raymond managed to find out where their daguerrotypes were hidden, and destroyed them. Now all that's left is their good selves, which stayed here after they died – and always will, probably, until they knock the building down.'

Jim said, 'It's no use, Eleanor. Nothing can persuade me to stay here. Nothing.'

They gathered around the graves at Rolling Hills cemetery, over a hundred of them – families, friends, fellow students and the media. It was a humid morning, and the sky was a strange reddish color, as if it had been filmed through a strawberry filter, or as if something freakish were about to happen.

Bobby's and Sara's families stood together, dabbing their eyes. Dr Ehrlichman gave a speech about promising lives cut short – the same speech that he always gave when West Grove lost one of its students, whether they had died in an auto wreck, or cut their wrists, or overdosed on smack.

'Who can predict what they might have been . . . what they might have achieved? Who can tell where the highway of fate might have guided their footsteps?'

At the end, Jim stepped forward. He was feeling tired and strained, and the burned prickles of his hair were stuck to his forehead with perspiration, but he had promised to say a few words on behalf of Special Class II.

'I didn't personally know Bobby or Sara, but I know what their fellow students thought of them, how much they loved and respected them, and how much they're going to miss them. Here's a poem that I was going to read in class next week, and which we were all going to discuss. I can't say what Bobby and Sara would have thought about it, but I think it's very appropriate for their passing. "Farewell" by Henry Thompson:

'One day the day will dawn which is my last
And that day I will never see the curtains drawn
To keep the night at bay; because the night
Will have consumed me. But do not mourn.
The path down which I ran to greet my mother,
The gate on which I swung when I was five.
Without me, you can go yourself to see them
And thus remember that I was alive.

'And you can see the beaches where I sang and danced
The hills on which I lay and watched the sky
And you can read the words in all my letters
And touch each page, because my ink is dry.
I need to know that, when I'm gone, those places,
Those fields and woods and orchards filled with flowers
Are still as bright as when I walked amongst them
Before I felt the shadow of the hours.

'Farewell, then. Now the telephone is ringing
Unanswered in the cold and empty hall.
And letters lie unopened on the table
And through the window rain begins to fall.
Whisper my name just once when you go walking
Up on the windy downs above the sea.
Whisper my name just one more time
For that will be the only trace of me.'

As he spoke the last few lines, tears ran freely down Shadow's cheeks, and Sue-Marie took out a pink tissue and honked her nose. Bobby's father and mother tossed handfuls of earth on to his casket, and then Sara's father and mother did the same to hers. Everybody remained by the graves for a while, some of them throwing in roses, many of them standing with their heads bowed and their eyes closed.

Jim assembled Special Class II and led them down the sloping driveway to the parking lot, where their bus was waiting.

'I can't believe they're both gone,' said Delilah, walking beside him. 'I keep thinking that I'm going to see them tomorrow, sitting in class, just like always.'

'Well, they'll be with us in spirit,' Jim told her. 'We'll have a discussion tomorrow about losing people, and how to express your emotions in words. If you can describe how you feel on paper, it really helps to ease the pain, believe me.'

Delilah looked up at him, squinting one eye against the sun. 'Can I ask you something, Mr Rook? When you look at us, when you look at Special Class II, do you think we're really dumb?'

Jim smiled and shook his head. 'The only dumb people I know are the people who refuse to learn English, because they think they're too cool, or they know enough words already.'

'I saw a new word today. Well, I'm not too sure if it is a word, or just somebody's name.'

'Oh yes, what was it?' He was only half paying attention, because he could see Karen walking diagonally between the gravestones so that she would meet up with him.

'Nemesis. It was scratched on the back of the seat in front of me, on the bus.'

'It means somebody who relentlessly seeks revenge. But it is a name, too, in a way. It comes from Nemesis, the Greek goddess of retribution.' He paused, and looked at her. 'Funny thing to scratch on a bus seat.'

'It was carved real deep. It must have taken hours.'

Karen came up to join him. 'That was a very sad funeral.'

'Yes, it was.'

'Why don't I give you a ride back to college?' she suggested. 'You don't have to go on the bus, do you?'

'No . . . I guess the Wild Bunch will be OK without me. They all seem pretty subdued after that.'

He stood by the bus door, counting all of Special Class II as they climbed aboard. Sue-Marie was the last. She was wearing a very short black dress and grape-jelly-colored lipstick.

'Are you going to sit next to me, sir?'

'Actually, Sue-Marie, I've accepted a lift from Ms Goudemark. We have some curriculum problems to discuss.'

Sue-Marie gave him a sultry look that could have burned holes through paper. 'Curriculum problems? Pity.'

It was all that Jim and Karen could do to stop themselves from laughing out loud. Jim had to press his hand over his mouth as Sue-Marie climbed the steps, wiggling her bottom, and the doors closed behind her with a sharp pneumatic hiss.

'She really has the hots for you,' said Karen, as they walked across to her pale-blue Mustang.

'If only I were ten years younger.'

'If you were ten years younger she wouldn't lust after you.'

Jim climbed into the passenger seat. 'You're not jealous, are you?'

'Jealous? *Moi?*'

She inserted the key into the ignition, and she was just about to start the engine when Jim saw something moving on the opposite side of the parking lot. He laid his hand on top of hers and said, 'Wait.'

'What?' she asked him. 'Did you forget something?'

'No. *Look!* Can you see that? Over there, just past those bushes!'

Karen frowned in the direction that Jim was pointing. 'I can't see anything. What is it?'

Jim felt as if all the blood was draining out of his face. Lurching across the parking lot, less than a hundred yards away from them, was the camera creature – Robert H. Vane. In broad daylight he looked just as terrifying as he had in the dark, his hunched-up body draped in black, his legs moving in that jerky, crippled, spider-like gait, as if he was right on the verge of toppling over. In spite of his awkwardness, though, he was moving disconcertingly fast, and he was heading directly toward the bus.

Fourteen

'What's the matter?' asked Karen. 'Jim, what's wrong?'
'Can't you see that? Look!' Jim struggled with his seatbelt and heaved himself out of the car.

'Jim, what is it?'

'Call nine-one-one!' Jim shouted at her. 'Fire department! Now!'

He started to run toward the bus, shouting hoarsely and waving his arms. The camera creature took no notice of him, but continued to clatter across the tarmac. He looked far bigger than he had before, and taller, with his humped black body and his stilt-like mahogany legs.

'Get out of the bus!' he screamed. 'Everybody get out of the bus!'

The bus driver had already started the engine and released the brakes. He was slowly inching out of his parking space, his hand flat on the steering wheel.

'Stop! *Stop!* Open the door! Everybody get out of the bus!'

He could see the faces of Special Class II staring at him out of the windows. Randy, and Delilah, and Edward, and Sally Broxman, twisting her hair. He felt as if he were running through treacle, and that his voice was slowed-down and blurred.

'*Sttoooopppp! Everrrybooody ggettt outtttt offff the busssss . . .*'

The camera creature suddenly stopped, his legs unsteadily jabbing for balance. Two arms emerged from underneath the black cloth, throwing it right back over his humped-up shoulders. It was then that Jim glimpsed for a split second what Robert H. Vane had become. A bone-white skull, almost square, with only a few strands of greasy, iron-gray hair. A face dominated by a huge dark lens, like a single eye. He raised one hand, except that it wasn't a hand, it was a blackened metal trough. It was impossible to tell where the man ended and the camera began; they were biologically intermingled.

Jim sprinted toward him, panting with effort, determined to tackle him and bring him down. But the camera creature was too quick for him. Jim still had more than twenty yards to cover when there was an ear-splitting *crack* and the entire world was bleached into nothingness – bus, sky, yucca trees, parking lot – followed by a wave of heat that sent Jim staggering backward. One foot got tangled up with the other, and he fell heavily on to the ground, knocking his head and grazing his hand.

When he managed to look up, he saw that the bus was on fire, blazing fiercely from front to back. The camera creature took a few three-legged steps back, then dropped the cloth to cover his head and body, and began to stalk quickly away. Jim had to let him go: the bus was a mass of rippling orange flames and he could hear screaming and shouting as Special Class II tried to escape.

He ran up to the front of the bus, one arm raised to protect his face. Behind the door he could see Ruby struggling to get out, her face contorted with panic. He tried to get closer, but the heat was roasting. Along the side of the bus, he could see Randy and Roosevelt beating at the windows with their fists, trying to break the glass.

He turned around. Several people were running toward him. 'Hammer!' he shouted. 'Tire iron! Anything! We have to get them out!'

He stripped off his coat and bundled it around his left arm, covering his hand. He edged toward the door, keeping his right hand lifted to shield his face. The sleeve of his coat began to smolder, but the heat was just about bearable. Edging forward just a little more, he reached out and grabbed the emergency door handle, and yanked it down.

The door juddered open, and Ruby tumbled out on to the tarmac, her hair smoking. Jim dragged her away from the bus, and Sara Miller's mother came up and put her jacket around her. Ruby was followed by Brenda, Vanilla and Freddy, all of them gasping from smoke and heat. Then – hacking and gagging even more wildly – came Roosevelt and George.

Jim waited a few moments longer, to see if anybody else would make it out, but that seemed to be all. 'Sonny!' he shouted. 'Sue-Marie!'

There was no answer. He tried to edge a little nearer, so that he could jump up on to the bus. But the front tire, which had been furiously smoldering up until now, suddenly burst into flame, and gouts of fiery rubber began to shower across the steps, like lava.

'Jim!' shouted Dr Ehrlichman. 'Jim, you get back here! That bus is going to explode!'

Jim ignored him. He turned to one of the funeral directors and said, 'Give me your coat!'

'What?'

'Your coat! Give me your coat!'

The funeral director pulled off his coat and reluctantly handed it over. Jim immediately draped it over his head. He crouched down, took a deep breath, and then vaulted on to the steps.

Inside, the bus was full of boiling black smoke, and he could see only inches in front of him. The driver was tilted over the wheel, his face sweaty and maroon. Jim heaved him out of his seat and rolled him down the steps. Then he groped his way down the aisle. Almost at once he found Randy, hunched on the floor, wheezing for breath. He dragged him along to the doorway, grunting with effort, and pushed him down the steps, too. He didn't have time to be ceremonious about it, or to worry about the flames from the blazing tire.

Coughing, breathless, he went back again, and this time he collided with Sonny, Sue-Marie and Edward, all holding hands.

'This way!' he said hoarsely, and led them toward the door. 'Just get the hell out!'

They stumbled down the steps. Jim, his eyes watering, peered toward the back of the bus. There must be two or three more students, at least. He inched his way back down the aisle, his hand held over his face. The heat was so intense at this end of the bus that he felt as if he were walking through a blast furnace. He could smell the hairs inside his nostrils burning, and the soles of his best black shoes were melting, so that every step was sticky.

Five rows from the back he found Delilah lying in her seat, semi-conscious. He leaned across and shook her. 'Delilah! Delilah! Wake up! You have to get out of here!'

He shook her again, violently, and this time she opened her eyes, blinked up at him, and coughed. On the back of the seat in front of her was the word NEMESIS, carved deep.

'Delilah! You have to get out!'

He managed to pull her out of her seat. 'What?' she mumbled. 'What's happening?'

'That way,' he said, pointing through the smoke toward the front of the bus.

At that moment there were two sharp explosions, one after the other, as the rear windows smashed. Oxygen rushed hungrily into the bus, and the last three rows burst into raging orange flame. The vinyl seat covers peeled away like dragon skin, and the foam upholstery dripped in monstrous blazing blobs. Even the composition floor started to burn.

Jim thought: that's it, nobody left alive. I have to get out of here.

Just as he was about to turn back, however, he saw shadowy movement amongst the flames. He peered through his wide-apart fingers. Nobody could have survived a holocaust like this. It wasn't possible.

But then two figures emerged from the fire, and they were both on fire, too. Pinky and David, trudging toward him as slowly as if they were climbing a mountain. Pinky's hair was alight, and her dress crawled with flame. Her face was blackened and cracked like barbecued pork, and her lips were livid scarlet. Both of her arms were raised in unbearable pain, in the drumming-monkey gesture that people adopt when they are burning alive.

David was close up behind her, his arms raised monkey-fashion, too. He kept nudging Pinky forward because both of his eyeballs had burst and his eye-sockets were nothing but glutinous holes. He had no hair on his scalp, only shiny black scales, like a turtle.

Pinky stopped. Jim thought she might be staring at him, but he couldn't tell if she could see him or not. David stopped behind her, and the both of them stood in the aisle for what seemed like a minute, burning. Black fatty smoke rose from the tops of their heads, as if they were human candles.

Pinky's lips moved, and she said something. It sounded like *please*, but it could have been anything. Jim raised his hand toward her, unable to touch her, but desperate to show her that he cared for her. Without another word she collapsed on to the floor, and David collapsed on top of her. The fire from the composition flooring engulfed them both.

Jim groped his way toward the front of the bus. He reached the top of the steps, hesitated for a moment, and then hurled himself sideways out of the door, right through the flames from the burning tire. He hit the ground and rolled over and over.

Somebody immediately grabbed his left arm, and just as quickly, somebody else grabbed his right. Whoever they were, they were very strong, because they dragged him away at a fast trot, his heels bouncing on the tarmac. They dragged him all the way to the grass bank at the side of the parking lot, and then they slowed up, and gently laid him down.

He looked up and blinked. His eyes were still watering and the sun was shining brightly so that all he could see of his rescuers was black silhouettes.

'Are you OK, sir?' one of them asked him.

He shielded his eyes with his hand and saw that it was a young black firefighter, in a helmet and rubbers.

'Yes,' he coughed. 'Thanks.' He coughed again, and again, and then he started coughing so much that he had to sit up.

As he did so, he saw the bus, burning like a Norse funeral ship, on its way to Valhalla.

'Pinky,' he croaked. 'David. They didn't stand a chance.'

'You did everything you could, sir, believe me.'

The bus exploded with a devastating roar. A huge ball of orange fire rolled up into the morning sky, followed by another ball of black smoke. Fragments of paneling and window frames and metal tubing were blown high up into the air, and then began to clatter down again, like tuneless bells. A blazing wheel dropped on to the tarmac only thirty feet away, and bounced, and then went rolling downhill with a firefighter running after it.

Karen pushed her way through the crowd and knelt down beside him.

'Jim! Jim! Are you OK?'

He coughed and nodded and coughed. 'Smoke,' he said, pointing to his chest.

She put her arms around him and held him close. 'You're crazy,' she said. 'You could have been killed.'

He couldn't answer. His throat was raw and he couldn't catch his breath. All he could think about was Pinky and David slowly walking toward him, both burning. He knew that he would see them now for the rest of his life.

That, and the word nemesis.

Lieutenant Harris came into the recovery room and, without being invited, pulled up a chair. He was wearing a particularly garish necktie, with purple lightning flashes on it. He took out his handkerchief and mopped the sweat from his upper lip.

'So . . . how are you feeling, Mr Rook?'

'Better. Sore throat. But at least I can talk.'

'They tell me you did a great job back there. Saved a lot of lives.'

Jim coughed and shook his head. 'I should have saved all of them.'

'I know how you feel. But you did everything you could. When it's somebody's day to die, even the Lord God Himself can't help them.'

Jim reached for a plastic cup and drank three mouthfuls of warm water. 'Did you talk to any witnesses yet?'

'Seven or eight so far. But we'll be interviewing everybody who was there. The CSU and the fire department investigators are checking the wreckage even as we speak.'

'Did any of the witnesses tell you that they saw a very bright flash of light?'

Lieutenant Harris nodded. 'Yep. They *all* did. That's one of the theories. A freak lightning strike. Happens on golf courses sometimes.'

'Nobody saw . . . any kind of a figure?'

Lieutenant Harris licked his thumb and leafed through his notebook. 'Nope. Nothing like that.' He paused, and then he said, 'Why? Did you?'

'I saw something, yes. Something which makes me sure that this wasn't lightning.'

'Oh, yeah? What was it?'

'I think it's connected with Bobby Tubbs and Sara Miller, the way they died.'

Lieutenant Harris looked at him suspiciously. 'We're not talking about spontaneous human combustion again, are we? I looked into that real thorough, and there are *no* genuine cases of people bursting into flame spontaneously. The only time that people have burned to ashes is when their clothes have caught fire because they're drunk, and they've been sitting too close to a naked flame. The clothes have acted like a wick, and their body fat has acted as a candle.'

Jim said, 'This wasn't anything like that. This was a single blast of intense heat and light, like the magnesium-powder flashguns that old-time photographers used to use.'

Lieutenant Harris sat and waited, as if he expected him to say more.

'That's it,' said Jim.

'That's it? It was an old-time photographic flashgun? Set off by whom, exactly?'

'Somebody who wanted to show me who was boss.'

'Can you give me a name? Can you explain how he did it? Can you tell me *why* he did it?'

Jim coughed, and cleared his throat. 'I don't think it would help. In fact, I think it would make things worse. I just wanted you to know that I'm ninety-nine per cent sure how it happened, and who did it. I'm also ninety-nine per cent sure how Bobby Tubbs and Sara Miller were murdered, and why, and who killed them.'

Lieutenant Harris opened and closed his mouth, like a goldfish. 'You're not trying to tell me that it wasn't Brad Moorcock?'

'No. no. It *was* Brad Moorcock, in a way. But in another way, it wasn't. But you'd be better off keeping him locked up, if only for his own safety.'

'I see,' said Lieutenant Harris, although he patently didn't. 'But you're trying to say that these two cases could be connected? The bus today, and Bobby and Sara last week?'

'Connected, yes. But not the same perpetrator, no.'

164

Lieutenant Harris mopped his face again, and then the back of his neck. 'Is that all you're going to tell me?'

'For now, yes. I still have to make sense of it myself.'

Lieutenant Harris stood up. 'Listen, Mr Rook. Most of my colleagues think that I'm off to the races, talking to you. They don't believe in the world beyond, and they certainly don't believe that there's any way of getting in touch with people who are dead and buried. Me, I keep an open mind about that. But I do think that you have some kind of rare ability and I'm willing to play along with you if it means that I get to the bottom of things.

'However, if I find that you know something that could materially affect my investigations, and that you're holding out on me for reasons best known to yourself, then I'm going to throw your ass in jail and I'm going to make sure that you stay there for a very, very long time, with nothing to eat but stale Saltines, and nothing to drink but flat root beer. *Comprendo?*'

All Jim could do was cough and nod.

Early that evening, when Jim returned to his apartment, the sun was shining on the wall above the fireplace, and on the portrait of Robert H. Vane. It lit the brushstrokes in lurid orange, as if the painting were on fire.

Jim stood and looked at it. Tibbles came in from the kitchen, still licking her whiskers from finishing off her bowl of mashed sardines. She climbed up on her hind legs, holding on to the knee of his black funeral pants with her claws.

'Are you satisfied?' Jim challenged Robert H. Vane.

Beneath his black cloth, Robert H. Vane remained silent. Jim couldn't even catch him breathing.

'Pinky and David, what did they ever do to you?' he demanded. 'Pinky believed in Paradise and David believed in God, and what did you do? You destroyed them, and you destroyed their beliefs, and all for what? To show me that I couldn't get rid of you? To show me that you can come sneaking out of that picture whenever you feel like it, day or night, and ruin people's lives, and that there's nothing I can do to stop you?'

He stepped right up to the painting, with his feet in the fireplace. 'Are you trying to make me feel weak and helpless? Well, congratulations, I do! I feel utterly useless, if you must know! But I'm going to get my revenge for what you did today, believe me, and you're going to come down from that wall, and I'm going to make sure you never hang up here again.'

He was still standing in front of the painting when there was a cautious rapping at the door, and Eleanor stepped into the room. She was wearing a long black gauzy dress, with nothing underneath, and very high black sandals with criss-cross straps.

'Mr Mariti? Oh, it's you, Jim! Sorry . . . the door was open. I thought you were moving out.'

'I've changed my mind. I have a score to settle first.'

'Score?'

'Didn't you see the news today? A bus caught fire at the Rolling Hills cemetery, with over a dozen college students on it. *My* students. Two of them were burned to death.'

'Oh my God,' said Eleanor. She came up to him and took hold of his hand. 'Oh my God, that's terrible! You must be devastated.'

Jim didn't take his eyes off the painting. Eleanor looked up at it, too. 'You don't think that . . .'

'I don't *think*, Eleanor. I *know*. I can *see*, remember, and I saw him there. Robert H. Vane. Nobody else saw him, but that doesn't matter. You can't arrest an evil spirit. You can't arraign a painting for homicide. I don't like to admit it, but you were right. The only person who can bring him to justice is me.'

'What are you going to do?'

'I'm going to have to find out how Raymond Boschetto

kept him trapped inside the painting. Whatever he did, it only worked so long as Raymond was alive. I'll have to go a stage further and work out how to keep him in there forever . . . or how to destroy the painting so that it can't come back.'

'Raymond didn't even give me the slightest hint. He said the less I knew about Robert H. Vane, the safer I would be.'

'Well,' said Jim, 'I have all of Raymond's books here, and all of his notes. It looks like I've got some homework to do.'

'Have you eaten?' asked Eleanor. 'I have some chicken and basil casserole, if you'd like some.'

'Why not?' said Jim. 'I'll open a bottle of wine, too.' He took off his glasses and rubbed his eyes. They were still sore from the smoke. 'I don't think I could sleep tonight, anyhow.'

Eleanor gently touched his cheek with her fingertips, almost as if she were intrigued to discover that he was real. 'I'll stay up with you.'

'OK then,' he said. The last of the sunlight faded from the painting. 'Let's see if we can trap this monster before the sun comes up again.'

Fifteen

They cleared a space on the dining-room table, and ate their supper with Raymond Boschetto's books and diaries stacked all around them. Jim found over thirty books on early photography, as well as books on precious metals, and how silver had been used since the times of the Ancient Greeks for magic rituals and mysticism.

'Silver is a moon metal, associated with the occult, with darkness, and the unconscious. It is in opposition to the gold of the sun, which is symbolic of light and life. The purity of silver and its connection to the moon made it the perfect metal for the making of talismans and amulets, and Mohammed himself forbade the use of any other substance.'

Jim reached across the table and took hold of the medallion that Eleanor wore around her neck. 'Is this silver?'

She nodded. 'The Benandanti gave it to me when I agreed to move in here. It warns me if evil is approaching. It tingles, that's the best way I can describe it.'

'Does it work?'

'It goes crazy whenever I get close to that portrait. *Fizzes*, almost. So yes, I guess it does. You see that face on it? That's a fool. Fools are supposed to be highly sensitive to evil, like dogs and cats.'

'I see. I guess that explains why I'm so sensitive to evil.'

Eleanor took hold of his hand. 'You're not a fool, Jim. You're incredibly brave. You put other people first.'

'Oh, well. Maybe you're right. As Blake said, "if a fool would persist in his folly, he would become wise."' He poured them both another glass of Barolo. 'But don't get me wrong; I'm not doing this because I want to, believe me. I'm only doing it because nobody else can.'

Eleanor cleared the dishes and stacked them in the dishwasher, while Jim started to read Raymond Boschetto's diaries. There were forty-one of them altogether, bound in brown leather. Jim had to put on his reading glasses, because Raymond's writing was tiny and crabbed, and he had crammed every single square inch of every page, even if it meant writing vertically up the margin.

Most of the diaries were nothing but a daily record of what Raymond had eaten (fresh figs and prosciutto with *scamorza* cheese) or the books he had read (*The Sacred Magic of Abramelin the Mage*, *Discourse of the Damned Arts*, *Faustbuch*). But in some passages, he ranted on furiously about the Benandanti and Robert H. Vane and how his whole life was being taken up by this 'impossible and dangerous commission.'

Little by little, however, Jim began to understand why the painting of Robert H. Vane was hanging here, in this apartment, and why the Benandanti had been unable to get rid of it. Raymond used the words 'shadow-self' to describe the dark side of Robert H. Vane's personality.

Robert H. Vane did many good and charitable works in the last years of his life, but he was physically weak and prone to frequent bouts of ill-health. I have no hesitation in ascribing this sickliness to the taking-away of his *shadow-self*, and its entrapment on a silver photographic plate, which happened when he posed for his own daguerrotype self-portrait. A man with *no* evil in him whatsoever may be saintly, but he will always be vulnerable to any kind of attack, be it a virus or another man with wicked intent.

Vane died of pneumonia in the spring of 1861. His remains were first buried in a private plot on the

Rancho Nuestra Senora, which belonged to a friend of his, a farmer named John Wakeman, but after three months his body was exhumed and moved to an unmarked plot. Mr Wakeman complained that Vane was 'not at rest' and that after his interment his daughters and his fruit-pickers had several times seen him in the distance, walking through the orchards as if lost.

So Vane's *good* self, while dead, remained restless, and it was plain from the multiplicity of arsons and murders by fire in the Los Angeles area that his *shadow-self* was also still at large. He was still taking portraits and still collecting on his silver plates the evil selves of those who unwittingly consented to pose for him – and there were many.

However, the daguerrotype is a very cumbersome process, and a great deal of heavy equipment is required to take each picture. By the latter part of the century, plate cameras were out of date for everything except for formal groups, and Vane was finding it increasingly difficult to take pictures without attracting attention. He would gatecrash weddings and sporting events and take crowd scenes in the streets, in order to garner as many souls as possible, but he knew that the Benandanti were always looking for him, and he had to be more and more careful.

In 1909, after years of persistent and diligent investigation, the agents of the Benandanti at last discovered that Vane's *shadow-self* was using an outbuilding at Long Beach as his hiding place and storehouse for his daguerrotype plates. The agents broke in and destroyed every daguerrotype plate that they could find, including a daguerrotype of Vane himself.

But over the next two and a half years, the burnings and the murders continued unabated, and the agents realized that Vane's *shadow-self* must be hiding elsewhere. After a spate of arson attacks in Malibu, they discovered more daguerrotype plates and – at last – the *painted* portrait of Vane. They destroyed the plates, but they found that the painting was indestructible. It simply couldn't be disposed of, not by any earthly means. They incinerated it. They broke it to pieces, and separated the pieces by many miles. Once they took it as far as Mexico, and buried it, but each time the painting turned up intact, in the very place where it had been before.

For that reason, the Benandanti had to concede that they could do nothing more than watch over it, while they tried to discover how to break the spell that protected it. I say 'spell' because I can think of no other word to describe the extraordinary supernatural force which Vane had used to safeguard his painted image.

The Benandanti agents destroyed Vane's camera equipment, and from 1912 onwards, one Benandanti after another volunteered to keep a watch on the portrait, to make sure that Vane was unable to climb out of it and collect more evil souls.

In 1935, when the Benandanti Building was erected, this particular apartment was set aside for Robert H. Vane's portrait and whoever had elected to watch it. The Benandanti believed that even if they had not yet succeeded in destroying the painting, they had successfully protected generations of Southern Californians from this merciless scavenger of souls.

But early in 1965, the Benandanti began to receive disturbing reports from the Mid-West of people being mysteriously burned to ashes, and farms being razed. Their agents undertook investigations in Iowa and Nebraska and soon discovered that somebody had been on the road taking 'old-time photographs'. Not just recently, but for twenty or thirty years – traveling all the way from Maine to Miami.

171

Eventually they found a picture taken just outside Cedar Rapids, Iowa, of a white Ford van bearing the legend *Robert H. Vane, Old-Style Family Photographs*. The picture was dated October, 1964. All the years that the Benandanti had believed that his *shadow-self* was hiding inside his portrait, Vane had been touring the country, gathering evil selves by the score.

He could easily leave and return to the painting, without being seen. He was, after all, *dead* (although he hadn't yet passed over to the world beyond) and so he was capable of appearing and disappearing at will.

Jim sat back. '*This* is why the Benandanti wanted me to have this apartment.' He passed over the diary and watched Eleanor as she read it. 'Vane is invisible, when he wants to be. Nobody can see him, except me and people like me. If there *are* any people like me.'

Eleanor said, 'I'm sorry.'

'What's the point in being sorry? Four young people are dead and being sorry isn't going to bring them back to life.'

Eleanor picked up another diary and riffled through the pages. 'Does Raymond say how he trapped Vane here?'

Jim opened the diary for 1965 and turned to September. 'Here – this is when he first agreed to move in here.'

'"I was asked today by X to take over the guardianship of Robert H. Vane's portrait, despite what the Benandanti now know about his invisible comings and goings. I declined. I knew what a thankless and tedious task it would be, and unquestionably dangerous, if I attempted to thwart him in his gathering of souls."'

The following week, however, Raymond had written the following:

Out of curiosity, I undertook some research into the

172

matter of portraits and paintings, and how they have
been used down the centuries as places of concealment for people's spirits. I discovered that Urbain
Grandier, the priest who had been accused of inducing
the Satanic possession of nuns in Loudun in 1634, had
asked for his portrait to be painted in the days before
his execution. For years afterward, a figure answering
Grandier's description was seen around the streets of
Loudun, and nine of those who had tortured Grandier,
or who had tried him or testified against him, all died
horribly of strangulation in their beds.

A cardinal from the Vatican was sent to investigate
these murders: Cardinal Vaudrey. He questioned the
artist who had painted Grandier's portrait, and the artist
told him that Grandier had insisted that he mix
powdered silver oxide into his paints, as well as the
ground-up dust from 'a dry cap of skin', which is
likely to have been Grandier's caul.

Cardinal Vaudrey attempted to have the painting
burned, but it refused to ignite, even when soaked in
oil. He threw it off a bridge into the river Vienne, but
the next day it was leaning against the wall in the
house where it had been stored before.

The cardinal was now convinced that he was dealing
with the works of Satan, so he decided that he would
have to *imprison* Grandier inside his portrait so that
he could never escape. The only way in which he
could do this was to *reverse* the ritual of exorcism. In
other words, he would have to make sure that the evil
spirit stayed *inside* the portrait, instead of forcing it
out, as he would have done if he were exorcizing it.

But the cardinal's dilemma was that he would be
obliged to perform this ritual every single day, twice
a day, for as long as he lived (and then pass on the
duty to another exorcist, and so on, *ad infinitum*). It
was the moon that made this necessary. Every time it

circles around the earth, the moon's gravitational force acts on silver to draw out any evil that might be stored in it – in the same way that it pulls the oceans, and causes the tides to rise.

So, if I were to accept the duty of keeping Robert H. Vane trapped inside his portrait, I would have to perform the same ritual of exorcism, day after day, night after night, for the rest of my life. I would be fighting a never-ending battle with the moon.

The next entry was very short.

This is the choice that I am faced with. I have sought guidance in prayer. I have argued with myself. I know what I will have to sacrifice: my freedom, my life, my happiness. In the end, however, I know that I have no option. If I refuse to guard the portrait, hundreds of people will die – thousands. Every night, the country will be swarming with *shadow-selves*, carrying out whatever acts of evil they want to, and the fires that burn across America will burn more fiercely than the fires of hell.

'Well,' said Jim. 'Now we know what we're really up against. Raymond died, and when Raymond died, the exorcisms stopped, and Vane was free to climb out of his portrait. He's started taking pictures again, too. He must have taken a picture of Brad Moorcock, because that was who that wino saw, breaking into the Tubbs' beach house. Not the real flesh and blood Brad Moorcock, of course, but Brad Moorcock's evil self, taking his revenge on Sara Miller for dumping him.'

He stood up. 'It all fits. Raymond died just over three weeks ago, and it was three weeks ago that Brad's fellow students began to notice that he was acting out of character. He was so *nice* all of a sudden that they couldn't believe it. And, of course, the reason was that he had no evil in him any more – *none*. He was one hundred per cent Good

Brad. All of his evil self had been caught on a photographic plate, by Robert H. Vane. But that evil self is just like a vampire now, hiding inside a daguerrotype instead of a coffin, and just like a vampire he can only come out at night, when the moon draws his evil out of the silver.'

'So what are you going to do now?' Eleanor asked him.

'Step one: I'm going to find out where Robert H. Vane keeps his daguerrotypes.'

Brad shuffled into the interview room, wearing bright-orange prison pajamas, and handcuffed. He looked exhausted and unshaven, and he sat down at the table with his head bowed.

'Brad?' asked Jim. 'How are you holding up?'

'I saw the bus burning on TV,' said Brad. 'That was horrible.'

'That's one of the reasons I'm here. I think that the bus fire may have something to do with the way that Bobby and Sara were killed.'

Brad lifted his head and stared at him. 'Huh? How do you figure that?'

'I can't explain exactly, not yet. But I want you to know that you didn't kill Bobby and Sara and I believe I can prove it. Well you *did*, but it wasn't really you. Not the you that's sitting here, talking to me now.'

'I'm sorry, Mr Rook. I don't understand.'

'Well, let me put it this way. Have you been feeling different in the past three weeks? Happier? Friendlier? Much less irritated by your friends and fellow students?'

Brad shrugged. 'I guess. I don't know. It hadn't really occurred to me.'

'At any time, in the past three weeks, have you had your photograph taken?'

'Yes, I have. After we won the game against Santa Cruz.'

'Who took it?'

'It was just some guy with a van, with a tent rigged up at the side of it.'

'Where was this?'

'Right outside the college, on West Grove Drive. He had a sign saying that he took old-style photographs. Some of them were hung up outside and they looked cool – you know, like real old "wanted" posters.'

'Could you describe him? The photographer?'

'Unh-hunh. It was pretty gloomy inside of that tent, and most of the time he kept this black cloth over his head. He asked me to stand in front of this background, and *bam*, he took this flash picture, and after that all I could see was stars.'

'But who took your money? And your name and address?'

'A woman. I guess she was his assistant or something.'

'Can you describe her?'

Brad thought for a while, and then slowly shook his head. 'I don't know why, but I can't remember what she looked like. I get the feeling that she was *dark*, but that was all.'

'Was she tall? Or short? Do you remember what her voice sounded like?'

'No, I'm sorry. It's like a total blank.'

'Can you remember anything she said? Anything at all?'

'She said . . . No, I can't remember.'

'Try, Brad.'

Brad pressed his fingertips against his forehead, his eyes tight shut. 'She said . . . "Have your picture taken, young man, have your worries taken, too." Something like that.'

'Did you ever get the picture?'

'Sure. About a week later. It's at home.'

'You didn't happen to notice where it was mailed from?'

'No. Is that important?'

'It could be. Did anybody else have their picture taken?'

'Just me. Danny Magruder was going to have his done, too, but his girlfriend showed up to give him a ride, and he took a rain check.'

'Thanks, Brad.'

He stood up to leave. Brad said, 'Are you going to get me out of here, Mr Rook? I can't take much more of this place.'

'I'm doing my best, Brad.'

'I didn't kill Sara, I swear on the Bible. Nor Bobby, neither.'

'I know that, Brad. All I can ask you to do is have faith.'

Because of the tragedy at Rolling Hills cemetery, Dr Ehrlichman considered closing West Grove Community College until the end of the week. But Nita Kherevensky, the college counselor, strongly advised that he should keep it open. The students needed to talk, and hug, and share their grief together.

'Ve haff to express our painfulness, and to esk itch ozzer vy did zis happen? Vy, vy, vy?'

'If you ask me,' said Raananah Washington dryly, 'she's just vying for attention.'

When Jim walked into Special Class II, he was surprised to see that everybody had showed up, even Randy, who had been badly bruised when Jim threw him down the stairs of the bus. Others were patched up with plasters, or had their hands bandaged, and Roosevelt was sporting a piratical eye patch.

As Jim put down his books, the class all rose to their feet, and clapped him. He stood for a moment with his head bowed, and it took all of his self-control not to cry. After a little while he raised his hand for silence, and they sat down.

'Usually,' he said, 'when something terrible happens, we can't make any sense of it. Auto wrecks, accidental drownings, overdoses, house fires – all we can do is grieve, and tell ourselves that the Lord works in mysterious ways, and try to carry on.

'What happened yesterday, however, when we lost Pinky and David, that wasn't just some random, inexplicable act of God. Your bus didn't catch fire by accident. There was no lightning, in spite of the fact that many witnesses saw flashes of bright light. There was no ruptured fuel line.'

The class looked at each other, quizzically, and Shadow mouthed: 'Wha'? Wha's he talkin' about?'

Jim paused for a moment, but then he carried on. 'What I'm going to tell you now may sound crazy, and if you choose not to believe me, then that's your privilege. But I'm telling you because it's true, no matter how bizarre it may sound. Also, I desperately need your help to stop it from happening again.

'Some of you may have heard that I have the ability to see things which most people can't see. I almost died when I was a boy, and ever since then I can see dead people as clearly as I can see you. I can also see forces and presences which might be described as demons.

'Yesterday, your bus was attacked by the spirit of Robert H. Vane, the same Robert H. Vane that we have been studying in class.'

'Oh, *right*,' said Roosevelt, slouching back in his chair.

'Is this some kind of a test?' asked Philip suspiciously.

'Come on, sir,' Edward protested. 'Robert H. Vane died over a hundred and fifty years ago!'

Jim waited until they had quietened down. Then he said, 'That's right, Robert H. Vane died in 1857, and his body is buried somewhere in Los Angeles, in an unmarked grave. But the evil side of his spirit lives on. He's hiding inside a portrait of Robert H. Vane that's hanging on the wall in my apartment. I think he's frightened that I can discover a way to destroy him, although I haven't yet. Because of that he's determined to destroy *me* first.'

He looked around the classroom. 'Unfortunately that also appears to include anyone I care about, which means you.'

Most of Special Class II were very superstitious. They believed in the Blair Witch, and zombies, and every urban legend about homicidal hitch-hikers and killer bees in the toilet. All the same, Jim knew that he was stretching their credulity to the limit.

But they had nearly died yesterday, when their bus was ablaze, and Jim had risked his life to save them, and for

178

that reason alone they sat in respectful silence and listened to what he had to say.

He told them everything that had happened to him since he had moved into the Benandanti Building, and everything that he had discovered from Raymond Boschetto's diaries. He even told them about Brad, and the fact that only Brad's shadow-self was guilty of taking his revenge on Bobby and Sara.

Roosevelt put up his hand. 'That shadow-self, that's still part of Brad, though, right? So, like, *part* of Brad is guilty of killing them, isn't he?'

'Yes, you're right. But not the part of him that's sitting in police headquarters waiting to be arraigned. That part is totally *good*. And there's another thing to consider. If Brad hadn't had his photograph taken, and the evil part of his personality was still inside him, he would still be the conceited pain in the ass that he always used to be, yes. But it's highly unlikely that he would have killed Bobby and Sara. His *good* self would have kept his *bad* self in check . . . the same as it does with all of us, all the time. All of us are a balance between good and evil.'

'Kind of like *Dr Jekyll and Mr Hyde*,' Edward suggested.

'Kind of like that, yes. Except that Brad's evil self can come out whenever it wants to, even when Brad's in jail – just so long as his daguerrotype stays intact.'

'You said you needed our help,' said Freddy. 'I mean, what can *we* do? We can't see no dead people. I think I'd dump in my pants if I did.'

'I need four or five you to help me. An A-Team. The next time Robert H. Vane climbs out of that painting, I'm going to follow him. I'm going to find out where he hides his van, and where he stores his daguerrotype plates, and I'm going to destroy them.'

Special Class II looked at each other uneasily. 'Isn't that kind of illegal?' asked Sue-Marie.

'Robert H. Vane has been dead for a hundred and fifty years. How's he going to make a complaint?'

'What about his assistant?' asked George. 'This woman that Brad paid his money to when he had his picture taken? Like, if Vane has turned into some kind of a mutant, she must be driving his van around for him, and taking care of all his equipment and stuff.'

Jim said, 'I don't know who she is, or why she's helping him. But she's an accessory to murder, don't forget, so I don't think *she'll* be making any complaints, either.'

There was a long, bewildered silence while the class tried to assimilate what Jim had asked them to believe, and what he was asking them to do. He could see it on their faces. *Supposing he's lost it. Supposing he's some kind of basket case. I mean, the way that bus caught fire, that* had *to be lightning, right? Like, what was more believable – lightning, or some spooky invisible creature that was half-man and half-camera?*

Then, very slowly, Shadow stood up, and held up his hand as if he were pledging allegiance to the flag. 'I just want to say that this is the weirdest shit that I ever heard in my entire life, and if anybody else had told me this shit, I would've paid them to take a taxi straight to the nuthouse. But I believe what you say, Mr Rook, because I believe that you don't tell no lies, and if you want anybody to come along with you and trash this dude's doo-doo-type collection, I'm with you.'

Randy raised his hand, too; and then Freddy.

'Anybody else?' Jim asked them. 'I'm not going to say it won't be dangerous, because it might be. But I don't see any other way of protecting ourselves. Yesterday it was Pinky and David. Tomorrow it could be any one of you.'

Edward put up his hand, and then – to Jim's surprise – so did Sue-Marie.

'Sue-Marie, I'm not sure that this is going to be suitable for girls.'

'You're not going to sexually disallow me, are you, sir?'

'Well . . .' said Jim. 'So long as you don't expect to be treated any differently from any of the boys.'

'Sir . . . Pinky was my best friend.'

Jim looked at her and he could see that she was close to tears. 'Sure. I know that. Thanks for volunteering.'

Shadow said, 'This camera dude killed Pinky and David, man, and we're going to show him that *nobody* can mess with Special Class II, no matter how long they been dead. Even if they been dead since dinosaur days.'

Jim said, 'OK . . . I'm going to end this class by reading a poem for Pinky and David. I'd like you all to stand up, if you would, and close your eyes, and think of Pinky and David, and their parents, and their brothers and sisters, and everybody who is grieving over their loss. It's by Kenneth Bright, and it's called "Cold Memory."

'The stars shine sharpest on the bitterest nights
And voices carry clearest when the hoar-frost bites.
And that is why, when all these years have passed, and all
    these years
In cold midwinter I remember them
And see them standing all around, my friends and loved ones,
    such a company
With all our hurts forgiven, and our pain long past.

'As snow begins to fall between the trees
I see them gather, quietly, such a company.
For ghosts appear in snow, and only snow, and in the cold
To take on snowy mantles, and to breathe like smoke
And take each other's hands, all friends and loved ones, such
    a company
With all our words forgotten, and our love long past.
I long for each successive winter, and its darkest day
To see them all again, now closer still by yet another year,
    and such a company.'

He closed the book. Vanilla said, 'Amen.'

Sixteen

Jim felt hungry around eleven o'clock that evening, and microwaved himself a can of chili con carne. He had only just finished eating when the doorbell buzzed. He went to open it, wiping his mouth on a torn-off piece of kitchen paper. Outside in the corridor stood his A-Team: Shadow, Randy, Edward, Freddy and Sue-Marie. They were all wearing dark clothes and woolly hats, and Shadow was wearing a hood, although he was so conspicuously tall.

'This is some building, Mr Rook,' said Freddy. 'Doesn't Scratch Daddy live in this building?'

'If I knew who Scratch Daddy was, I'd probably be able to tell you.'

'Only the coolest mixer in the universe.'

Sue-Marie wandered into the living room and circled around it with her mouth open. 'This is really *amazing*,' she said. 'It's like Castle Dracula.'

'Is that chili you've been having for supper, sir?' asked Randy, sniffing the air. 'Do you put crumbled corn chips in your chili? I always do. Gives it extra texture, you know? My uncle puts cigarette-ash in his, did you ever hear of that?'

'I . . . ah – this chili came out of a can. I didn't have time to cook it from scratch.'

Shadow walked across to the portrait of Robert H. Vane. 'So this is where he's hiding, yeah? That's one seriously strange picture, that is.'

They gathered around it. Jim said, 'I don't know for sure

if he's going to come out tonight. We may have to wait two or three nights, or even longer – there's no way of telling. But I get the feeling that he needs to keep on taking new pictures of people, rather like vampires need blood. He's been trapped for nearly forty years, after all. He may need fresh supplies of evil images to build up his strength.'

Edward asked, 'Mr Rook – you said in class that you have this ability to see dead people and demons and such. When Vane comes out of this picture – *if* he comes out – will we be able to see him, too?'

'I don't know for sure. It's possible. I've never come across anything like this before. The thing that's hiding in this painting is not a spirit in the usual sense of the word, he's only one side of Robert H. Vane's personality. And then, of course, he's mutated: I never saw anything like it. Legs like a camera tripod, an eye like a giant lens, and a hand like a flashgun.'

'Half-man, half-machine,' said Randy. 'That's like *Robocop*. Or maybe Seven of Nine, from *Star Trek*.'

'Randy, hallo?' said Sue-Marie. '*Robocop* and Seven of Nine are *fiction*, OK? Robert H. Vane is really real.'

Jim picked up a tangled length of string, with small Christmas bells attached to it, as well as a can opener and two bunches of keys. 'I'm going to hang this string right across the painting. If Vane *does* decide to climb out of it, we should be able to hear him.'

'And then what?'

'We follow him. That's all we can do.'

At that moment Tibbles walked into the living room, and stopped, and looked around.

'What happened to your cat, sir?' asked Sue-Marie, horrified.

'Mr Vane here tried to incinerate her, but he only half-succeeded.'

Tibbles went around and suspiciously sniffed all the students in turn. She seemed to approve of them, because she climbed up against Shadow's leg and started to nuzzle his knee.

Jim massaged her ears. 'She looks pretty gruesome at the moment but her fur's growing back. It's a miracle she wasn't killed.'

'Maybe it wasn't so much of a miracle,' put in Edward. 'She's a cat, after all, and animals don't have an evil side to their personality, do they, in the same way that humans do? Like, they can't tell the difference between right and wrong.'

Shadow unhooked Tibbles from the leg of his cargo pants. 'Ow! She may not be evil but she sure knows how to dig her claws in.'

Jim showed the A-Team around the apartment. Sue-Marie adored the bathroom, and practically invited herself around for a shower. Randy poked around the kitchen, flicking through cookbooks, and helping himself to a large spoonful of Jim's left-over chili. Shadow looked through his CD collection, and kept sorrowfully shaking his head.

'Man, I gotta come round here and sort out your tunes. I mean, what's this Fountains of Wayne, man? You need some Choppa and some Kingpin Skinny Pimp and you definitely need some Ying Yang Twins.'

Edward sat down at the dining-room table and looked through Raymond Boschetto's books. 'These are really rare, sir, some of these photographs of early Los Angeles. Look at this one: *An Orange Tree that Died Overnight, Simi Valley, 1889.* And who are those weird people in hoods, standing around it? They look like Ku Klux Klan.'

'Raymond Boschetto collected hundreds and hundreds of strange photographs,' said Jim. 'I think he was looking for any pictures that Robert H. Vane may have taken. Any images of pure evil.'

'God, you have some totally freaky pictures in this apartment,' said Sue-Marie. She came and stood very close to him, so that her left breast pressed against his arm. 'I don't know how you can sleep here, sir. *I* couldn't. Not without somebody to hold me.'

Jim looked down at her and she looked back at him and blinked her sooty eyelashes, as if to say, 'What?'

'OK,' said Jim. 'I have plenty of Coke and Gatorade and donuts and I can grill some hotdogs later if anybody's hungry. I suggest we sit here in the kitchen and keep our ears open in case Vane tries to climb out.'

'We're not going to keep watch?'

'Not directly. You've already experienced what Vane can do with his flashgun. If he climbs out of that painting and finds that we're standing in his way, it's going to be cremated students on the menu.'

'Human ash,' said Randy. 'That might be good in chili.'

They sat around the kitchen table and talked for more than two hours. They discussed their favorite movies, their favorite TV programs, their favorite music. They talked about what they were going to do when they graduated from college. Shadow was confident that he was going to build 'a style empire.' He was going to produce hip-hop records and DVDs and manage sports personalities, as well as designing men's fashion and generally being an international icon of all that was cool. Sue-Marie had a hazy but very sincere idea that she wanted to 'fly around the world like Princess Di used to, helping people with no education and no food.' Edward had plans to design computer software that would give people completely invented lives, complete with childhood photos, school qualifications, credit ratings, and comprehensive details of vacations they had never been on. 'Fantastically useful if you're a fraudster, right, or a bigamist, or your real life is so boring you just feel like banging your head against a wall.'

The Italian clock in the living room chimed three thirty, and they all checked their watches. They had already drunk eleven cans of Coke, three-quarters of a bottle of Gatorade, and eaten most of a double pack of Oreos.

'Looks like Vane the Pain's going to be a no-show,' said Freddy.

Jim rubbed his eyes. 'Let's give him till four. Then I think we'd better call it a night.'

'Maybe he knows that we're waiting for him,' said Sue-Marie.

'He probably does,' Jim agreed. 'I think he's aware of everything that's going on around him. But I also think that he's hungry. He has a lot of time to make up for. A whole lot of souls to collect.'

'Well, I don't mind waiting,' said Randy, scraping the last of Jim's chili out of the pot, and licking the spoon. 'Next time, though, I'm going to bring some supplies, and cook us all a gumbo. Everybody here like chicken gumbo?'

'I'm a vegetarian,' said Edward.

'That's OK, you can eat the gumbo and leave the chicken on the side of your plate.'

Freddy suddenly raised his hand and said, '*Sssh!* Did you hear something?'

They stopped bantering and listened. All Jim could hear was the fridge muttering and the air-conditioner rattling and muffled laughter from somebody's TV, turned up too loud.

'What was it, Freddy?' asked Sue-Marie.

'I don't know . . . sounded like ker-*lunk* . . . like a door closing.'

Jim said, 'Wait here.' He left the kitchen and went soft-footed to the living-room door. He had left it two or three inches ajar, so that he could hear the bells on his booby-trap tinkling if Vane tried to climb out of the painting.

Jim stopped behind the door and listened again. Nothing. Very slowly, he eased it open. It creaked slightly, and he hesitated, but there was no sound except for another roar of laughter from the neighbors' TV. He glanced back toward the kitchen, and his A-Team were all watching him, their faces tense. 'It's OK,' he said hoarsely. 'I don't think there's been any movement.'

He pushed the door wider and put his head around it. The only illumination in the living room came from a single table lamp with a brown glass Tiffany shade. Nothing appeared to have been disturbed. The rug was rucked up, exactly as it was before. The cushions on the couch were still indented where Tibbles had been sleeping on them.

He walked into the room and approached the painting. Robert H. Vane was still standing there, with his black cloth draped over his head. But then Jim saw that the string of bells was broken in the middle, and the bells themselves were melted into tiny, twisted blobs. He lifted up one end of the string and saw that it had been burned through.

With a chilly sense of failure, he realized what had happened. Robert H. Vane's image was only a painted surface, and so it had remained in the frame. His shadow-self must have been concealed in the silver oxides underneath. It had already climbed out of the painting, and had crept out of the apartment without them being aware of it. The ker-*lunk* sound that Freddy had heard was the front door closing behind him.

'Guys!' Jim shouted. 'Shadow! Sue-Marie! Edward!'

His A-Team came crowding through the door. 'What's happened?'

Jim held up the string. 'Vane got out. Look at this – he's melted all the bells, so that they wouldn't ring. That noise we heard, that was him leaving.'

'He can't have gotten far,' said Freddy. 'Come on, if the guy's got a tripod instead of legs . . .'

'You haven't seen how fast he can move,' Jim told him. He made a scurrying gesture with his fingers. 'He's quicker than a spider.'

'Urgh,' said Sue-Marie. 'I really have a thing about spiders.'

'Let's see if we can catch up with him,' Randy suggested.

'I mean, why not? What else are we going to do?'

'OK – if you want to go for it.' Jim grabbed his car keys from the table and the six of them bundled out of the apartment, tripping noisily over Raymond Boschetto's shoes. 'Hey, is this yours, sir?' asked Shadow, picking up a brown and white loafer with white tassels, a real going-to-the-races shoe.

'Previous tenant's. I've never been that snazzy.'

Shadow lifted up his dark glasses and looked him up and down. 'Yeah,' he agreed.

They all jogged along the corridor and Freddy pressed the button for the elevator. When it eventually arrived they wedged themselves into it and stared at their multiple reflections as they slowly descended to the lobby. 'Remember,' said Jim, 'if we see him, all we're going to do is follow him. I don't want any confrontations. He's far too dangerous for that.'

'We could use some guns,' said Shadow. 'Once we catch up with him – *pow!* – all we have to do is put a cap in his head.'

'That would be first-degree homicide,' said Edward.

'The guy's been dead for a hundert an' fifty years! How could that be homicide? Besides, he's half-guy and half-Instamatic, ain't he, and nobody never got arrested for Instamaticide.'

Once they had reached the lobby they pushed their way through the revolving doors and out on to the street. Even though it was well past three in the morning, and there was a stiff ocean breeze blowing, the night was unusually cold for this time of year. A sheet of newspaper scuttled across the street and Jim felt a momentary frisson of fear. But he couldn't see any sign of Robert H. Vane.

He coughed and said, 'Lost him, I'm afraid. I think we'll have to call it a night.'

But Freddy said, 'Look – that van over there! That's *his* van, ain't it?'

Half-concealed by shadow, a dark-brown van was parked in an archway on the opposite side of the street. Jim could just make out the gilded letters *Old-Time Photography*. The van must have just started up, because smoke was blowing out of its exhaust.

'You're right,' said Jim, 'let's get after him.'

He had left his Lincoln at the end of the block, with two wheels up on the curb. They ran toward it and climbed in – Sue-Marie and Edward in the front, and the other three in the back.

'Ain't no space for my *knees*, man,' Shadow complained.

Jim started the engine and the Lincoln bounced heavily off the curb. In his rear-view mirror he could see that the van was backing slowly out of the archway, and so he waited for a moment to see which direction it would take. It turned west, toward the ocean, so he had to spin the wheel and do a U-turn to follow it, with the Lincoln's suspension bucking and its tires howling on the pavement like cats. Sue-Marie held tightly on to Jim's thigh to stop herself from sliding across the seat, but she still managed to press herself against him, even when they straightened up.

The van drove fast. There was hardly any traffic around, so Jim kept as much distance between them as he could. They passed 10th, 9th and 8th, and then, without making a signal, the van turned northward on 7th.

'Drives real good for a dead guy,' said Freddy.

Randy sniffed and shook his head. 'Nah, that woman's driving him, I'll bet. Look – she just ran a red light. And another one. That's just the way my sister drives.'

The van turned left on to Pico, and then right again into Palimpsest, a street of shabby flat-fronted apartment buildings and cheap hotels. It carried on for two hundred yards and then – without making a signal – it drew into the curb and stopped. Jim stopped his Lincoln, too, and immediately killed his lights.

They sat and waited. The van had parked outside a three-story 1920s building with large metal-framed studio windows. The white distemper on the front of the building was flaking like dead skin and the windows were all covered with black paint. Faintly visible above the doorway was the inscription DELANCEY ANIMAL HOSPITAL, FOUNDED 1922.

'What do we now, sir?' whispered Sue-Marie. Even if she had screamed it at the top of her voice, nobody in the van could have heard her, but they all felt subdued and conspiratorial.

'We wait, I guess.'

'Maybe we should go back to your apartment and smash up that painting now,' Edward suggested. 'If we did that, Vane wouldn't have any place to come back to, would he? I mean, Dr Van Helsing used to put garlic in vampires' coffins, didn't he, while they were out sucking blood, so they wouldn't have any place to hide when the sun came up.'

'Good thinking,' Jim acknowledged, 'but somehow I don't think it would work. From what I've read, Vane's painting can't be destroyed and it can't be thrown away.'

'Hold up,' said Freddy. 'The door's opening.'

The driver's door of the van opened halfway, hesitated, and then opened wide. A figure climbed out, wearing a black windbreaker with a hood, black jeans and black boots. The figure made its way to the back of the van, and from the way it walked, Jim could see that it was a woman.

She opened the rear doors. The interior of the van was lit by a single red bulb, like a photographic darkroom. All that Jim could see at first was folded bundles of black cloth, and what looked like an old-style photographic enlarger, complete with bellows. But then something stirred, and heaved itself up. A stilt-like mahogany leg stuck out, and then another. Very slowly and awkwardly, Robert H. Vane climbed out of the back of the van, and stood for a moment on the pavement, tugging his black cloth over him, so that his head and his body were completely concealed.

'There – that's him!' said Jim.

Freddy looked at Edward, and Edward looked at Sue-Marie.

'Who?' asked Randy.

'Robert H. Vane! He's right there, standing by the back of the van! Can't you see him?'

'You're serious?' asked Shadow.

Jim turned to them. 'I swear to you that he's really there. Right now, he's standing in the street right by the back of the van. Three legs, like a tripod, and a black cloth hung over him.'

Randy circled his fingers around his eyes and peered through them like make-believe binoculars. 'I don't see him, sir. All I can see is that woman.'

'Me too,' said Sue-Marie.

'In that case, I'll just have to ask you to make a leap of faith. He's there. He seems to be finding his balance. OK . . . now he's making his way toward the steps . . . he's climbing the steps . . . he's waiting for the woman to close the van doors.'

'This is *so-o-o* weird,' said Sue-Marie. 'I feel like we're in a dream or something.'

'We are,' said Jim. 'There's more to life than what we can see, after all.'

He watched as the woman in black climbed the steps and unlocked the front doors of the one-time animal hospital. Robert H. Vane went inside, and she followed him and closed the doors behind her.

'What do we now?' asked Edward.

'We wait some more.'

'But they could be here for hours.'

'In that case, we wait for hours. Bobby and Sara and Pinky and David, they don't deserve anything less. For their sakes, we're going to nail this bastard for good and all.'

Shadow clenched his fist and said, 'Yeah.' But then he thought for a while, and added, 'We could still use some guns. Glock nine millimeter. *Pow!*'

Jim turned around in his seat. 'You can't see him, Sonny. What are you going to shoot at?'

'All right, then. Uzi fully automatic. Spray the room, *ba-ha-ha-ha-ha-ha!* You've got to hit him then.'

'We'll see,' said Jim. 'You may be right, and that's the only way to kill him.'

'Yeah,' said Shadow. 'I know a guy in West Hollywood, he can get us anything we need. Glocks, Uzis, Ingrams. He does a great line in Rolex watches, too.'

They only had to wait for fifteen minutes before the front doors of the animal hospital opened up again and the woman looked out, checking the street. They ducked their heads down but they were too far away for her to see them.

She went back in, and came out a few seconds later carrying two flat wooden cases.

'Daguerrotype plates,' said Edward immediately. 'That's how they used to carry them around. I saw it on the Internet.'

The woman stowed the cases in the back of the van. As she was doing so, Robert H. Vane appeared in the doorway and began to make his way clumsily down the steps.

'He's coming out,' said Jim. 'He's going to the van. He's waiting for her to open the other door. That's it, he's climbing inside.'

'How does she know he's there?' asked Randy. 'Like, if we can't see him, how can she?'

'Maybe she has the same ability as I do,' said Jim. 'I know it's pretty rare, but I can't be the only one.'

The woman closed the van doors, locked them, and walked back to the driving seat. It was 3:59 A.M. She started the van and drove away, turning right at the end of Palimpsest Street, and heading east.

'Aren't you going to follow him?' asked Freddy.

'No,' said Jim. 'No point. If we follow him tonight, we might be able to stop him from taking a few more pictures, but we need to find out how to stop him forever. Let's go inside.' He opened his glove box and fumbled around for his flashlight.

'Inside? You mean . . . inside that building?'

'Where else?'

'Supposing somebody sees us and calls the cops?'

'Then we'll tell them that we're on a college field trip. Landmark buildings of Venice.'

'Of course! At four o'clock in the morning, all dressed like terrorists.'

They walked along the street until they reached the DeLancey Animal Hospital. Freddy looked up at it apprehensively. 'This has to be the scariest building I've ever seen. You couldn't make a building look scarier than this, could you? Blacked-out windows, flaking paint. And it *smells*, too. Can you smell it? Like sewers or something.'

'It's a building, that's all,' Edward reassured him.

'Yeah, but what's in it?' asked Shadow. 'The evil dead, right? Or the dead evil. One of those two.'

'Let's just see if we can get the doors open,' said Jim.

He climbed the steps to the front doors. They had originally been painted olive green, but years of weathering had made them as scaly and fissured as alligator skin. There was a corroded brass knocker hanging on the left-hand door, in the shape of a snarling coyote. It looked to Jim like the coyotes he had seen in Native American carvings. They were always positioned to face toward the east, where evil spirits come from. There was something unsettling about this knocker. When he turned away from it, he thought that it quickly moved its head, as if it were alive.

He checked the locks. Three five-lever mortise locks. No chance of breaking in with a Visa card. There was no access to the back of the building, either. He stepped back and looked up at the facade. It might be possible for somebody with baboon-like agility to climb up on the porch and break one of the windows. He turned around to his A-Team and said, 'Does anybody have a head for heights?'

Freddy came forward, smacking his hands together. 'You're thinking of gaining entrance through that window, sir? Absolutely no *problemo*. I was always getting locked out when I was a kid, and we lived four storeys up. Here, Randy, give me a boost, will you?'

Randy linked his hands together, and Freddy clambered up him as easily if he were a stepladder. Randy said, 'Ow!' when Freddy stood on top of his head, but in a matter of seconds Freddy had swung himself up on to the top of the porch. He reached across to the studio window and tapped at a large rectangular pane at the bottom.

'Tire-iron!' he called down in a stage whisper.

Jim loped back to his Lincoln and took out his tire-iron. He threw it up to Freddy, and without any hesitation Freddy smashed the window pane and knocked out the jagged shards of glass. He climbed across to the window ledge, and within seconds he had disappeared inside the building.

'That guy should be a professional burglar,' said Edward admiringly.

They waited for a short while, and then they heard the locks being turned. The front doors opened, and Freddy beckoned them inside.

Seventeen

Inside the animal hospital it was gloomy and airless, and the odor was even stronger. It wasn't sewers, even though it smelled equally unhealthy. It was more like rotting fur coats, and vinegary red wine and chemicals. Although the windows were all painted black, a faint orange illumination filtered down the staircase from a skylight in the roof. The bare-boarded floors were gritty with dust and broken glass.

Jim shone his flashlight right and left. The old reception desk was still standing in one corner, a large walnut affair as big as a grand-piano. On the wall hung a faded picture of a German shepherd with its tongue hanging out, and the slogan *Happy Again!*

They crossed the hallway and Shadow opened the door marked Waiting Room. It was empty, apart from two tilted-over chairs. They tried the room opposite, which must have been a consulting room when the hospital was open, because an old-fashioned examination table stood in one corner, and there were yellowing medical charts still pinned to the walls.

'No daguerrotypes here,' said Jim. 'Let's try upstairs.'

'I didn't see anything in the room I broke into,' said Freddy. 'Only some empty cages.'

Jim went up the first two flights of stairs and the A-Team followed. He briefly shone his flashlight into the room where Freddy had entered the building, but Freddy was right. All it contained was three tiers of wire cages, with their doors

195

hanging open. He came back across the landing and tried the door opposite. He rattled the doorknob but it was locked.

'Sonny,' he said to Shadow, 'you have the biggest feet.'

'And?' said Shadow defensively. 'I still got the coolest shoes.'

'I meant, you have the biggest feet so you're obviously the best person to kick this door open.'

'Oh. OK, sir. Gotcha.'

Shadow took two paces back. Then he kicked the door hard, right by the handle. There was a splintering crack and part of the architrave split, but the door didn't budge. He stepped back and kicked it again, and then again. At the third try, it flew wide open, and slammed against the wall.

They went inside. The room was dark and musty, and lined on three sides with wooden filing cabinets. Jim counted thirteen of them. He went across to the nearest cabinet and shone his torch on the label. *Escondido County Fair, September 23 – 25.*

'That was only a week ago,' said Edward.

Jim pulled open the top drawer. Inside, carefully stored in brown padded envelopes, he found thirty or forty daguerrotype plates, about 6 x 8 inches, each of them framed in black-painted wood and covered with a protective layer of glass. Each envelope was stenciled with a name, or names. *Peter T. Reynolds, Julie Inkster, Dan Forsman, Lanny Peete, Corey Kite, Nancy Lopez.*

'Here they are,' said Jim, carefully drawing one of the plates out of its envelope. 'The pictures that Robert H. Vane has been taking since Raymond Boschetto died.'

'That's a daguerrotype?' asked Freddy, frowning at it. 'It looks just like a dirty mirror to me.'

'That's because you have to look at it from an angle, so that the dark areas look light and the light areas look dark.'

He shone his flashlight obliquely across the plate, and they suddenly saw a serious-looking young man with curly hair and glasses. 'You're right, in a way, though, to say that it looks like a mirror. In a daguerrotype, your picture's always laterally transversed, the same way as it is in a mirror.'

The drawer below was marked *West Grove and Westwood, September 1 – 4*. 'This was the time he must have taken Brad's picture.' He opened the drawer, and there it was, *Bradley Moorcock*, between *Elroy Herber* and *Vince McNally*.

The first filing cabinet was full; but only the top drawer of the second cabinet had any daguerrotypes in it, and all of the remaining cabinets were empty. 'Still,' said Jim, 'he's taken a hell of a lot of pictures, considering he's had less than a month to do it.' He looked around. 'He must be planning to fill them all up. A repository of evil selves.'

Randy said, 'He's going to go apeshit when he finds out that we've smashed them all up.'

Jim opened the middle drawer, lifted out an envelope marked *Daniel John Hausman* and carefully took out the glass-framed daguerrotype inside. He checked it with his flashlight, angling it this way and that. Unexpectedly, it appeared to be blank. There was no image on the silver at all, only faint grayish blotches. Maybe it had faded. Daguerrotypes were very sensitive, even after they had been fixed with a salt solution, or washed with gold.

He picked up another envelope. *Philippa Ostlander*. This daguerrotype plate was blank, too. He pulled out another, and another. None of the plates in the middle drawer had images on them.

Edward had been watching him, and he took one of the plates and examined it himself. 'There's no picture.'

'They're not here at the moment, that's why.'

'I don't understand.'

'They're out there, somewhere, in the city, doing whatever it is that evil selves do. Like Brad Moorcock, getting his revenge on Sara.' He paused, and then he said, 'What time is it?'

'Twenty after four.'

'What time does it get light?'

'I don't know. Around five, I guess. That's when my older brother always goes jogging.'

'In that case, we have to get out of here, and we have to get out of here *now*.'

'I thought we were going to break up all of these daguerrotypes.'

'We can come back later and do that. Right now, I think it would be a very sensible precaution if we left.'

He replaced all of the blank daguerrotypes and closed the drawer. As he did so, however, he thought he heard the sound of a door closing, somewhere downstairs. He lifted his hand to indicate that they should all keep quiet.

'What is it?' asked Sue-Marie.

'I don't know . . . I'm going to take a look.'

He went to the door and shone his flashlight on to the landing.

'Anything?' asked Randy.

'I don't think so. Just the wind, probably, closing one of the doors that we opened downstairs. All the same, I think we need to get out of here before it starts growing light.'

'This is *great*!' said Edward excitedly. 'This is just like being Dr Van Helsing.'

'This is not at all great,' Sue-Marie retorted. 'This is totally scary.'

'You seen those vampires on *Buffy*?' said Freddy. 'Like, you go to bean them, right, and they just disappear in a cloud of bats.'

'Come on,' Jim urged them. 'We can come back later this morning, when the sun's up, and all of these shadow-selves are back where they belong.'

He crossed the landing. As he did so, he saw somebody coming up from the first flight of stairs from the hallway. A young man, dressed in gray. The young man reached the turn in the staircase and stared up at him. His face was silvery-black and his eyes were phosphorescent white and his hair was white, too.

Another figure came climbing up, and then another, and another, and they were all dressed in varying shades of gray and black, and they all had silvery-black faces and white eyes. There must have been twenty of them, at least, and they crowded on the stairs looking up at Jim and his A-Team and saying nothing at all.

Jim thought of Bobby's and Sara's ashes, lying in heaps, and their barbecue-blackened bones, and their skulls grinning at each other face to face.

He thought of their photographic images imprinted on the closet wall. Images created by a light so bright that it could penetrate brick.

'We . . . we haven't come here to hurt you,' he announced in a loud, clear voice.

The silvery-black figures didn't answer, but continued to look up at them, their black hands holding on to the banisters.

'If you allow us to leave quietly, without any trouble . . . well, we'll leave quietly, without any trouble.'

'Mr Rook,' whispered Sue-Marie, 'who are these people?'

'You can see them?'

'Of course I can see them! Who are they?'

'They're the people from the blank daguerrotypes. It's nearly daylight, so they're coming back.'

'Holy shit,' said Randy. 'What are we going to do?'

'Take them on,' said Freddy. 'Did you ever see my kung-fu?'

'You can't take them on,' said Jim. 'They're made of light, that's all. They're photographic images. More than that, they're completely evil.'

As he spoke, the young man at the head of the silvery-black people began to climb up the second flight of stairs. The others followed. Although they appeared as negatives, Jim could recognize women as well as men, and older people as well as young. They made no sound as they came up the stairs apart from the faintest metallic rustling.

'Please!' Jim appealed to them, raising both hands. 'These young people have done nothing to you! You can go back into your frames . . . we promise not to harm you! We'll just go away and leave you in peace and forget we ever saw you!'

The silvery-black people didn't seem to hear him, or else they weren't interested in what he had to say. They continued to climb the stairs, and as they came nearer, Jim could even *smell* their evil. It was like dust scorching on a hot electric fire. The pupils of their eyes were expressionless white dots, and Jim could see their black teeth and their seal-gray lips.

'Please!' he repeated, but the silvery-black people had nearly reached the landing and he knew they weren't going to stop – and they weren't going to be merciful. They were incapable of mercy. Any kindness that they possessed was still in their physical bodies, and God alone knew where *they* were.

Jim swiveled around to his A-Team. 'The window!' he shouted at them. 'We can get out the way Freddy got in!'

He pushed Sue-Marie toward the room where the empty cages were. Randy, Shadow, Freddy and Edward came scrambling close behind them. Jim just managed to drag Randy through the door by his arm when there was a flash of light on the landing as bright as an atom bomb.

'Jesus!' said Freddy, blinking like an owl.

There was another flash, and another, and then there was a flickering storm of flashes. Jim slammed the door shut and twisted the key. He could hear the paint crackling on the other side.

Freddy was first out of the broken window, then Sue-Marie. The barrage of flashes continued, and even though the door was closed they created a jerky strobe effect, as if Jim and his students were in a Keystone Kops movie, desperately trying to escape from a speeding locomotive.

Shadow was the last out before Jim. As he climbed out of the window, he said, 'You don't have to worry about being snazzy, Mr Rook. You the man.'

'And you don't have to worry about sucking up to me. Just move your ass or I'll fail you on twentieth-century poetry.'

Jim maneuvered one leg through the window and found his footing on the ledge outside. At that instant, the door burst open, and there was a million-kilowatt burst of light that dazzled him completely. He blindly threw himself sideways, toward the top of the porch, and Shadow managed to grab his sleeve to stop him from falling down to the sidewalk. For a moment he clung on to the guttering, his legs dangling, grunting with effort. Then Edward reached up and guided his feet down on to Randy's shoulders.

Randy said, 'Ow! Watch the ears, OK?'

Shadow swung down and dropped on to the steps. Then the six of them stood on the sidewalk outside the animal hospital and looked up at the window. They saw two or three more glimmers of light, but then nothing. The sky was turning pale, with a swirl of strawberry-colored clouds in it, and a cleansing truck was making its way toward them on Palimpsest Street, spraying the gutters. Jim hadn't smoked in years, but he really could have used a cigarette.

'Are we still coming back here?' asked Edward. There were dark circles under his eyes and his hair was all messed up.

Jim nodded. 'I don't think we have any choice. Who knows what those shadow people have done tonight? If they're anything like Brad, they've been cremating anybody they don't like. And who knows what they're planning to do tomorrow night, and the night after that?'

'I freely confess, I was crapping myself,' said Freddy. 'I don't think I'm ever going to be scared of anything ever again. Those shadow people – jeez. They're worse than ghosts.'

'"I am half-sick of shadows,"' Jim quoted. 'Come on,

let's see if we can find someplace open for breakfast. I'm buying.'

They went to the Truck Stop on Santa Monica Boulevard, a cheerful 1950s-style diner with red-and-white Formica tabletops and a jukebox. Randy, Freddy and Edward ordered scrambled eggs with bacon and grilled tomatoes and links, but Shadow stuck to maracuya-flavored bio yogurt because 'my body is a sacred place of worship,' and Sue-Marie could only prod a pancake around her plate because she was still feeling trembly. Jim drank two cups of intensely black coffee, and then he ate the rest of Sue-Marie's pancakes, drowning in maple syrup, for the energy.

'We'll go back to Palimpsest Street around one o'clock,' said Jim. 'I'll bring hammers and sulfuric acid from the college laboratory, and protective gloves. We'll take out all the daguerrotype plates, smash the frames and pour acid on to the images. Vane probably has unused plates stored in that building, and mercury, and all his fixing salts. We'll destroy those, too.'

'What's going to happen to the people in the pictures? I mean the *real* people, like Brad?'

'I don't know,' Jim admitted. 'But I don't think we'll be destroying the evil part of their personalities. We'll be releasing them, that's all, setting them free. With luck, they'll find their way back to the bodies in which they belong.' The waitress came past with the coffee jug and he held up his cup for her. 'Let's hope so, anyhow.'

'That still doesn't solve the problem of what we're going to do about Vane the Pain himself,' said Edward.

'No, it doesn't. But I think that Vane really *needs* these evil images. I think they give him strength. If we destroy them, I believe that will make him very much weaker. I just have to find a way to finish him off, for good and all.'

'Maybe you should try to keep him trapped inside the painting, the same way that Raymond what's-his-name did.'

Jim shook his head. 'I thought of that. But that means I would have to hold a reverse exorcism, twice a day, for the rest of my life. For starters, I don't even know how to hold a forward exorcism – and so far I haven't found any description of it in Raymond Boschetto's diaries.'

'What about this woman who drives him around?' asked Sue-Marie. 'If you could find out who she is, and stop her from doing it, Vane wouldn't be able to go out and take any more pictures, would he?'

Jim said, 'You're right. I've been thinking a whole lot about her. I can't understand how he found her, or how he persuaded her to help him. He's a monster, after all. What kind of a woman is going to help a creature like that?'

Freddy wiped tomato catsup from his chin. 'Next time, Mr Rook, we should follow her, and put her out of business. We should wreck his van. Like, without a van to get around in, and somebody to drive it, what can Vane do?'

'He's still very dangerous,' Jim replied. 'I didn't see any sign of his van when he came to the cemetery and set fire to the college bus. He can get around, believe me, even without a van. He's quick – and to most people, of course, he's invisible.'

'No harm in boosting his wheels, though,' Randy suggested, his mouth full of sausage.

'You're right. But it's time you all got yourselves home. You can take a shower and sleep for a couple of hours. I'll meet you back in college at twelve thirty.'

Jim went back to the Benandanti Building. Mr Mariti nodded to him as he crossed the hallway and said, 'You look like ten miles of bad road, Mr Rook.'

'Thanks, Mr Mariti.'

Tibbles was waiting for him right behind the front door, and she stayed two or three inches behind him wherever he went, so that he kept tripping over her.

He walked across to the fireplace and looked up at the

painting. He knew that Robert H. Vane was back inside it now, or at least his spirit was, or whatever it was that Robert H. Vane had turned into.

'What are you, Robert H. Vane?' Jim asked him out loud. 'What do you really want?'

Tibbles rubbed his ankles and purred. She knew what *she* wanted: cut-price tuna, squashed with the back of a spoon.

After he had fed her, Jim stripped off and took a shower, turning the faucet marked 'Torrent'. The noise from the plumbing was deafening, like a subway train hurtling down a tunnel at high speed, and the water pressure was so powerful that he had to lean against the shower cabinet to stop himself from being beaten down to the floor.

When he had finished, he climbed out, wrapped a large blue towel around his waist and went into the kitchen to make himself some more coffee. He switched on the portable television on the kitchen counter.

'. . . Nine people died last night in eleven unconnected fires in the Santa Monica and West Hollywood districts. In one, TV actress Kathy Mulholland was burned to death in her automobile as she stopped at a traffic signal on the Pacific Coast Highway. In another, the head of Cellcorp mobile phone systems was found dead in a seven-hundred-dollars-a-night suite at the Palms Marina Hotel, along with an unnamed woman . . .'

Jim stood with the kettle in his hand watching the news as fire after fire was reported, and in each case the victims had been burned 'almost beyond recognition.' He was still standing there when a slight movement made him glance toward the doorway. Eleanor was standing there, staring at him, white-faced. She was wearing a short black dress and black pantyhose, with very high black patent shoes. He was so startled that he almost dropped the kettle in the sink.

'Eleanor! Jesus! You frightened me.'

'I'm sorry, I didn't mean to. I heard noises, that's all, so I came in to make sure that everything was OK.'

Jim switched on the kettle and defensively tightened his towel. 'You probably heard the shower. It's like Niagara.'

Eleanor came into the kitchen and circled around him. 'So, how did it go last night?'

She stood very close to him. In her black patent shoes she was almost two inches taller than him, which he found strangely disturbing.

'Well, we almost got ourselves killed, but we found out where Vane is storing all of his stuff.'

Her green eyes widened. 'You're not hurt, are you?'

'No, thank God. But it was close. We were still searching through the daguerrotypes when their images returned – their shadow-selves. And their shadow-selves can do what Vane can do. They can set off flashes of intensely bright light, and incinerate anything that happens to be in the way.'

'Were there many of them?'

'Twenty at least. We had to make a quick exit out a second-storey window.'

'So where was this?'

'An old animal hospital on Palimpsest. It looks like it's been empty for years.'

'You didn't have time to destroy any of the plates?'

Jim shook his head. 'No – but we will. We're going back later today.'

'What about Vane himself?'

The kettle boiled and Jim poured water into the cafetière. 'My students asked me that. I don't know what the answer is, not yet. But you know –' he tapped his forehead – 'I'm working on it.'

'You're not worried, when you go back, that Vane will try to stop you?'

Jim looked at her. There was an expression on her face that he couldn't read at all. Was she being provocative? Or was she trying to warn him?

He said, cautiously, 'He'll have to get there somehow, if he's going to stop us.'

Eleanor said nothing, but she didn't take her eyes off him and she didn't blink.

'He travels around in a van, advertising old-style photos. That's how he gets people to pose for him. But if he's going to stop us . . . first of all he has to know what we're going to do, and second of all he has to arrange for his van to take him there.'

Still Eleanor said nothing. Jim slowly pushed down the plunger on the cafetière, and said, 'Coffee?'

'No, thank you. I find it difficult enough to sleep as it is.'

Jim filled a large mug with a sepia picture of Harry Houdini on it. 'The van . . . it's driven by a woman. She was dressed all in black when we saw her last night. She reminded me of you, maybe taller. You wouldn't have any idea who she is?'

'None, I'm afraid.'

'Maybe your friends the Benandanti might know?'

'If they do, they've never mentioned her to me.'

'It's just that we can't work out how Vane persuaded anybody to act as his assistant. What kind of a woman would agree to drive him around like that? We don't know if he's even capable of talking. He's a living nightmare, after all.'

Eleanor shrugged. 'When you look around you, Jim, you can see strange relationships everywhere. But when you realize what each partner is looking for in those relationships – sometimes it's love, sometimes it's nothing more than sharing the same taste in music – they don't seem nearly so strange after all.'

Eighteen

As Jim walked along the crowded corridor to Special Class II, he caught sight of Vinnie Boschetto coming the other way. Vinnie was wearing a red-and-yellow shirt with parrots on it, so he was hard to miss. He turned on his heel and tried to hurry out of the doors that led to the swimming pool, but Jim caught up with him and grabbed his belt at the back.

'Where the hell are you going, Boschetto?'

Vinnie raised both hands in surrender, dropping test papers all over the pathway. 'Jim, believe me, I'm so sorry.'

'You're sorry? Two of my students were burned to death, right in front of my eyes!'

'Jim, honestly, I never thought it would come to this. It's tragic.'

'For Christ's sake, you knew what you were dealing with! You almost got me burned to death, too!'

'We had no idea that Vane was going to get so angry! We thought that you would find a way to deal with him. Come on, Jim, you've handled stuff like this before! Spooks, demons, things that go *arrggghh* in the night . . .'

Jim seized the lapels of Vinnie's shirt and screwed them around so tight that he pulled off the two top buttons. 'You bastard. You and your goddamned Benandantis. You deliberately offered me that apartment cheap, didn't you, knowing that I was going to come face to face with a creature that could have cremated me? I could be dead by now – nothing but ashes, like Pinky and David.'

'Jim . . . what could I do? We were desperate! Uncle Raymond died of a heart attack and we had nobody to keep Vane in check.'

'Oh, yeah? Why didn't you volunteer?'

'I wouldn't have known where to begin. I'm a history teacher, Jim, that's all. I don't have any knowledge of religious rituals, like Uncle Raymond, and I don't have any psychic powers, like you. How was I supposed to deal with an invisible thing that hides in a painting and steals people's souls?'

'So you tricked *me* into doing it?'

'I'm sorry. When I heard that you were coming back to West Grove I thought you were going to be the answer to all of our prayers. I'm sorry it all went so wrong. If only there was something I could do to make amends.'

Jim released his grip on Vinnie's shirt, although he was still shaking with anger. 'I can't even ask you to call on Pinky's and David's parents, can I, and tell them the real reason why they died. That would only make things worse.'

'Jim – buddy – whatever you want me to do, I'll do it. We had no way of knowing that Vane would attack you, or attack your students. He's been trapped in that painting for more than thirty years . . . We just didn't want him to get out and start taking pictures again.'

'You mean you wanted me to take care of him for you, without even bothering to warn me what I was up against?'

'I'm sorry!' Vinnie repeated. 'We simply thought that once you'd seen Vane appear, you'd work out for yourself what he was up to, and discover a way to stop him. Did you see the news? Those shadow-selves of his have been starting fires all over. Before we know it, they're going to start forest fires and burn down half of Los Angeles County.'

Jim shook his head in disbelief. 'You know what I should do? I should just walk away from this, and let you handle it yourself.'

'Jim, you can't! We're right on the brink of hell here. Not just us, but hundreds of people – thousands, even.'

'I know,' said Jim. 'There's no way I'm going to let Pinky and David die for nothing, and there's no way I'm going to let Vane take any more pictures.'

Vinnie watched him for a while, saying nothing. His test papers started to blow across the grass but he ignored them. 'So what are you going to do?'

'Last night we followed Vane – me and some of my students. We found his studio, where he's hiding all of his daguerrotypes. We're going around there later to trash them. You can come along if you like, as part of your penance.'

'Jim, you don't know how bad I feel.'

'Vinnie, before this is over, I'm going to go out of my way to make sure that you feel a hell of a lot worse.'

Jim's first class was at 10 A.M. When he walked in, it was obvious that his A-Team had already told the rest of Special Class II what had happened last night, because they were all tense and expectant – and quiet, for a change. Raananah Washington came past the open door, stopped, and looked inside, just to make sure that Special Class II were actually there. Jim called out, 'Good morning, Raananah!'

When she had gone, he turned to the class and said, 'It seems like you've all been updated. Last night we found out where Robert H. Vane hides his daguerrotypes. Today we're going to hit back at him. The A-Team are coming back to Vane's studio with me, and we're going to be doing some serious damage. But that still won't solve the problem permanently. We have to find a way to destroy Vane himself.'

Ruby put up her hand. 'Mr Rook, I was talking to my grandmother yesterday about evil spirits.'

'Oh, yes?'

'My grandmother told me that when she was a little girl in Dominica, in Santo Domingo, there was an undead spirit that used to walk around her neighborhood. It used to strangle cats and dogs and steal food and sometimes it stole children, too, and their bones were found in the forests, their bones all gnawed like they was eaten. My great-grandmother wouldn't let my grandmother go out after dark, in case the undead spirit caught her. They used to call it *El Espejo* – the Mirror – because when it came after you, and you looked at its face, all you could see was yourself.'

'How creepy is that?' said Jim. 'Did they manage to exorcize it?'

'My grandmother said that in the end two priests came from Rome and helped them to hunt him down. The priests carried a large mirror with them, and they caught *El Espejo* in a dead-end street, and they made him look in the mirror at his own face. My grandmother has a saying, you know? "Evil can't bear to look at itself." *El Espejo* fell down paralyzed and the priests buried him. Inside his casket, they fixed a mirror, so that if he opened his eyes he couldn't see nothing but his own face.'

'Maybe that would work with Robert H. Vane,' said Jim.

'Yeah,' said Shadow, tilting back his chair. 'Maybe it wouldn't, either. That spirit your grandmother was talking about, that didn't fry people alive, did it? Robert H. Vane could turn us into charcoal before we got within twenty yards of him, and that goes for any one of those doo-doo-type gooks, too.'

'Anybody else got any ideas?' asked Jim.

'What about this reverse exorcism?' suggested George. 'Maybe Father Foley could help us.'

Father Foley was the priest who ministered to the needs of West Grove's Roman Catholic students. Jim hadn't talked to him in a long time – not since one of his students had been haunted by night terrors about demons from hell – and he remembered that he was very skeptical when it came to the supernatural. 'Demons are nothing but our own guilt, Jim.'

Jim said, 'I guess I could try . . . But I don't think Father Foley is very enthusiastic about exorcisms. In fact, I don't think the Roman Catholic Church as a whole is very enthusiastic about exorcisms, not these days. You need to show them at least one of the five proofs of demonic possession, and before we can do that we have to show them Robert H. Vane himself.'

'So what are the five proofs of demonic possession?' asked Edward.

Jim counted them on his fingers. 'One, you have to talk in unknown languages. Two, you have to know things that are distant or hidden. Three, you have to be able to predict future events. Four, you have to have an abhorrence of all things holy. Five, you have to show unusual physical strength.'

'That sounds like Freddy,' said Edward. 'You can't understand a word he's talking about and he knows if you have money, even if you've hidden it in your locker.'

'No, but his socks are holey,' said Roosevelt.

They left West Grove in two cars shortly after 1 P.M. Jim took Vinnie in his Lincoln, along with Sue-Marie and Edward, while Shadow followed close behind in his shiny black Ford Explorer, with Randy, Freddy and Philip, who had volunteered to join them. There was a forest fire burning up in the canyons, and the day was gloomy with smoke and fine particles of ash. There was a strong smell of burning in the air, too, and Jim hoped that it wasn't an omen.

Vinnie kept shaking his head, saying, 'I never thought it would come to this.'

Jim said, 'It's too late now, Vinnie. You can't turn the clock back. Let's just see what we can salvage.'

He could hear the bottles of concentrated sulfuric acid rattling in their plastic milk crate in the trunk. 'This is what happens when you allow yourself to take evil for granted,' he added. 'So long as Vane was safely trapped in that painting, the Benandanti forgot about him, didn't they? But all these years they should have been scouring every religious library in the world, searching for a sure-fire way to get rid of him for good.'

Vinnie reached inside his shirt and lifted out a small brass cylinder, hanging on a chain. 'It's not *they*, Jim. It's *us*. I'm a member of the Benandanti, too. This is the caul I was born with, all rolled up.'

Jim glanced at it, and wrinkled up his nose.

Vinnie said, 'You'd be amazed how many Benandanti there are. Politicians, businessmen, top people in the entertainment business. We're all devoted to stamping out evil, wherever it is.'

'Except that you grew complacent, didn't you, when it came to Robert H. Vane. And because of that, God knows how many people have been burned to death.'

'Yes,' Vinnie admitted.

Jim drew up outside the DeLancey Animal Hospital on Palimpsest Street and Shadow pulled up close behind him. Jim and Vinnie and the A-Team all climbed out of their vehicles. They looked up and down the street to make sure that there were no police cars around, and then Freddy climbed the steps to the front door of the hospital and took out his lock-pick. Meanwhile Randy lifted the crate of sulfuric acid out of Jim's trunk, while Shadow carried the canvas bag full of hammers and screwdrivers that Jim had borrowed from Walter the janitor, and Sue-Marie carried a shopping bag full of bright-red industrial gloves.

It took Freddy less than a minute to pick all three locks. He pushed the door open and said, '*Ver-wull-ah*, as they say in France. Beats climbing through windows.'

Jim checked the street again for any police cars, and then they trooped inside, closing the door behind them.

'Hell of a place,' said Vinnie, with a shiver. After the warmth of the midday sun, the animal hospital was distinctly chilly, and it smelled even more unpleasant than it had last night. They had brought five flashlights with them, and their beams criss-crossed the hallway and illuminated the reception desk and the picture of the happy German shepherd.

'Hell of a place is exactly right,' said Jim, and started to climb the stairs.

They went directly into the room where Robert H. Vane kept his filing cabinets. Jim pulled the first drawer right out and lowered it on to the brown linoleum floor. 'Take out every drawer, go through every single daguerrotype one by one. Break the glass frame, and then pour acid over the surface. Tilt the plate from side to side, so that the whole image is burned off. When you've done that, pass the plates to Roosevelt and Mr Boschetto here, and they'll cut them up with shears so that they can't be re-plated and reused.'

Sue-Marie hunkered down next to the drawerful of daguerrotypes in her very short fringed leather skirt. She took a plate out of its envelope and peered at it closely. 'Sir, I can't see no picture on this one.'

'You have to hold it at an angle,' Jim explained.

She squinted at it one way, and then the other. 'I still can't see nothing.'

Jim went across and looked at the plate, too. He shone his flashlight across it, at a diagonal, but Sue-Marie was right. The murky silver surface had no image on it at all. 'Odd,' he said, and took another plate out of its envelope. That, too, was blank.

He was suddenly filled with an overwhelming feeling of dread. 'Pull all of these drawers out!' he barked. 'Check all of these daguerrotypes!'

The A-Team took out plate after plate.

'Blank!' said Edward.

'Blank!' said Randy.

'Nothing on this one, neither!' said Shadow.

Jim found an envelope with a name he recognized. He opened it up and took out the daguerrotype, but that was

213

blank, too. Soon the floor was strewn with empty brown envelopes, and blank daguerrotypes were scattered all around them.

'What?' asked Vinnie apprehensively.

'They're not here,' said Jim. 'The shadow-selves, whatever you want to call them. We can't destroy them because their images are out and about someplace.'

'I thought they could only go out at night,' said Roosevelt. 'You know, like vampires.'

'*Out*, yes,' said Jim. He slowly stood up, listening. Edward noisily took another plate out of its envelope. Jim put his finger to his lips and said, 'Ssshh!'

'What is it?' asked Philip. He looked even paler than usual, which made his spots look even redder.

'I don't know,' said Jim. He was sure he had heard the faintest of rustling noises, the same noise that he had once heard in a darkened attic, when the rafters were clustered with bats. He moved cautiously toward the half-open door, opened it a few inches wider, and listened again.

'They're downstairs,' he said.

'You mean the shadow-selves?'

'Can't you hear them? They can't go out during the day – the sunlight would fade them away to nothing – but it's dark in here. All the windows are blacked out.'

'Oh, Jesus,' said Freddy. 'We're going to get barbecued.'

'They must have known we were coming!' said Vinnie. 'How the hell did they know we were coming?'

'I'm not sure. But we have to get out of here, and quick.'

He went out on to the landing. There was nobody on the stairs, but he could definitely hear shuffling and breathing. He crossed over to the banisters and looked down into the hallway.

He hardly ever swore. He had always believed that swearing was the sign of somebody who didn't know how to express themselves. But he swore then, even though he did it under his breath.

The hallway was crowded with silvery-black faces, all looking up at him with foggy white eyes. There must have been over a hundred of them, spilling out of the doors of every downstairs room – the waiting room, the surgery, the reception area. There was no way for Jim and his A-Team to get to the doors. They wouldn't even be able to make it halfway down the stairs before they were incinerated.

He turned around. His A-Team were standing right behind him. 'We'll have to do what we did last night – climb out of the window!'

Vinnie said, 'What? What is it, Jim? What's down there?'

'Look for yourself.'

Vinnie peered over the banisters. He said nothing, but when he looked back at Jim his face was aghast.

'Satisfied?' Jim asked him. 'Now let's get out of here!'

Shadow went over to the opposite door and opened it. As he did so, however, five or six silvery-black people appeared inside the room. Shadow immediately slammed the door shut. 'Mr Rook, we can't get out that way! It's cramful of gooks!'

'Let's try the back of the house!'

Roosevelt tried another door, and then another, but both of them were locked. He opened a third door, but that room was crowded with shadow-selves, too, black-faced and white-eyed, and they took a threatening step forward. Roosevelt pulled it shut as fast as he had opened it, but he shouted out, 'I can't lock it! There ain't no key! They're tugging at the handle and there ain't no key!'

Jim said, 'Back in here, quick! We'll just have to break another window!'

He beckoned everybody back into the room with the filing cabinets in it. Vinnie was the last, except for Jim, and he was sobbing with panic.

'Vinnie!' said Jim. 'We're going to get out of here, all right?'

Vinnie stared at him wild-eyed. 'They're going to cremate us alive! We're all going to die!'

215

'Pull yourself together, will you? We have kids to take care of!'

'I'm sorry! I'm so sorry! We didn't know that anything like this would happen! I swear it . . .'

Jim pushed him roughly into the room. He was just about to follow him when a slanting bar of sunlight crossed the wall at the side of the staircase. It disappeared almost instantly, but it was definitely sunlight. For a split second Jim couldn't think what it was, but then it came to him. Somebody must have opened the front door!

Treading very cautiously, he went back to the banister rail and looked down into the hallway. The silvery-black shadow people were still there. In fact there were more of them than before, jostling together like cockroaches. They were all looking up at him, and some of them were baring their black, negative teeth. He kept his hand half-raised in front of his face, in case they started flashing their lights at him, but they seemed to be waiting for something.

He stepped nearer to the banister and saw what it was that they were waiting for. Right in the middle of them crouched the hooded black figure of Robert H. Vane. His tripod legs were extended so that they were even longer and spindlier than they had been before, which made him twice the size.

Vane took one step forward, toward the bottom of the staircase, and then another, and another. His legs were so long that he crossed the hallway in two steps, and the third took him halfway up the first flight of stairs. He was followed closely by the swarm of shadow-selves, so that the awkward clattering of his feet was accompanied by the same metallic rustling as before, only much louder this time.

Jim ran back to the filing cabinet room and shut the door behind him. There was no key, so he tugged Randy by the sleeve and said, 'Put your shoulder against it! Hold them back as long as you can!'

He turned to the window. Shadow and Freddy were

216

wrestling with claw hammers, trying to pry away a protective wire-mesh screen. Jim hadn't noticed it before, because it was painted black, just like the glass.

'How long is that going to take to get off?' he demanded.

'Doing our best, sir! The screws is all rusted and painted over.'

'Well, hurry! Vane's here, and he's coming upstairs!'

'Vane?' Vinnie almost shrieked.

'This was a trap. Vane must have known we were coming.'

Jim picked up a hammer and hit the side of the wire-mesh frame, trying to dislodge the screws. He hit it again and again, but all he managed to do was distort it.

'Mr Rook!' Randy shouted. 'Mr Rook! They're pushing against the door!'

'Shadow! Go help him! Vinnie, you too!'

'They're going to burn us alive!' screamed Vinnie. 'We don't stand a chance, they're going to burn us alive!'

'Just shut up and help to keep them out!' Jim yelled.

The door began to shake as the shadow-selves threw themselves against it. Randy, Shadow and Vinnie pressed against it as hard as they could, and Edward joined them, while Jim and Philip carried on smashing at the wire-mesh frame that covered the window.

But then there was a blinding flash all around the edges of the door, and an unbearable blast of heat. The A-Team staggered back into the room, flapping and clutching and blowing on their hands. The door was kicked from outside, and then kicked a second time. In a swirl of noxious black smoke, the door swung wide open, its paint still blazing and dripping on to the floor in rivulets of fire. Outside stood Robert H. Vane, with the black cloth drawn back from his square, bone-white head. Jim could see now that it was only his right eye that had mutated into a huge black lens. His left eye was gray, and disconcertingly normal, although he stared at Jim as if he were short-sighted, or drugged. His mouth hung open on one side, like a stroke victim, and his teeth were crowded and spotted with black decay.

Jim stepped in front of his students and spread his arms protectively. None of them spoke. Robert H. Vane heaved himself into the room, and stood facing them, with six or seven of his silvery-black shadow people trying to force themselves around his legs.

'So – ahem! – this is the showdown,' said Jim. He was trying to sound challenging, but he had a catch in his throat and he had to keep clearing it. 'This is where absolute evil starts to take over the world, is it? And – ahem! – woe to anybody who tries to stand in the way.'

Robert H. Vane's bellows-like chest rose and fell. '*I do nothing,*' he whispered. His voice reminded Jim of a sack with a dead dog in it, being dragged across a rough path. '*All I do is show the human race what it really is.*'

'Oh Jesus, oh Jesus, he's going to burn us alive!' moaned Vinnie.

'The human race isn't all evil,' said Jim. 'There's good and there's bad in every one of us, except for you.'

'*I am purity,*' whispered Robert H. Vane.

'You?' said Jim. 'You're pure evil, that's what you are. You and all of these shadow people that you keep trapped in your daguerrotypes. The *good* Robert H. Vane is lying in his grave, and all that's left is his ugly side, which is you.'

'*I am the purifier.*'

'Don't make me laugh. You're a walking contagion.'

Vinnie gritted his teeth. 'For God's sake, don't provoke him, Jim, he's going to cremate us!'

'*I am the beauty of simplicity, and objectivity, of uncontaminated good and uncontaminated evil.*'

Jim stared at Robert H. Vane's lens-like right eye and suddenly understood what utter evil really was. It was like waking up at night and finding the bedroom to be seamlessly black, without even the faintest chink of light. *I look,*

*I judge, I take what I want and I destroy what I don't want.
Because I alone have the right to do so.*

Robert H. Vane raised his right hand and it was like a
trough, rather than a hand. A trough like an old-fashioned
flashgun, but filled with the brilliant energy of evil instead
of magnesium powder. Vinnie was right. He was going to
cremate them, reduce them all to nothing but ashes and
burned bones.

But what had Ruby's grandmother said? *'Evil can't bear
to look at itself.'*

Robert H. Vane took one more unsteady step closer. Sue-
Marie had her eyes tight shut and she was making a high-
pitched squeaking noise. Shadow was rapidly muttering a
prayer. Even Edward was reciting Psalm 23: 'Yea though
I walk through the valley of the shadow of death I shall
fear no evil, thy rod and thy staff . . .' Vinnie just kept
sobbing and snorting.

One of Robert H. Vane's brass-bound feet caught the
edge of a daguerrotype plate, and it gleamed briefly in the
corner of Jim's eye. *'Evil can't bear to look at itself.'*

'A-Team,' said Jim, as clearly as he could. 'Simon says
pick up a daguerrotype. Now.'

'What?' said Sue-Marie, opening her eyes.

'Just do what I do! And do it now!'

Without another word, Jim bent down, picked up two
daguerrotype plates, and held them in front of Robert H.
Vane's lens, one above the other. Edward did the same,
and so did Shadow, Philip and Randy. Only Vinnie looked
confused.

'Vinnie!' shouted Jim. 'Pick up some plates! Hold them
like this!'

Still Vinnie didn't understand. Jim was just about to
help him when Robert H. Vane let out a scream that
sounded like a horse caught on a barbed-wire fence. He
lurched backward on his tripod, his lens dipping and
turning as he tried to escape his own reflection. But in

each of the fourteen daguerrotype plates that Jim and his A-team were holding up, all he could see was the murky, distorted image of a man who had grown into something unspeakably hideous.

Vane shook his head and tried to turn himself around, but his tripod legs were caught on the skirting boards, and he tripped on the scattered daguerrotypes. Behind him the silvery-black shadow people collided with each other in their confusion, and twitching snakes of static electricity crawled from one to the other.

'*That is not me!*' screeched Robert H. Vane. '*That is not me! That is not me! I am beauty!*'

Jim brandished his daguerrotype plates nearer and nearer to the lens of Robert H. Vane's right eye. His students did the same, until Vane was almost surrounded.

It was then that Vane ignited his flash. The light was so bright that Jim thought for an instant that there could be no darkness anywhere in the world, not even inside his own skull. The heat, too, swamped him totally, as if somebody had thrown a bucketful of blazing gasoline all over him. His fingernails, unprotected by the daguerrotype plates, felt as if they were on fire. Beside him, Vinnie didn't even have time to scream. His hair flared up, his flesh shriveled, and then there was a sharp crack as his bodily fluids evaporated. He collapsed on to the floor with a hollow knocking of bones.

But it was Robert H. Vane who caught most of his own flash. Reflected back to him from fourteen silver daguerrotype plates, it shattered his lens, roasted his face, and set fire to the black cloth that covered his back. He pitched backwards, his tripod legs blazing, his arms furiously thrashing. The shadow-selves shrank away from him on to the landing.

'*I am ... I am ... beauty!*' he raged. He lifted his flashgun again, trying to hold it steady with his left hand.

Jim shouted, 'Watch out!' At the same time Vane set off

another flash, even more blinding than the first. Sue-Marie screamed as the heat burned her fingers, and Freddy yelled, 'Shit!' But they held their daguerrotypes tight, and most of the flash bounced back.

Robert H. Vane exploded with a soft, pressurized *whooommfff!* Fiery pieces of fabric and wood were thrown across the room, and his body collapsed in the middle of his burning legs.

Jim dropped his daguerrotypes and frantically blew on his fingers to cool them down. His corduroy pants were scorched at the bottom and his shoes were smoldering, because the daguerrotypes hadn't shielded him completely, but it had been enough.

He looked down at the blazing ruin of Robert H. Vane's shadow-self. His A-Team stood around him, and for the first time in his life he couldn't think of anything to say.

But then there was a rustling sound from the doorway. It was crowded with silvery-black images; the dark side of ordinary men and women. Static electricity flickered on the ceiling like summer lightning, and there was a threatening smell of ozone in the air, as if a thunderstorm were just about to break.

'This sucks,' said Freddy. 'How are we going to get out of here?'

Nineteen

'Maybe they won't hurt us, now that Vane's gone,' said Edward. Maybe . . . if we kind of leave the premises quietly . . . let them get back to their plates . . .'

'Are you kidding me?' said Shadow. 'They may look like an old-time minstrel show, but those mothers are seriously pissed.'

Jim took a step toward the door. The shadow-selves didn't budge. In fact, they began to press even more closely into the room. The crackles of static grew increasingly loud and violent, and showers of sparks began to dance around their hair and fingertips.

'What are they doing?' asked Sue-Marie, huddling herself close to Jim's shoulder.

'Building up their energy is my guess,' said Jim. 'I think they want to blitz the lot of us in one damn great flash.'

'We should break the windows,' said Philip. 'If they can't stand the light—'

'That's right!' Roosevelt interrupted. 'I saw that in a Dracula picture. They pulled down the drapes and Dracula got totally frizzled.'

'We can't get to the glass, man,' said Shadow. 'That screen is totally impenetray-table.'

'Maybe we should football charge them,' Randy suggested. 'All get together and go for it.'

'Oh, sure, and all end up like a KFC party bucket.'

One of the shadow-selves stepped toward them, followed by another, and another.

'Oh God,' said Sue-Marie.

The leader was tall and looming, with wild shoulder-length hair. He gave an aggressive shake of his head, and his eyes flashed with brilliant white light. He shook his head again, and this time the flash was even brighter. Jim, blinking, heard a slowly rising whine, like the whine of dozens of flash battery packs. It was the shadow-selves, building up their power.

'The plates!' Jim said. 'Pick up the plates again, and use them as shields!'

But Shadow said, 'No way, man! I am sick of this shit! There ain't no black-faced gooks going to barbecue me!'

'Sonny!' Jim shouted. But Shadow trampled forward, over the daguerrotype plates, and pushed the leading shadow-self back against the wall. Then he pushed the next, and the next, and then he was forcing his way out on to the landing, elbowing his way through the crowd of shadow-selves, yelling all the time at the top of his voice.

'You get out of my way, you freak! You hear me? You just get out of my face!'

He was halfway across the landing when there was a dazzling flash of light. Jim saw everything in reverse, so that Shadow looked white and so did the shadow-selves who were jostling all around him. There was another flash, and then a whole succession of flashes, as if Shadow was a celebrity arriving at a movie premiere. But with each of these flashes, Jim could feel a tremendous blast of heat.

Shadow shouted out, 'No!'

Jim saw that his hair was alight, and smoke was billowing out of his hooded top. But he kept on shoving his way through the crowds of shadow-selves until he reached the door on the opposite side of the landing.

Shadow was burning now, and flames were jumping up his back. But he pushed his way into the room, past the rows of wire cages, waving his arms around like a fiery windmill and yelling at the shadow-selves that were milling around in his way. His words weren't even intelligible now – they were nothing but screams of pain and desperation.

He forced his way toward the window. Three or four of the shadow-selves clung to his blazing clothes, trying to stop him, but he twisted himself from side to side and shook them off. Then, without any hesitation, he lowered his head and threw himself right through the black-painted glass. The window exploded, and Shadow disappeared in a roaring gout of fire.

Instantly, as if accompanied by a fanfare of golden trumpets, the sun blazed into the room, and right across the landing. The shadow-selves let out a dreadful, orchestrated shriek, and shrank away from the sunlight with their hands clamped over their eyes. They couldn't even make it to the darkness downstairs. They dropped to the floor, one on top of the other, like slugs showered with salt. Jim and his A-Team stood in the middle of the room, close together, watching in disgust as the shadow-selves writhed and shriveled. Their silvery-black sheen turned to viscous gray, and then to albino white, and then they faded altogether, the way that all photographic images fade in the sunlight. Their grinning black teeth were the last to disappear.

Jim went cautiously to the door and looked around. The landing was deserted. There was nobody in the animal hospital but them. Even the smoking heap that had once been Robert H. Vane had faded away, leaving nothing but a few fragments of a broken camera: a blackened lens, a shutter mechanism, and a few brass hinges.

'We did it!' said Edward. 'Or Shadow did it, anyhow.'

'Shadow!' said Randy.

They hurried downstairs, opened the front doors and went outside. There was a crowd around Shadow already. He was lying on the sidewalk with a blanket draped over him. His face was scarlet and black and badly charred, and a thick delta of blood was running from the back of his head into the gutter.

224

Jim knelt down next to him. 'Sonny?' he said hoarsely, but Shadow's eyes were closed.

'He just fell,' said a white-haired man in a flappy pair of khaki shorts. 'The window went bang and out he came, burning like a space shuttle.'

'I called nine-one-one already,' added a young man in a long red apron.

'Is he dead?' asked Sue-Marie, standing close behind him.

Jim felt Shadow's wrist. He couldn't feel a pulse. 'I think so,' he said.

'What happened in there?' asked a fat woman in a flowery dress.

Jim slowly stood up. His face was smudged with smoke and his hair was sticking up like a cockerel. 'I think you could call it a tragedy,' he said.

Lieutenant Harris came into the interview room, accompanied by Detectives Mead and Bross. They all pulled up chairs and sat and looked at Jim as if the very sight of him made them feel tired.

'To be frank,' said Lieutenant Harris, 'we don't believe one single word of it.'

Jim nodded. 'I didn't expect you to. I don't believe it myself.'

'The problem is, there is no other explanation. Not unless all of you are certifiably insane.'

'That's one possibility, of course,' Jim agreed.

Detective Mead said, 'It's going to take a few days to get a complete report from the CSU, and even longer before the ME's finished. But it doesn't look as if you or any of your students were directly responsible for the deaths of Vincent Boschetto or Sonny Powell.'

'It looks like two more cases of spontaneous human combustion,' said Lieutenant Harris.

Jim looked at him narrowly. Lieutenant Harris didn't even blink.

'The ME has already decided that Bobby Tubbs and Sara Miller were victims of SHC, and so we'll be releasing Brad Moorcock. Apparently all of the recent burnings in the Santa Monica and West Hollywood areas have also been caused by SHC. The theory is that solar flares have had something to do with it. That, and the very dry summer. People have literally been microwaved to death.'

'Solar flares?' said Jim.

'It could have been "shadow-selves,"' said Detective Mead. He looked as if somebody had just told him that his mother had died.

Lieutenant Harris said, 'Pending further investigation ... Well, Mr Rook, you and your students are free to go.'

He drove the A-Team back to West Grove first. It was evening now, and most of the college building was in darkness. They stood together in the parking lot, all of them exhausted, all of them numb from what had happened to them, and clutching themselves as if they were feeling the cold, but all of them strangely reluctant to leave. In the end, Jim had to say, 'See you tomorrow, right? We can talk this out in class. Share it with everybody else.'

Sue-Marie said, 'Nobody will ever know what we did, will they?'

Jim put his arm around her shoulders. 'That's the fate of all really good people, Sue-Marie. They don't get prizes. They don't get interviewed on TV. They just get the satisfaction of knowing that they've made the world a safer place to live in.'

Freddy came up to Jim and gave him a low five. 'Thanks, Mr Rook. I think you taught me some kind of lesson today, even though I'm not exactly sure what it is. I just believe that I'm going to be a better person from now on, that's all.'

Edward shook Jim's hand as well. 'I learned something, too. The more you find out, the more you don't know.'

Randy said, 'Shows you, doesn't it? What you see in the mirror, that's not what you necessarily are.'

Jim smiled and said, 'Too right. "Man's mind is a mirror of heavenly sights."'

He watched them all leave. He was still standing by his car when Karen appeared with Perry Ritts. Karen came over while Perry stood a few feet away, looking impatient.

'Oh, Jim – we heard about Vinnie and Sonny. It's terrible! Are you OK?'

'Sure, I'm fine. A little burned at the edges, but otherwise OK.'

'What actually happened, Jim?' Perry asked loudly. 'They didn't say too much on the TV news.'

'Sorry, I'm not at liberty to tell anybody – not yet. But the police are ninety-nine per cent sure that it was an accident.'

'An accident? Jesus! Vinnie got burned to ashes and what's-his-name jumped out of a second-storey window – that sounds like a pretty bizarre accident to me. Come on, Jim. You were there. What *really* happened?'

'There was a clash between reality and illusion, Perry, that's all. A conflict between the way things look, and the way they really are.'

Perry waved his hand dismissively. 'You know your trouble, Jim? You talk like you're deep but you're so shallow you don't even come to my ankles.'

Jim took hold of Karen's hand and squeezed it. 'Yes,' he said. 'You're probably right.'

Jim let himself into his apartment and tripped over Raymond Boschetto's shoes. Tibbles had been asleep on the couch but now she opened her eyes and yawned at him.

He went over to stroke her, but he had only taken two steps across the room when his eye was caught by the painting. The black cloth had disappeared. There – half-smiling, with a fine, prominent nose and long, shining hair – was the face of Robert H. Vane, daguerrotypist, as he must have appeared before he took his self-portrait. His eyes looked intelligent and kindly.

Jim approached the painting and felt it with his finger-tips. It hadn't been retouched. The paint on the face was dry and cracked, just like the rest of it.

'So,' Jim said under his breath. 'Nothing is permanent. Things *can* be put right.'

He looked around the living room. There was no doubt about it, the atmosphere had subtly changed. There was almost a feeling of relief.

After he had fed Tibbles, though, he picked up the brown envelope that he had salvaged from the animal hospital – the one marked with the name he had recognized – and went across the corridor to press the buzzer at Eleanor Shine's door. He waited for a while and then pressed it again.

Eventually, Eleanor opened it. She was wearing a long black satin wrap, and her hair was tied severely back in a glossy French plait. 'Jim!' she said, sounding almost surprised.

'Do you mind if I come in?'

'Of course not. I was just about to take a bath.'

He walked into her apartment. It was identical to his, except that the door to the kitchen was on the left, instead of the right. It was decorated much more severely, with black drapes and a gray carpet and white walls, and modern German furniture made of black leather and chrome. There was a bookcase, filled with identical black-bound books, and a Bang & Olufsen CD unit. On top of it stood a white statuette of a naked woman dancing, and a white Wedgwood urn, but there were no flowers, no pictures on the walls, and no mirrors.

'You haven't seen the news, then?' Jim asked her.

'The news? Why? What's happened?'

'There was an incident at the old DeLancey Animal Hospital on Palimpsest Street. A college teacher was burned to death and a young student threw himself out of a window.'

Eleanor sat down on the black leather couch. Her wrap

slid back, revealing her white leg, right up to her hip. 'That's tragic,' she said.

'Yes,' said Jim, 'it was.' He circled the room, swinging the brown envelope from side to side. Eleanor watched him, her eyes hooded.

'Do you want a drink?' she asked him at last. 'You look as if you could use one.'

'No, thanks. I can't stay for long.'

'Did they say how it happened . . . this incident?'

Jim came around the end of the couch and sat down so that he was facing her. 'No, they didn't, and they never will. Not publicly, anyhow. There are some things even a nation that believes in UFOs won't swallow.'

He laid the envelope down on the glass coffee table beside him. Eleanor didn't look at it. She kept her eyes fixed on Jim, as if she were afraid he was going to jump at her without warning.

Jim said, 'What happened was that somebody wasn't what they appeared to be. Somebody betrayed somebody, so that when somebody arrived at the animal hospital, somebody was waiting.'

'Am I supposed to understand that?'

Jim picked up the envelope. 'You know what's in here, don't you? It has your name on it, after all. *Eleanor Shine, Benandanti Building*. And it's dated the day after Raymond Boschetto died.'

He opened the envelope and drew out a black-varnished wooden frame, containing a silvery-gray daguerrotype plate.

'See? Blank. No image. Because the image is sitting right here, right in front of me.'

'I still don't understand what you're talking about.'

'Yes, you do. When Raymond Boschetto died and Robert H. Vane realized that he was no longer trapped in his portrait, he came climbing out to look for somebody to help him . . . somebody to set up his old-time photographic business. Somebody to drive him around, and take care of him.

'The nearest person he could find was you. You lived right across the corridor. He might have been a monster, but there was nobody to disturb him while he prepared himself, and Raymond Boschetto had all the daguerrotype plates and all the chemicals that he needed.

'What happened? Did he knock at your door and take a picture before you knew what was happening? Or did he blind you with one of his flashes, drag you in here, and *then* take it? And what happened to the good Eleanor, the real Eleanor? Did he kill her?'

He stood up, walked across to the bookcase, and picked up the Wedgwood urn. He opened the lid and there were brownish-gray ashes inside. 'This is the real Eleanor, isn't it? The good Eleanor? You – you're nothing but Eleanor's shadow-self. Her evil side. I'll bet you never open those drapes in the daytime.'

'You're demented,' said Eleanor, turning her face away.

'Am I?' said Jim. He went right up to her and wiped his finger across her cheek. He left a black mark all the way from her nose to her ear. 'Make-up, to hide the fact that your face isn't white at all, it's black, like a negative. Hair dye, because your hair isn't black, it's dead white. Contact lenses, to conceal your eyes, and white enamel, to conceal your black teeth. You've been lying and scheming ever since I moved in here, haven't you?'

Eleanor furiously rubbed the make-up on her cheek. 'You stupid little man! You should have been grateful to the Benandanti for giving you such an apartment and kept out of things that were none of your concern!'

'That's right,' said Jim. 'Vane thought that I wasn't going to be any trouble at first, didn't he, and that I couldn't stop him from climbing in and out of that painting whenever he wanted to. Then he realized that maybe I wasn't such a patsy after all, and he tried to frighten me by setting fire to my students' bus. Well ... he under-estimated me, my dear, and most of all, he underesti-mated my students.'

Eleanor waited until he had finished and then she gave him a slow hand-clap. 'Well done,' she said. 'So what are you going to do now?'

He held up the daguerrotype. 'I'm going to give you a choice. You can either return to this plate, and stay there, or else I'll destroy it, and you'll never have any place to hide. Now that Vane's gone, the Benandanti won't continue to pay for you to stay here, and sooner or later you'll have to leave – and go out into the daylight.'

'You are *evil*,' Eleanor spat.

'The decision is yours. I'll give you twenty-four hours to think about it.'

He took the daguerrotype and walked out. Eleanor stalked after him and slammed the door behind him.

Back in Special Class II the next day, they bowed their heads in two minutes' silence for Shadow, and there were tears.

Jim said, 'Sonny was brave and selfless, and if it weren't for him, I wouldn't be standing here today – and neither would Sue-Marie or Roosevelt or Edward or Randy or Philip. We owe him our lives, and it's a debt we'll never forget.

'Only you in this class know what a great evil we fought against, and how we beat it, and only you in this class know how much it cost us. Here's a poem by John Forbes White to remember Sonny by. "Set Against the Wind."

'And with his window wide he faced the storm
Blinded by lightning-strikes and deafened by the scream
Of winds that had been raised for his discouragement.
Yet even when the rain assailed his soul
Cascading cold through every crevice of his doubt and fear

He sang of clearing clouds, and turning west
To see his friends returning by the shore.'

Later, as he unlocked his apartment door, he heard somebody calling, 'Mr Rook! Mr Rook!'

He turned to see Mr Mariti shuffling along the corridor
as fast as he could.

'Mr Rook, you don't see Ms Shine today?'

'No, I haven't. Why?'

'The plumber, he has to fix a washer in her bathroom.
But she is not there. But all of her clothes are there, everything. And lights on. And TV on. But no Ms Shine.'

Jim hesitated, and then he said, 'Let me take a look.'

Mr Mariti opened Eleanor's apartment door with his pass
key, and Jim followed him in. He was right: the apartment
looked exactly as it had last night. They walked from room
to room, but there was no sign of Eleanor anywhere.

It was only when they came to the bedroom that Jim realized what had happened. The black drapes were still drawn
across, and he saw that their hems were actually tacked to
the floor. But they had been slashed six or seven times with
a kitchen knife, so that the sunlight flooded in. The kitchen
knife was lying on the carpet, and next to it was a black satin
wrap, as fluid as a puddle of oil. He picked it up, and pressed
it to his nose, and breathed in. It smelled of lilies and vertigo.

'Ms Shine?' asked Mr Mariti. At that moment Tibbles
walked in, looked around, and sniffed.

'I think she decided to leave,' said Jim, hanging the wrap
on the end of her bed.